ORIGINS: THE ROAD TO POWER

A Target Prequel

RICKY BLACK

RICKY BLACK
BOOKS

MAILING LIST

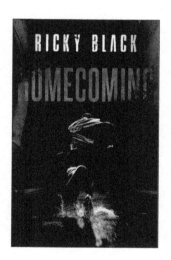

If you want more information regarding upcoming releases, or updates about new content on my site, sign up to my mailing list at the end of this book — You'll even receive a novella, absolutely free.

BEGINNING

CHAPTER ONE

Monday 10 March 1997

HE JUST NEEDED a few more seconds

His arm stretched out, the stacks of twenty and fifty-pound notes within reach. He grinned as he grabbed the money.

'Lamont!'

Lamont Jones jerked awake, vaulting from the bed. Stretching and wiping his eyes, he quickly trundled downstairs. Carmen Jones sat at the table, a middle-aged black woman with long black hair and great bone structure, just barely hanging onto the looks that had once enticed many men.

'Good morning, Auntie.'

Carmen ignored her nephew, looking over him with a critical eye. Lamont was gangly, with similar cheekbones to his Aunt, and messily curly hair. A jagged scar at the bottom of his chin slightly marred his features. He was long-limbed with a quizzical nature and dark, rosewood eyes that showed a vulnerability that intrigued those around him. Auntie was immune to it.

'Get back upstairs and wash your face. You look disgusting,' she said.

Lamont hurried to obey, heading back downstairs afterward. Auntie had lit a cigarette, the disgusting smoke wafting around the kitchen. He was just getting over a chest infection and the smoke tickled his lungs. If Auntie noticed, it didn't show.

'Get started on breakfast. Your sister will be up soon and I don't want her to be late.'

Lamont busied himself turning on the hob, then went to the fridge for eggs and bacon. Auntie watched, eyes narrowing.

'Comb your hair too. You're a mess.'

The usual anger simmering within, Lamont ignored Auntie. She did this daily and rising to it would only make things worse. Instead, he skilfully prepared and served breakfast, made her a cup of tea, and then went to wake his sister. Marika Jones snored softly, the quilt pulled over her head.

'Rika . . .' He gently rocked her. 'Rika, you need to wake up.'

'Mhmm.' Marika stirred, looked at Lamont and then closed her eyes again. Mumbling, Lamont yanked away the quilt.

'Oi, what are you doing?'

'You've got school today.'

'I'm tired. I wanna go back to sleep.'

'Don't make me get Auntie.' He would never utilise this threat, but it often paid dividends.

'I don't care. I'll tell her I'm ill.' Marika pulled the quilt back over herself.

'Fine.' Lamont left to take a shower. Auntie normally timed him, so he made sure he was out within minutes to avoid her complaints about him using all the hot water. Like everything else in the house, the shower was top of the line but Auntie still found fault. Dressing for school in a worn pair of jeans and a baggy shirt, he threw on a pair of cheap trainers with damaged soles. Marika was drinking a glass of milk in the kitchen, beaming when he re-entered the room.

'Hurry, Rika. Are you going to school by yourself, or with Danielle?' Her friend's mum had a car and usually drove Marika to school. He had wanted Marika at his high school so he could keep an eye on her, but Auntie hadn't cared, choosing to send her somewhere else.

'Marika isn't going to school today. She doesn't feel well,' said Auntie.

'She's lying, Auntie.' Lamont glared at his sister, whose smile widened.

'You don't dictate to me. My niece said she is ill, so she isn't going to school.' Auntie lit another cigarette. This time, she unlocked the back door and stood outside.

'How often do you think you're gonna get away with this?' Lamont hissed. Giggling, Marika continued sipping her milk and dismissed him. She seemed to take several days off school a week. Whereas Lamont attended school every day even when he was ill, she took liberties.

Lamont could do nothing about it. He had no say in the household. School was his way out and because of that, he soaked up everything taught to him.

Grabbing a jacket and his school bag, Lamont left the house. He embraced the air of Chapeltown, or the *Hood* as it was affectionately known. A diverse, multicultural suburb in Leeds, Chapeltown had a reputation for violence. Lamont saw beyond that. There was beauty in the Hood, a certain energy that sometimes made the hairs on his arms stand on end. He couldn't explain it, but he felt it.

Lamont headed towards the main road, his steps halting when he saw the group of boys skulking on the corner. They smirked when they saw him.

'Look who it is; *Trampy Lamont*,' one of them, a lanky kid named Tower, called out. He came from a big family and had several brothers. He was always throwing his weight about and targeting Lamont. They'd fought before, but his friends always jumped in when it looked like he would lose.

Lamont sighed, knowing he couldn't avoid them. If he tried to run, they would either chase him or spread the word that he was a coward. He froze as the group approached.

'Where'd you get them trainers from? Africa?' Tower stood in front of Lamont. His friends guffawed as if he had told the funniest joke in the world.

'Nah, even the Africans wouldn't wear them,' Another boy piped up.

'Look how his toes are nearly poking through! And look at them trousers,' Tower continued. Lamont stood, hands in his pockets, taking the insults. Tower was trying to bait him and he would not rise to it. Seeing that his strategy wasn't working, Tower tried another tactic.

'Gimme all the money you've got. Now.'

'I don't have anything, Tower.'

'Why do you talk like that?'

'I don't talk like anything.'

'Yeah, you do. You talk like a white man, all prim and proper. You're from the Hood. Act like it,' Tower snarled. 'Gimme your money. If I don't get a pound in sixty seconds, we're gonna rush you.'

Sighing, Lamont removed his school bag and jacket. Putting them on the floor, he faced the boys.

'Why are you taking your coat off? You wanna go?' Tower taunted. Lamont tensed, waiting for them to make the first move. Before Tower could do anything, another voice spoke up.

'I'll go with you.'

Tower and his cronies froze, recognising the harsh voice. Tower swore quietly as Marcus strolled towards them. Marcus Daniels was sixteen years old, but he was over six feet tall, with the build and the attitude to prove it. He glared at Tower and his gang, eyeing each of them. None met his gaze.

'Yo, safe, Marcus.' Tower's tone softened.

'Don't *safe* me. Why are you lot surrounding my brother?' Marcus asked in his slow voice. He was soft-spoken, his eyes constantly showing his true intent. They were full of malice and rage against the world. Anyone who knew him, knew Marcus was the real deal.

'Nah, we were just playing with him. Lamont's cool,' Tower back-pedalled. His boys slowly backed away.

'L, are they troubling you?'

Lamont needed only a second to reply.

'Nah. Like Tower said, we were just messing.'

Tower shot him a look, pursing his lips and tilting his head to one side.

'Are you sure?'

'Yeah, man. I'm sure.'

'You lot, go away. Trouble my bro, you'll have me to deal with,' Marcus promised. The boys hurried up the road.

'You should have let me stomp them out.'

'There's no point. It'll just make it worse next time,' replied Lamont.

'Doesn't matter. Sometimes you need to take the licks. People will never respect you if you don't stand up for yourself.'

Lamont knew Marcus meant well, but resented being spoken down to by anyone. It was easy for Marcus to preach about standing up for himself. Everyone feared him. Lamont was on his own most of the time and had no one to back him up.

'Whatever, man. Have you been out all night?' He changed the subject.

Marcus grinned. 'Had some business, then I stayed with Mia.'

Lamont laughed. Mia was Marcus's girlfriend, for lack of a better term. She lived with her older sister. Marcus was always around and if the rumours were true, had also slept with Mia's sister.

'What kind of business?'

'Don't worry your head about it, *schoolboy*.' Marcus reached into his jeans pocket and peeled off five, ten-pound notes. 'Keep hold of that. Don't let the witch see it.'

'I won't.' The first time Marcus had given him money, Lamont foolishly left it on his bedside table. The next day he awoke to the lash of the belt striking his legs and Auntie screaming that he was a thief.

'I'm gonna head home. Why don't you skip school and come with me?'

Lamont shook his head. 'I'm not missing school. I'll get with you later if you're about.'

'Let me know if Tower and his people trouble you again.'

'I will,' Lamont lied. Tower was an annoyance but the last thing he needed was people thinking he needed Marcus to fight his battles.

7

For the past few years, Marcus had lived with Lamont, his Auntie, and Marika. The son of a pair of hardcore drug abusers, his father was murdered trying to rob a drug crew, and his mother died of an overdose when he was six. Marcus had been in his fair share of foster homes. Moving in with Lamont had calmed him down, but the demon still lived below the surface.

Once he turned to walk home, Lamont quickened his pace. If he didn't hurry, he would have to get the bus. Folding the money Marcus had given him, he put it in his sock and was on his way.

———

Lamont was hurrying out of the school gates that afternoon when he heard someone call his name. Tower strode toward him with his gang following.

'Oi, don't think you're rough because you've got *Psycho Marcus* backing you. My brother will end him if he steps out of line, understood?' Tower pushed out his chest.

'I do,' Lamont said listlessly.

'You better. I want some money tomorrow. Don't try avoiding me either, because I'll come to your yard and smack up you and your sister, you get me?'

'Don't talk about my sister,' Lamont's tone became cold. Tower and his people picked up on it.

'Or what? What are you gonna do?' Tower said. Lamont glared, his eyes blazing. The sight of his stare made Tower feel uneasy. He glanced at his crew.

'Don't forget what I said. Come, you guys. Let's go.' They hurried away. Lamont took a deep breath, not realising he'd clenched his fists.

'Are you walking home, L?'

Lamont hid the smile that appeared on his face as Erica Anderson sashayed into view, two of her friends flanking her. Erica was tall, with skin the colour of dark honey. Lamont had liked her for the longest time, but painfully knew that he was in the friend zone. She had an older boyfriend, but often talked with Lamont, and would walk home with him.

'Hey, Erica. Yeah, I am. Are you?' he said, resisting the urge to fidget.

'Yeah. These two are getting the bus, but I'm meeting Leon at the park. Do you mind if I walk with you?'

'No, course not.' Lamont's smile widened. Erica's friends giggled, shaking their heads.

'Let's go then. See you two later,' Erica said to her friends. Walking with Lamont, the two of them crossed the road, walking down the long path that led to the park.

'Did you do Mr Silver's homework?' Erica asked as they walked.

'Did it on Sunday. Did you?'

'Yeah, did it at Leon's house. When he let me anyway. I swear, all he does is try to feel me up!'

'Bet that's annoying,' Lamont said, feeling a flash of anger as his stomach hardened.

'It's sweet. He's not a talker, so I guess it's his way of telling me what I mean to him.' Erica giggled, running a hand through her hair.

'Yeah, there's always that.'

'What were Tower and his boys saying? You looked mad.'

'Nothing. Just Tower being Tower.' Lamont didn't want to think about him.

'Okay. Just be careful. You know what he's like.'

'I'm always careful,' replied Lamont, smiling. Erica grinned back.

'What are you doing this evening?'

Lamont shrugged. 'Should be good. All the washing, or if I'm lucky, Auntie will let me do the ironing or cooking.'

'She treats you worse than a slave.'

Lamont had confided in Erica about Auntie's treatment. Once he even showed her the welts on his back from the belt. Marcus was his best friend, but he wasn't the easiest to converse with. Erica showed him the affection and sympathy that he needed.

'I'll be out of there soon,' Lamont said, his voice strong.

'How? How will you live?' Erica looked thoughtful.

'I'll get a part-time job and start college. I can't stay under that roof forever.'

Erica nodded. Lamont had mentioned his desire to leave home before. They walked along, talking about school life and playground dramas.

'Lavinia likes you. Do you like her?' Erica was referring to a girl in their year at school.

'She's all right. Not my type, though.'

'Really? So what's your type then?' Erica pressed.

You, Lamont wanted to say.

'I don't have a proper type. I just know that Lavinia's not for me. She's cool to talk to, but I don't have feelings for her.'

Erica smiled. 'Give her a chance. I bet she'd let you sleep with her.'

'I'm not interested in that,' Lamont lied. He was sixteen. It was all he thought about.

'You're not? Have you done it before?' Erica asked.

'Yeah. Loads of times,' Lamont's voice took on a boastful tone, the lie growing. He had virtually no experience with the opposite sex, other than a few kisses and fumbles. Between his mismatched clothing and being prey for every bully going, Lamont wasn't top of the social spectrum. Life had dealt him nothing. He was smart, but it was getting him nowhere. Lamont hoped adult life would change things for him, but struggled to see how it could.

'Really? Who with?' Erica leaned into him, her eyebrows raised.

'No one you know,' Lamont furtively replied.

'You're no fun. Did you enjoy it? I always do.'

Lamont's stomach lurched at Erica's words. He knew she had slept with Leon, but didn't want to hear about it.

'It was okay. Nothing special.' Lamont hated himself for lying, wishing he could tell Erica the truth; that she was the only girl he wanted to sleep with, mainly because of the kindness she had shown him. He couldn't. He had committed himself to the lie, and now he would have to see it through.

'You must not be doing it right. Talk to Leon. He's great at it. Suppose it's because he's older.'

'Yeah, must be,' Lamont grumbled. The park was coming into sight now.

'Gosh, you're so moody sometimes, L.' Erica linked arms with him and kissed him on the cheek. Lamont's face burned, his jeans tightening. She smelled amazing. Like apricots.

'Shut up,' He said good-naturedly, enjoying the contact. They crossed the road and trudged up the steps to the park. Lamont spotted Leon and his friends sitting on the swings. They were all hard-faced, towering over Lamont. Leon, a bullet-headed eighteen-year-old with facial hair and a sneer, looked him up and down. He disentangled himself from Erica.

'I guess I'll see you tomorrow at school then,' he said, not liking the way Leon and his friends were staring.

'Why don't you stay and hang out? Leon won't mind. His friends are cool.'

Lamont shook his head.

'Nah. Auntie will flip. I'll see you later.'

Lamont hurried away. Washing his hands and face as soon as he got in, he headed to the kitchen. Raucous laughter greeted him. Auntie and two of her friends sat around the table, smoking, drinking and laughing almost manically at some joke. They all looked up as Lamont entered.

'Good afternoon, Auntie,' The practised words rolled from Lamont's tongue with passable conviction. She stopped laughing.

'Don't stand around talking. Grab the dustpan and brush and sweep the stairs. Come back when you're done. I've got more for you to do.'

Lamont did as instructed. It was tedious work, bending over to sweep the stairs causing him backache. He didn't know why he couldn't use the big brush but the last time he had asked, Auntie had hit him in the head with it.

When he finished, he looked into Marika's room, where she draped on her bed reading a magazine. She looked at Lamont haughtily when she saw him.

'What do you want?'

'Where did you get that magazine?'

'Auntie bought me it. For being so good today.' Marika grinned. Lamont clenched his fists.

'You little faker. You could've at least swept the stairs for me.' Marika made a face.

'Whatever. Is Marcus in?' He continued.

'He's in his room. Think he's sleeping,' Marika replied, turning back to her magazine.

Lamont left, picking up the dustpan and brush. Emptying the dirt into the bin downstairs, he washed his hands again, put the dustpan away and went back to Auntie for further instructions.

When all his chores were finished, Lamont flopped onto his bed, spent. He was sure that Auntie made up jobs for him to do. She seemed to get a kick out of watching him sweat. He had homework, but before he started, he needed to relax. Yawning, he stared up at the ceiling, gathering his thoughts.

Lamont dreamed of a time when he would be on his own. He would be a working man, free to live his life any way he wanted. The thought was daunting, yet something he did for himself now. Other than the roof over his head, Auntie provided nothing for him. He did everything. He had tried making money getting part-time jobs in the past, but Auntie always seemed to scupper his hustle.

School was nearly finished now. If all went well, he would not have to suffer much longer.

'L?' There was a heavy knocking at the door.

'Come in, Marcus,' he called out. Marcus sauntered into the room, smirking when he saw Lamont lying down.

'The fuck are you doing, thinking and strategising and shit!' he laughed.

'Just trying to get my mind right.'

'Get money, you get your mind right. Money opens doors,' Marcus said matter-of-factly. To him it was that simple.

'When I finish school, I'll get money,' Lamont assured his friend. Marcus made a face.

'When? Any job you get, it's gonna take time to make real cash,'

Marcus pointed out. Lamont didn't respond. Marcus had touched upon the flaw in his life plan. Whatever job he ended up in, it would take time to build up. He would need to be patient.

'Forget that, anyway.' Marcus scratched his head. 'We're going out.'

'Nah, I'm tired,' Lamont replied, stifling another yawn.

'I'm not asking. I'm tired of seeing you sitting up here, night in, night out. Throw on some aftershave too; we're gonna be around women.'

CHAPTER TWO

Monday 10 March 1997

MIA GREETED Marcus with a long kiss at the door. Lamont averted his eyes when he started feeling her up. Eventually, they broke apart.

'L, this is Mia. Mia, this is my brother, L,' Marcus introduced them. Mia was curvy and caramel skinned, with a round baby face and slightly slanted hazel eyes. She kept her hair in neat crotchet braids and wore light pink lipstick.

'Nice to finally meet you, L. Marcus's mentioned you before,' Despite her friendly tone, he saw the way she looked at his clothing. He forced himself to stay respectful.

'Same, Mia. He talks about you all the time.'

Marcus chuckled, disguising it as a cough when Mia shot him a glance. They all headed into the main room. Lamont expected a mess, but the room gleamed. The TV alone was bigger than Auntie's, and the sofa looked to be top of the range. An older girl who Lamont guessed was Mia's sister glanced at them, wearing a jumper and a pair of cut-off shorts. Her gaze lingered on him for a second, then she went back to reading.

'This is my older sister, Rochelle. Shelle, this is Lamont. He's Marcus's friend.'

'Nice to meet you, Rochelle.'

She gave him another glance, dismissing him without a word.

'Ignore her; Rochelle's always on her period.' Marcus put his arm around Lamont. 'C'mon, what do you want to drink?'

'Just some juice or some water please,' Lamont replied. Marcus and Mia shared a look and sniggered. Even Rochelle tried to hide a smile.

'A real drink. You think we came here to sip Kia Ora?' Marcus laughed louder. Lamont wet his dry lips. He'd never tried alcohol before. Marcus strode into the kitchen, returning with a bottle of Courvoisier and four large glasses.

'Come, Shelly. Have a drink with us.' Marcus poured a liberal amount into one glass.

'I don't want a drink.'

'Have one or I'll take your little magazine and rip it up.'

Tutting, Rochelle held out her hand and took the glass. She downed it and handed it back.

'Happy?'

'Over the moon,' Marcus shook his head at Rochelle, then turned to Lamont and Mia. 'Come on.'

Mia took her glass. Lamont picked up his, trying to not make a face. He sniffed the glass, his nose curling from the strength alone.

'Just down it in one, L,' said Marcus. They toasted, and both poured it back. Lamont swallowed the alcohol, then launched into a huge coughing fit. His chest and throat felt like they were on fire. Marcus guffawed.

'Lightweight. Here, the second one will go down nicely.'

———

By the time Lamont finished the second drink, he was leaning big time. The room swayed around him, and he struggled to focus. He heard Marcus and Mia giggling; the sound distorted. His head pounded, and he could feel the liquor in his belly. He felt free of the usual woes he seemed to carry around. Lamont wished Erica was nearby so he could tell her the truth about his feelings. Somewhere amid his thinking, Mia and Marcus disappeared. Only Rochelle remained, now watching television.

'Do you mind me watching with you?' Lamont cringed at how foreign and magnified his voice sounded. Rochelle shrugged.

'Tell me about yourself,' Lamont said, wanting to make conversation. She glared, turning back to the TV.

'There's no need to be rude,' The liquor made him confident. 'I'm trying to get to know you, that's all.'

Rochelle gave him another look, this one seemed devoid of aggression or attitude. It was deeply speculative.

'You're much more attractive when you're quiet,' she said flatly. Her words punctured Lamont's vibe. He closed his eyes and rubbed his head, wishing he'd declined the liquor.

'Do you mind if I have some water?'

———

They didn't stay long. Marcus and Mia came downstairs a while later with rumpled clothing. Marcus counted out some money and threw it on the coffee table, then he and Lamont left.

The chilly night air removed whatever vestiges of alcoholic influence remained for Lamont. He swayed slightly for a few steps, then became steadier on his feet. Marcus prowled alongside him, tense, eyes flitting in every direction. The Hood was his jungle, and he always had to be on point.

'Where did you disappear to?' Lamont asked. Marcus laughed.

'Where do you think? I went to see my girl, not to sit around watching *London's Burning*.'

'Why did you bring me?'

'Because, you sit in that house all day, reading books and cleaning up after your Auntie like *Cinderella*. I just wanted you to loosen up.'

'Fair enough.' Lamont smiled. As tough as Marcus was, he cared about him, and it was touching.

'What did you think of Rochelle?'

'She seemed nice.' Lamont picked his words carefully. Rochelle was stunning, but closed off, and it made him wonder why. He recalled her comments about his looks, ignoring the sudden heat rushing through him.

'I'd love to hit that.' Marcus rubbed his hands together.

Lamont paused. 'Wait, I thought—'

'I know what you thought. I let people believe it. Truth is, Mia's always watching me. Rochelle's sexier,' Marcus went on. 'Still, Mia knows her role. She lets me store shit in the yard, and she gives a blowjob that'll curl your toes.'

Lamont listened, happy to walk along and let Marcus ramble about blowjobs.

'You should bang Rochelle. Get her to take your cherry,' Marcus said offhandedly. Lamont stopped in the middle of the street.

'What are you talking about?'

Marcus laughed. 'I know you're a virgin. Doesn't matter. Just lose it ASAP. Do that and you might develop some game.'

Lamont stuck a finger up at his friend, and they began walking again. He didn't know how Marcus had worked it out. He'd never confided in his friend about anything to do with girls, but Marcus was more perceptive than he gave him credit for.

They had almost reached home when Lamont's stomach churned worse than ever.

'Oh shit!' he groaned, doubling over and throwing up. Marcus chuckled as he retched two more times, holding his stomach, groaning like someone had hit him.

'C'mon, lightweight. Let's get you inside and get you some water.' Marcus was still laughing like a madman. He held out his hand. Lamont grabbed it. They walked the rest of the way in silence.

———

The next day, Lamont was still messed up from the alcohol. Shaking it off, he traipsed to play football as he did several times a week. A man named Nigel Worthington held the sessions. Nigel was a broad-shouldered man who had always been around the Hood. He'd had a promising football career until a bad tackle put an end to that. Undeterred, Nigel refused to sit around. He started his own business and began coaching some local kids for free on the side.

Lamont changed into the provided uniform and dutifully completed the rigorous callisthenics they performed at the beginning of the session. They completed press-ups, sit-ups, sprints and a whole other medley of exercises. Lamont loved the discipline, and he loved pushing himself. It also remained the only time Auntie allowed him to have any fun. By the time they finished, everyone was sucking in air.

Nigel allowed them to drink some water, then laid out a succession of football drills for them to complete. The rules were simple. Everyone had to take part and if one person didn't, all the kids were banned from playing the end-of-session match. As the kids came down hard on anyone who didn't take part, this rarely happened.

Once the drills were over, Nigel selected two captains and they picked the teams. Once done, Nigel blew his whistle, and the match was up and running.

Lamont received the ball and went past two players like they weren't even there. He wanted to go all the way, but forced himself to pass to another player, who scored. It was a one-sided match after that. Lamont got two goals and set up three more. Playing football was the only time he felt accepted. Everyone knew his background but on the football pitch it didn't matter that he wore cheap clothing. All that mattered was his performance.

Once they had tidied up and the other kids had gone, Lamont was alone with Nigel. He was about to leave when Nigel called him back.

'I'll give you a lift, Lamont. You don't need to walk.'

'It's not far,' Lamont quickly said.

'I don't mind. Give me two minutes to put these cones away and we'll set off.'

Lamont quietly sat in Nigel's Volvo listening to *Phil Collins*. He only recognised the particular song because he'd heard it on the radio countless times. It surprised him that Nigel was a fan.

'How are you doing, Lamont?'

'I'm doing fine,' he replied. Nigel had never offered him a lift before, nor had he ever asked how he was doing. He wasn't rude, but his focus was teaching them to play football, not trying to pry into their lives.

'You played well today. You've taken on board everything I've taught you. You were really implementing some good one-touch football and your movement off the ball is amazing.'

'Thanks.' Lamont didn't know what to say. He had joined the football sessions with an inflated ego, believing he was the best. Nigel refused to start him for any matches, but he never complained. When given the opportunity, he scored hatfuls of goals, before being dropped again. He almost quit, but finally realised the point Nigel was trying to make.

During the next match, he waited to start and when he came on, set up two goals and kept the ball moving with some tight passing. After that his relationship with Nigel improved.

'Have you ever thought about taking it further?' Nigel asked.

'Taking what further?'

'Football. You could go far. Seriously,' Nigel continued. 'You have the traits teams look for when selecting young talent. You could get to the top.'

Lamont's eyebrow rose. He was good, but didn't think he had anywhere near the talent needed to play professionally.

'What do you think? I know it's daunting. I'd be there to help you out though. I have good contacts and I'm certain I could get you a trial. What do you say?'

Lamont sensed Nigel meant well, but didn't like the fact he was pressuring him into a decision. Auntie would never agree to it, anyway, and she was still his legal guardian.

'I'd need to have a think about it.'

Nigel frowned, slowly nodding.

'No problem. That's no problem at all. Let me know when you've decided. I'll set everything up. You won't need to worry.'

Lamont wondered about Nigel's angle. *Was he offering to be his agent? Was Lamont his ticket to the big time?*

'How are things with your Auntie?' Nigel glanced at Lamont as they stopped at a red light.

'Fine,' he mechanically replied. He had shut down now. He gave the same answer to teachers when they'd enquired about Auntie.

'Good. That's excellent. I'll shut up and get you home now.'

———

The next night, Lamont was reading a book when there was a loud knock at the front door. Auntie and Marika were out. Lamont smiled when he saw his friend standing there.

'Yes, L!' Levi Parker greeted him. Auntie didn't allow his friends in the house, so he shut the door and they sat outside.

'Easy, Levi. What's up?'

Levi beamed. He was the same age and size as Lamont, but more confident, living well thanks to the drugs his older brother sold. He wore his hair in neat, thin cornrows and rocked a sports jacket and tracksuit bottoms with Nike's and a thin gold chain.

'I've got some real good news, L. We're gonna make some money!'

'Doing what?'

Levi glanced around.

'Can you leave here?'

'Auntie said to stay until she got back.'

Levi frowned. 'Stop by my Nana's yard when you can. I've got summat to show you.'

———

Once Auntie returned, Lamont headed out to see Levi. He lived two streets down so he didn't have far to walk. A few of the elders in the Hood were milled around, talking in loud voices and laughing. They greeted Lamont warmly, and he was polite in return. Some had been friends of his parents and occasionally told him stories about them; stories Auntie was too lazy to share.

Knocking on Levi's door, he waited for an answer.

'Lamont! How have you been?' said Nana Parker, warmly greeting him. She was in her sixties and seemed to be perpetually cold. Every time he saw her, she wore a thick cardigan and warm clothing, even in the summer.

'Hello, Nana P. Are you okay?' He made conversation for a few minutes, then walked up the stairs to Levi's room, knocking on the door.

'Come in, L!' Levi called out. It startled Lamont to see Levi sitting on his bed smoking. Next to him was the biggest bag of weed Lamont had ever seen.

'What's that for? Are you gonna smoke it?'

'Course not. We're gonna sell it. Craig's gonna hook us up. Are you in?'

Lamont wasn't stupid. He knew how things worked in the Hood. More people were selling drugs these days, and there was a lot of potential profit. Craig Parker had started out selling weed and now moved heroin and crack for one of the local shot callers. He made enough money to show off and also pay his Nana's bills. Their father had run out on them, their mother was too strung out on drugs to be a good parent. Craig had stepped up at an early age to feed his family, and Lamont admired that.

'No, I'm not in.' Despite his obvious struggle, he didn't want to become just another black kid selling drugs. He had worked too hard and taken too much crap at school to give in now.

'You need the money more than I do. Your Auntie's got you living on some real slave shit, man. What else are you gonna do? I wanna go fifty/fifty with you, L.'

'I just can't do it.'

Levi sighed, shrugging.

'I just wanted to help you. Here, try this.' He held out the spliff. Lamont shook his head.

'No thanks.'

'C'mon L, you don't go to prison for having a couple' burns.' Levi sucked his teeth and took a deep toke. He tried holding it, but ended up coughing.

'Nicely done,' said Lamont, laughing.

'Whatever. Where's Marcus at these days?'

'Doing his thing. He's not at home much. He's out, or he's at Mia's.'

'Mia . . . I'd have her,' Levi said almost reverently.

'Yeah, she's nice.'

'Her sister's sexy too. I was chilling with Dennis, and he said Marcus is doing them both, and that he's got them on Spencer Place making money. That true?' Levi asked. Spencer Place was a road in Chapeltown, synonymous with prostitution. They knew people their age who had slept with the women who roamed there.

'No, it's not true. They're cool. I was chilling with them last week.'

'For real? Yo, you need to rush her sister. If it was me, I'd have made a move by now,' Levi bragged. Lamont just let him go on. He liked to listen, Levi liked to talk. Their personalities were in sync.

'Whatever, man. I need to go anyway, before Auntie complains.'

Levi finished his spliff and emptied the ashtray into the bin.

'Look, if you change your mind about selling, you know where I am. Got it?'

'Got it.'

———

Levi's offer remained on Lamont's mind for days, the temptation growing. He could work towards building his future. He could get out from under Auntie's tyrannical reign, get somewhere nice for him and Marika to live. They would be happy.

If he didn't get caught.

Weed was minor compared to some other drugs on the streets, but it was still illegal and people still went to prison for selling it. If Lamont was locked up, even if it was only in a young offender's institute, Marika would be at the mercy of their Auntie. He knew Auntie favoured Marika and wouldn't mistreat her. She would dote on her more. That was what he feared most of all; his sister becoming like their poisonous Aunt.

When school finished, Lamont and Erica walked to the park

together. Erica talked non-stop but he stared at the ground, wondering how much he could make.

Would Craig let them step up or would he leave them selling only ounces? Would Levi stick to a fifty/fifty split? Was it all worth it?

As he looked down, he noticed his well-worn Gola trainers. He fixated on them, imagining them as a fresh pair of Nike's, the sort Marcus wore. He'd said Lamont could borrow them, but he couldn't bring himself to share his friend's trainers.

'Lamont?'

Startled, he looked up. Erica wasn't next to him. He turned, noting that she had stopped walking now, looking at him with concern.

'Yeah?'

'Are you okay? You looked like you were in a trance.'

'I'm fine. Just thinking.'

'About what? You looked proper serious.'

'Nothing much. Just school stuff,' he lied. Judging by the raised eyebrow, Erica didn't believe him.

Leon and his friends were in the same place when they reached the park. Leon again glared at Lamont, but he wasn't intimidated this time. He smiled to Erica, said goodbye and turned to walk away.

'Oi!' Leon's booming voice called out. Lamont faced him.

'Yeah?'

'Come here. I wanna chat to you,' Leon ordered. Lamont held his ground for a moment, then ambled into the park. He felt the eyes of Leon's friends on him, but ignored them and concentrated on Leon. He swayed on the swing in a baby blue tracksuit with white trainers. Despite the hot sun, he wore his hood, trying to ignore the bead of sweat dripping down his forehead.

'What's up?' Lamont asked. Leon eyeballed him for another moment before he spoke. Erica draped over him, trying and failing to look relaxed.

'What's your deal?'

Lamont frowned. 'My deal with what?'

'Are you a puff?'

23

Leon's friends fell about laughing at the wit of their leader. Thankfully, Erica looked as embarrassed as Lamont did.

'Leon, leave him alone. He's my friend.'

'I know. You told me. I just wanna know if he's your gay friend or if he's after a piece. He's always around you.'

'Like I said, he's my friend. That's why he walked me up here. I came to see you but if you're going to act like this, then I'll leave.'

'What you gonna do? Get this tramp to comb your hair?' Leon cracked. His friends laughed harder. Enraged, Lamont moved towards Leon with his fists clenched.

'What? Are you stepping?' Leon rose, ready to fight, before Erica got in the middle.

'No! L, just leave it. He's being a prick,' she said, pushing him gently away. Leon's friends were on their feet, still glaring. Lamont didn't care. He'd had enough. Enough of people treating him like crap because of circumstances that weren't his to control. He hadn't asked for any of it.

'Fuck this,' he spat. Turning on his heel, he left, ignoring Erica's pleas for him to come back, the abusive taunts of Leon and his cronies.

Lamont's rage hadn't diminished by the time he arrived home. He slammed the front door as he stormed into the house.

'That you, Lamont? Who do you think you are, slamming my door!' Auntie shouted. Ignoring her, Lamont stomped upstairs and dropped his school bag on the floor.

'Oi, I'm talking to you? Did you hear what I said?' Auntie barged into his room. She glowered and he returned the look without flinching.

'I heard you.'

'Take that look off your face, before I knock it off,' Auntie warned. Ignoring her again, he continued to glare. Her eyes flashing, Auntie slapped him across the face, the sound ricocheting around the room. Lamont stayed where he was, willing himself to ignore the stinging feeling.

'Did you hear me!' she screamed. Still, he didn't say a word. His eyes desperately wanted to water, but he wouldn't allow it. He wouldn't give Auntie that satisfaction. Not this time. He was done being the victim. His hands balled into fists, but remained by his side. Auntie noticed.

'You wanna fight do you? You ungrateful piece of shit. Get your chores done before I call someone round to teach you a lesson. Is that what you want?'

The front door opened before Lamont could answer and they heard Marika's voice from the bottom of the stairs.

'Auntie, I'm home! Are you here?'

'Coming, sweetness,' Auntie called out with false enthusiasm. She gave Lamont an ugly scowl. 'We're not done, boy. Chores. Now.'

With that she left.

CHAPTER THREE

Tuesday 11 March 1997

LATER THAT NIGHT, Lamont left the house without telling Auntie. The mellow night air had people out in force, chilling and shooting the shit. It was one thing he loved about Chapeltown. There was a sense of community that you didn't get in other areas. Heading briskly along the roads, Lamont stopped at Levi's place.

'Yes, L. You good?' Levi greeted him.

'Can we talk?'

Levi nodded. 'Come. We'll go upstairs.'

The two boys traipsed to Levi's bedroom. Lamont had always liked it. It had everything; a colour TV, a PlayStation, and a CD player with two tape slots. The walls were adorned with posters of everything from *Wu-Tang Clan* to *Tupac*.

'What's up, man? You look stressed,' said Levi.

'I've changed my mind.'

'About what?'

Lamont stared at him until finally, his friend caught on.

'What changed your mind?'

'Look at me,' Lamont said, tone still solemn.

'What are you on about?'

'I'm broke, living with a woman that hates me, and everyone

thinks I'm some tramp. Like it's my fault my parents died.' All Lamont's frustration exploded from him. Levi watched in stunned silence as he vented about the altercation with Leon.

'Shoulda smacked them up, L. Never let anyone take you for an idiot.'

'That's the thing. Everyone takes the piss; all because of how I look. I'm sick of it. You want us to sell weed, we'll sell it. Tell me what you want me to do.'

Levi grinned. He wanted to sell for his brother but didn't want to do it alone.

'Gimme a couple' days to talk to Craig and set summat up.'

'Why so long?' Lamont wanted to get started as soon as possible. The quicker they started selling, the quicker he would make money.

'Craig's never here. He pays Nana's bills and gives her money for food and stuff, but he's always out and about, staying at different yards and shit.'

'Okay. Get at me as soon as you can.'

'I like this fire! Keep it up and we'll get rich!'

———

By the time Lamont slipped back inside, Auntie was already in bed. Quietly locking the door, he took off his trainers and padded carefully up the stairs. He was about to go into his room when Marcus's door opened.

'C'mere.'

Surprised, Lamont entered Marcus's room. Like Levi's it was kitted out with the latest electronics. Marcus also had a set of large dumbbells and some barbells. There were several Flex magazines tossed all over the place and a foldaway weightlifting bench in the corner.

Lamont stood awkwardly by the door. As cool as he and Marcus were, he didn't spend much time in Marcus's room.

'I need a favour.' Marcus rummaged in a drawer. For whatever reason he was shirtless, wearing only a pair of black tracksuit bottoms.

'What's up?'

'I'm doing a move, but one of my guys can't make it. I need you to step in. I'll pay you two hundred quid. Cash in hand.'

The money immediately swayed Lamont, but he held back.

'What kinda move?'

'You know what I do, L, so don't try playing dumb. You don't need to do anything. Stand there and let me and my dude handle it. Jump in if it goes wrong. Easy money.'

Lamont hesitated, thinking about what he could buy. Since his argument with Leon, he thought only about bettering his circumstances. He would not wallow anymore.

'L, we're family, so I'm gonna kick it up to two fifty. We need to go though. My boy's got us a car, and he's gonna be outside any minute. Are you in?'

Lamont took another second to think, but his mind was made up.

'I'm in.'

———

Marcus told Lamont to dress to blend in, so he picked out a pair of frayed black trousers and a black hooded top. He kicked on his black trainers and was good to go. They left the house. A Vauxhall Cavalier waited, a youngish boy with a rough-looking face behind the wheel. He nodded stoically at Marcus and stared Lamont down.

'Yo, this is, L. L, this is Victor, or *Big V*,' Marcus introduced them. They climbed into the car, and Victor drove away. Marcus stared out of the window. Lamont sat in the back, his heart hammering. He was going on his first ever move. He'd heard of them before. People went on moves for all kinds of reasons, mostly for money or fun. Lamont wanted to ask what they were doing, who they were doing it to. Most of all, he wanted to go home. He felt like Tre from *Boyz N' Tha Hood*, in the back of the ride and wanting to have the guts to tell Big V to pull over. He took a deep breath, remembering he was doing this for the money.

After a long drive, the car pulled to a stop on a random street.

Marcus and Victor climbed out. Lamont followed suit, not recognising the area.

'Keep a lookout, L,' Marcus instructed as he and Victor opened the car boot. Lamont watched in horror as he saw Marcus slip what looked like a gun into his trouser waistband. Victor gripped two worn-looking baseball bats. He handed one to Lamont.

'Here, put this on too.' Marcus threw a balled-up black item to Lamont, and he unravelled the balaclava. It clearly belonged to the guy he was standing in for and reeked of sweat. He put it on, tugging it down to ensure it concealed his face.

'Right then. L, take the back. Me and Vic will take the front. Anyone comes at you, smack 'em with the bat. Understand?'

Lamont nodded, trying to ignore the jitters in his stomach. He felt like if he opened his mouth he would throw up. Evidently his fear showed on his face because Victor finally spoke.

'He looks shook. Are you sure he's up for it?'

'He'll be fine. Come on, let's get in place.'

The trio hurried along. Slipping down two streets, they stopped in front of a dilapidated looking terraced house. It seemed to loom in front of Lamont like some haunted house from an old vampire movie. Imposing and eerily majestic.

Remembering his instructions, Lamont stumbled around to the back of the house. He listened out for noises and he didn't have to wait long. There was a loud crash, a woman's screams, then a scuffle. Trying the backdoor, he was startled to find it open. He hurried into the house toward the noise, entering the room in time to see Marcus hit a mousy-haired man in the face with the butt of his gun.

'Where's it at?' he bellowed.

'Mate, you've got the wrong house. There's nowt here,' The man moaned, blood staining his greying white vest. In the corner, Victor restrained a chubby, screaming woman.

'Shut your mouth!' He slapped her. The man tried to rush at Victor, but Marcus hit him again.

'I said, where is it? Don't play with me!' He hit the man a third time, then instructed Victor to hit the woman again. Victor threw

29

her on the floor and jabbed the bat into her ribs as she retched and coughed.

'That's enough!' Lamont shouted. Victor and Marcus both looked at him.

'Shut up. You know why we're here, so don't go acting like a punk.' Marcus turned back to his victim. 'I'm gonna ask you one more time, then my man there's gonna open up your missus! Where is it at?'

'It's u-upstairs,' the man finally stammered.

'Upstairs where?'

'Main bedroom. Under the mattress.'

'Yo!' Marcus got Lamont's attention, 'go get it. Don't come back down without it.'

Lamont's legs felt like lead as he willed himself to walk up the stairs. The hallway was a complete mess, the front door wide open, probably from Marcus's entry. When he reached the top, Lamont walked into one room. It was a cluttered, boxy mess. He checked it anyway and found nothing. He didn't know what they had come for, but assumed it was money or jewellery.

The next room was larger, though equally messy, with clothes and shoes strewn all over the place. He put down the bat and lifted the mattress. He found a carrier bag there, which he grabbed. Leaving the mattress where it was, he headed back downstairs and handed the wares to Marcus. Marcus peered into the bag.

'Did you look?' he asked.

'No, I didn't,' Lamont's voice was calmer than expected.

'Okay,' Marcus turned back to the blooded man. 'Listen, I'm gonna take this and that's the end. You wanna make an issue of it, I'm gonna come back and pop one in your woman. When the police come, don't tell them anything, or we'll be back.' Kicking the man again, he signalled for them to leave.

They ran down the roads back to the car. Lamont felt like he was in a dream. It all felt too surreal. He couldn't believe what he had just taken part in. Again feeling his stomach, he took deep breaths, trying to avoid being sick.

'L! Come on!' Marcus yelled. He got his bearings and began

running again. They climbed into the car and Victor sped off down the road.

'Right, slow down, Vic,' Marcus said when they were away. 'We don't wanna get a pull with this strap on us.'

Victor did as ordered. Lamont trembled in the back, still shocked at what had transpired.

'Oi, L?' Marcus called from the passenger seat. Lamont looked at him.

'Take the mask off, you plum.'

Victor laughed as he removed the smelly balaclava and threw it to the side.

'Where did you find this guy? He's a pussy!'

Marcus's face darkened.

'Pull over. Now.'

Victor pulled the car to the side of the road. Without warning, Marcus's arm shot out and he began choking him.

'Yo! What are you doing?' He spluttered, trying in vain to break Marcus's grip.

'L's my brother. Talk to him with respect or I'll end you. Understand! Well, do you?' Marcus's eyes popped, spit flying from his mouth.

'Yeah! Y-Yeah I understand! Let me go,' Victor yelled. Marcus released the hold.

'Good. Start the car. Pegz is waiting for us.'

Subdued, Victor drove to a park in Harehills. The three of them walked to the swings. It was pitch black now, the park deserted, save for two figures in tracksuits sitting on the swings. They stood when they saw them approaching.

'Yes, Pegz,' Marcus greeted him.

'Safe, Marcus. You get it?' Pegz asked. He was a peanut coloured man, very skinny, with shifty looking eyes. He appeared older than Marcus, and spoke with an obvious familiarity. His companion had his heavily muscled arms folded. He was so large he even made Marcus look small.

'Yeah. It's here.' Marcus held out the carrier bag. Pegz peered inside, taking the package from the bag and smiling. It was drugs

— a white block Lamont assumed meant it was cocaine. Pegz beamed.

'You're a legend, Marcus. Did Daryl give you any trouble?'

'Nah. We smacked him and his missus around.'

'That's my Don! What did we agree on? Two grand?'

'That sounds right.'

Pegz handed Marcus a stack of money. Marcus counted it, slapped hands with Pegz and they were on their way back to the car. Marcus handed them both their shares.

'Good work, L. For real.'

'How did he know the man's name?' Lamont said.

'Who?'

'Pegz. How did he know who you robbed?'

'Oh. That's his brother-in-law.'

'Are you serious?'

'Pegz has a baby to his sister. Some horrible little thing from Seacroft. Pegz is the one who told us where to go.'

'That's wrong though.' Lamont shook his head. Marcus glanced at him.

'This is the life. Everyone is looking for a come up. You just got two-fifty for standing in the corner looking like you were gonna shit yourself. Sit back and enjoy. Don't worry about the hows and whys.'

Victor laughed, but turned it into a cough when Marcus glared at him. When they reached Auntie's, Marcus turned to Victor and slapped his hand.

'Good work, man. Ditch the car. Store the tools for next time. I'll get at you tomorrow. Stay quiet too, okay?'

'I know the drill,' Victor assured him. He gave Lamont a nod and drove away.

'That was easy,' Marcus yawned. 'I'm gonna grab some food and maybe go to Mia's. You coming?'

Lamont wanted to be by himself, needing to process what had transpired.

'I have school tomorrow.'

'So what? You had school last time. Come and have another drink.'

Lamont shook his head. 'Not tonight.'

'Check you later then.' Marcus touched fists with Lamont and disappeared down the road.

When Lamont was inside, he brushed his teeth, stripped down and climbed into bed. His heart was still pounding. He lay there, thinking about everything that could have gone wrong. They could have been arrested, or badly hurt if more people had been at the house.

Lamont hadn't found the robbery itself difficult, but the casual violence unnerved him. Watching Victor hit the woman in the stomach had appalled him. He didn't want to be associated with that. He hid the cash he'd received, feeling ashamed for taking part. He hadn't harmed Darryl or his woman, but felt shame just the same.

So much had happened today. All the events seemed to hit him at once. He grew angry as he recalled the way Leon had treated him. The way Auntie attacked him. Lamont had made some money, but he was still in the same position as he was before the robbery. He was still a piece of shit, looked down on by everyone around him.

———

Lamont's mood continued into the next day. He kept his head down, but found himself answering the teachers back with more force than normal. Hurrying toward the gates after school, he found Tower and two of his friends waiting.

'Look who it is,' Tower laughed to his cronies when he saw Lamont. 'It's our favourite tramp.'

Lamont ignored them, keeping his eyes on Tower. Tower liked to bait him, but he wasn't vicious. He was just a bully who liked an audience. Lamont found himself strangely calm, weighing up the situation.

'You good though, L? You doing well? Because those trainers are leaning to the side!'

Tower and his friends laughed. He reminded Lamont of Erica's boyfriend, needing to poke fun at him to make himself feel better. Had he looked at Lamont — truly looked at him — he would have known that today wasn't the day to provoke him.

A small crowd gathered around now. It was the end of the day and everyone wanted to see the drama. No one really liked Tower, but they laughed anyway.

'Seriously though, L. It must be hard in your household. You're pathetic If I was you, man, I'd just kill myself.'

Lamont felt himself twitch, hands clenching and unclenching, a pounding in his ears. The crowd whispered to one another, pointing at him like he was in a zoo. He trembled, a lone tear rolling down his face. Tower noticed.

'Are you serious? Yo, he's crying!' he bellowed with laughter. Lamont was on the verge. Tower was in his face now. He patted Lamont on the head like a dog, and that was all it took. With a guttural roar from deep within the recesses of his soul, Lamont struck.

Tower was completely off-guard. The blow caught him flush on the cheek, distorting his features for a second, his face almost clay-like. He staggered back, eyes narrowing as he threw a sloppy return punch. Lamont stepped to the left and caught him with a hook, sending him to the ground. The bully tried scrambling to his feet, only to see stars as Lamont kicked him in the face. One of Tower's friends tried to intervene but tripped over his own feet. Lamont kicked him, keeping him down. Tower struggled to his feet, and Lamont whaled on him with lefts and rights.

The other two bullies flung Lamont to the floor and began kicking him. Lamont curled up, then lunged and tackled one of them. They rolled around, trying to pin him down, but he was unhinged, his hands free, lashing out in all directions, hitting anyone he could.

Finally, several teachers waded into the midst to break up the fight. It took two of them to contain Lamont, who struggled to get free. Physically dragging him away, they led him up the path and back into school.

That evening, Lamont sulked in his room. For his antics at school they had suspended him for a week. The head teacher threatened expulsion, but several kids came forward saying that Lamont had been provoked. This combined with his stellar attendance record and schoolwork led her to change her mind.

Lamont was calmer, but he didn't feel better. He thought he would after finally getting the better of Tower, but he felt hollow. Tower wouldn't take the beating lightly. He would probably make Lamont's life more hellish than it already was.

Lamont shrugged, his head bowed low. He needed someone. Someone he could talk to and unload on, but he had no one like that in his life. He hadn't spoken to Erica since leaving her in the park with Leon. She had tried speaking to him during the day but he had rebuffed her. He knew it wasn't Erica's fault that Leon had started with him, but she went out with him, which made her partly responsible.

There was a knock at Lamont's bedroom door. He ignored it. Auntie had ripped into him earlier, threatening to kick him out. After striking him several times, she ordered him upstairs. Lamont had been there ever since, stomach rumbling with hunger. He could have gone downstairs and made something, but his body wouldn't cooperate.

The person knocked again, louder.

'L, I'm coming in,' Marcus said. He walked into the room and shut the door behind him. 'Why are you sitting in the dark?'

'I like the dark. It's peaceful.'

Marcus shook his head and turned the light on, the glare making Lamont squint for a second. Marcus looked down at him, concern evident in his obsidian eyes.

'I heard about what happened today. Are you good?'

Lamont nodded. 'I'm fine.'

'I heard you spazzed on Tower and his boy's, bro. Word is you were brawling with like five of them, and then teachers came and you were fighting with them too!' Marcus sounded impressed.

'He pushed me too far,' Lamont replied.

'Tower's a prick, thinking he's connected. I'm gonna talk to his brother, and I promise he ain't gonna trouble you again. What did the witch say?'

'Usual line. *I'm a disgrace, blah blah.* She's threatening to throw me out.'

'How many times has she used that one? This place would turn to shit without you and she knows that. Let her say what she's saying.' Marcus paused. 'Are you sure you're okay?'

Again, Lamont nodded.

'I'm just saying . . . I know how I can be, but you're my brother. If there's anything you really need to talk about, I'm always gonna be here for you.'

Lamont smiled. 'I know, man. I appreciate it. I don't know what's wrong with me . . . Guess I'm just tired of it all. Is this the best it gets for me? Someone troubles me constantly, I finally stand up for myself, and I end up getting suspended from school? When's it supposed to change? When are things gonna get right for me?'

'Make them right, blood. Don't sit around waiting for it because I'll tell you something; people are so screwed up that you can't rely on things being right. Make them right by doing your own thing.' Marcus paused again. 'I've got another move if you're interested.'

Lamont shook his head. 'No thanks. It's not for me.'

'You sure? There's three hundred quid in it for you.'

'I'm sure. Thanks though. What you said; I think you're right.'

Marcus grinned. 'Read one of your books or something. Just kick back.'

'Yeah, I think I'll do that.'

CHAPTER FOUR

Saturday 15 March 1997

LAMONT WOKE early and tiptoed down the stairs. Marika had stayed at a friend's house the night before, and Auntie was sleeping in, so neither were in his way.

Making himself some juice, he did some press-ups on the kitchen floor, then ate breakfast. When he finished, he tidied up and rushed through the usual chores before taking a shower. He swiftly dressed and rooted around his room, collecting his hidden money.

Including what he had made working with Marcus, Lamont had saved over four hundred pounds. The goal of independence for he and Marika was still a while away. For now, Lamont was tired of looking how he did. It was time to change that.

Since going to live with Auntie, Lamont couldn't recall ever having new clothes. She bought a lot of his clothes from various jumble sales and charity shops. Her clothing was all designer, and even Marika had some nice pieces. With Lamont, she told him he grew too quickly for her to be buying him new stuff. He'd heard it so often he almost started to believe it.

Gathering his money and making sure the notes were neat, Lamont shoved them into his pocket and left the house, locking the door behind him. He hurried down the street and crossed the road, walking to town. It was a beautiful morning. It wasn't warm, but the breeze was pleasant on his face. By the time he reached the city centre, he was hungry again. Buying a sandwich and a drink, he ate quickly, standing against a wall opposite the St John's centre. When he finished, he went into a shoe store.

As soon as Lamont entered, he smelled the suede and the leather of the different trainers and shoes. When Auntie would take him shopping when he was younger, he wasn't allowed to even look in the shop's direction. As he had grown older he would go in with Marcus or one of his other friends, usually just to look. Now, he would buy.

Lamont navigated his way through some other shoppers and gazed at the Nike section of trainers. He noticed the shop staff watching him out of the corner of his eye. One stood near the exit in what she thought was a discreet manner. It galled him that they would just assume he was some scruffy thief. Nostrils flaring, he reached for the best pair of trainers he could see; a pair of white, grey and royal blue Nike Tailwinds. Signalling to one of the staff, he beckoned him over. The man came, but dragged his feet. He was bald and wiry, his black and white polo shirt and black trousers hanging loosely on his frame.

'How can I help?' he sounded bored.

'I want these in a size nine,' said Lamont. The man hesitated, sharing a look with another member of staff. The nerves Lamont felt walking in, dissipated. This person didn't know him; he would not let them look down their noses.

'Is that a problem? Do you not have any in stock?' Lamont raised his voice, causing people to look over. Abashed, it galvanised the man into action.

'Sorry, I'll go look now.'

Lamont watched the man hurry away. He glared at the woman standing by the door, and she turned away. After trying on the trainers, he paid at the till, hiding a smile at the look of shock that appeared on the retailer's face. He tried getting him to buy a host of other accessories, but he turned him down and left the shop with his head held high. He went to a few other shops buying various t-shirts and a few tracksuits.

Hands heaving with bags, Lamont went to Waterstones, his favourite bookshop. The second he walked in, he was as always enthralled by the books. He glanced around, mooching around the different sections and selecting two paperbacks along with a copy of *Prince* by *Machiavelli*. After paying, he treated himself to a taxi home.

As Lamont sat in the back of the car, lost in his own thoughts, he felt like a different person. He had new clothes, new books to read, and he was travelling home in style. It all seemed surreal, and he wondered if it was a sign, if fate was trying to tell him that crime paid. For years he'd toed the line, receiving nothing but scorn. He had turned to crime for the first time and now he seemed to be on an entirely different path. It was strange.

Lamont paid the driver around the corner from his house, climbing out with his bags. He unlocked the front door, then locked it behind him.

'Lamont!'

Ignoring Auntie, he hurried upstairs, hesitating outside his room.

'Lamont, come here right now!'

'Thinking fast, he opened Marcus's door and put the bags in there. Hurrying to the bathroom, he flushed the toilet and pretended to wash his hands.

'Didn't you hear me calling you?' Auntie was on him the second he entered the living room. She was smoking with a vengeance, taking full advantage of Marika being out of the house.

'Sorry, I needed the toilet,' he lied.

'Where were you?'

'I went for a walk.'

Technically, he'd walked into town, he rationalised.

'Who said you could do that? There's work for you to do.'

'I needed some fresh air, and I didn't want to disturb your sleep.'

Auntie glared. Finishing her cigarette, she beckoned Lamont to come with her. They traipsed upstairs and she barged into his room, looking around. Eyes narrowing, she turned back to him, eyes flashing with anger.

'Next time you wanna leave the house, tell me first. You're not a damn grown up yet.'

'Yes, Auntie. I will.' Lamont did his best to hide his glee. If Auntie had found the clothing, all hell would have broken loose. Once the clothes went into his battered wardrobe, she would be none the wiser. It wasn't as if she ever did his washing, anyway.

'Get downstairs and do your chores.'

'I did them this morning,' said Lamont. Walking past Auntie, he didn't even wait for her to say anything else as he headed to make a drink. Shopping was thirsty work.

———

Lamont resisted the urge to wear his new clothing when he ventured out later on that night. Marika wasn't back from her sleepover and Auntie had gone out. Not wanting to remain in the house, he roamed the streets.

Levi had contacted him earlier, ringing Auntie's landline to let him know he was still waiting for Craig. Lamont's intent to sell drugs hadn't abated. He would do whatever was necessary to leave Auntie and all her mess behind. Working with Levi would help him put something together.

Stopping at a paper shop, he bought a bottle of Ribena, sipping it as he slouched against a nearby wall. He was so lost in his thoughts that it took him a moment to realise someone was trying to talk to him.

The baby-faced teenager was Lamont's age, with skin the same shade as a peanut shell, closely cropped hair and harsh, dark eyes. He was stockily built, the outlines of muscle visible through the grey hooded top he wore.

'What's up, Shorty?' Lamont greeted his friend.

'Nothing, saw you chilling over here so I thought I'd come see how you were doing. Heard you got kicked out of school for stabbing someone?' Shorty raised an eyebrow.

'I got into a fight and ended up suspended. It involved no

knives.' Lamont couldn't even think where that rumour would have come from.

'Thought it sounded a little dodgy. How come you were fighting? You're usually trying to walk away when people trouble you.'

'They provoked me.'

'Always with the big words,' Shorty scoffed. 'Go on then; who provoked you?'

'Tower.'

Shorty's lip curled. 'Ninja's little brother? He's a geek. I hope you smacked him up.'

'I did all right.' Lamont wouldn't boost his ego and tell Shorty the whole story. He sighed, realising he would have to face everyone at school when he went back. He thought about the altercation with Leon. Even after fighting to be left alone, he would still have to deal with Leon's nonsense. He could walk another way home, but the road leading to the park was the quickest route. He could even take the bus, but pride wouldn't let him do that.

'L?'

Lamont jerked out of his reverie.

'Are you high? Why are you acting all spaced out?'

'I've just got some things on my mind. Do you know a dude called Leon?'

'Leon who? What's his surname?'

'I'm not sure. He's about eighteen, nineteen. Hangs around that park near Chapel Allerton. He's kinda light skinned, and he's got a bullethead.'

Shorty scratched his chin. 'Doesn't ring a bell. Is he troubling you?'

Lamont didn't reply. He hadn't asked Shorty because he wanted Leon hurt. He'd hoped he knew Leon and could talk to him.

'Is he?'

Lamont sighed again. 'He hasn't put his hands on me or anything. He doesn't like me being around his girl, and he's threatened me before.'

Shorty's eyes darkened as they analysed Lamont. They had stuck together since the age of five, where they were two of only a handful of ethnic children at their Primary school. By the look he gave him, Lamont knew how this would turn out. It never took much to set off Shorty.

'Where do you see this guy again?' Shorty's voice was even, but Lamont wasn't convinced.

'Chapel Allerton Park, near my school. He's always there with his crew.'

'How many of them?'

'Four or five usually.'

Shorty scratched his chin, his nostrils flaring. He nodded his head as if internally agreeing to something.

'When do you go back to school again?'

'Next week Wednesday,' Lamont replied. Shorty nodded again.

'Cool.'

———

Lamont left school next Wednesday, not surprised to see Shorty and another local goon. His name was Kieron, but everyone called him *K-Bar*. K-Bar was dark-skinned and bony, with thin shoulder length dreadlocks and dead eyes. He was Shorty's crime partner and though doleful, didn't need any excuse to cause trouble.

'L, c'mere,' Shorty called out. Looking left and right, he hurried across the road.

'What are you lot doing up here?'

Shorty laughed. 'We're gonna handle your problem. Come.'

Falling in step, Lamont followed Shorty and K-Bar towards the park.

Leon and his cronies sat in their usual spot, laughing and telling jokes. There were a few girls lingering around. Scanning their faces, Lamont saw none were Erica. Recognising him, Leon scowled.

'What are you looking at?'

Shorty cut his eyes to Lamont. 'Is he the one?'

Lamont nodded.

'Oi! I'm talking to you! Erica's not here to look after you now!'

Shorty rubbed his nose. 'I'll deal with this.'

Without missing a beat, he entered the park and strolled up to Leon. Sensing trouble, Leon's boys closed ranks, causing Lamont and K-Bar to stand at either side of Shorty, ready to back him up.

'Who are you?' Leon didn't like Shorty eyeballing him.

'You need to back off my boy. If I hear that you or any of these dickheads have been troubling him, I'll deal with you myself.'

Leon stood. He towered over Shorty, but the younger man didn't flinch.

'I don't think you know who you're dealing with.'

'No. I don't think you know who *you're* dealing with. L is off limits to you and your crew,' Shorty's voice was calm but he was definitely ready for war. Lamont knew the signs. He had seen Shorty in action before. He took a step back to give him space.

'Listen, little man, leave before I get mad. Take that tramp there with you. If I catch him around Erica again, I'll fuck him up,' said Leon.

That was enough.

Before Leon could react, Shorty levelled him with two swift hits, knocking him into the swing. The girls screamed and ran. Leon's friends waded in, but K-Bar pulled a knife, causing them to freeze.

'Back up. It's one-on-one, or I'm cutting everyone,' K-Bar's voice had enough conviction to cause the group to step back.

Leon was up now. He looked dazed, but the hits had hurt his pride more than anything. He charged Shorty, who saw the move coming and planted his feet into the ground. Grabbing Leon in a front headlock, he brought his knee up, catching him in the face. Bringing his elbow down on his spine, Shorty let the older boy crumple to the ground.

'That all you've got?' He taunted, panting slightly. When Leon tried to rise, he brought his foot back and kicked him in the head. Leon fell back and didn't move. Standing over him, Shorty looked to his friends, frozen with fear at the sight of Shorty's calculated assault on their leader. Without him they were powerless.

'Yo, when *Mr Untouchable* here wakes up, tell him to stay away from L. I'm warning you all once. Find someone else to touch, or we're coming back with more weapons.'

Shorty walked away. K-Bar followed without a word. Lamont snuck a glance at Leon's friends, then trailed Shorty and K-Bar.

————

'I don't think he'll be troubling you anymore, L.'

It had been less than an hour since the fight. The trio stood in the Hood, drinking bottles of Lilt and enjoying the sun.

Shorty was all smiles after beating Leon. Lamont had seen this reaction from his friend before. Violence didn't make Lamont happy, but he wasn't ungrateful. Shorty had beaten up Leon for bullying him. Shorty and Marcus were alike in that way; they cared for little, but protected anyone in their circle. He was lucky to have friends like them.

'Yeah. I think you put a stop to that.'

Shorty drained his bottle and threw it into the street. 'Dudes like him run their mouths because they've got people around them. Hit them a couple times, they crumble like he did.'

Lamont wasn't listening. His eyes were on the bottle that Shorty had thrown.

'Pick that up, man.'

Shorty was talking to K-Bar now. He evidently hadn't heard Lamont.

'Shorty.'

Shorty turned.

'What?'

'That bottle. Pick it up and put it in the bin, man. It's right next to it.'

'What?' Shorty frowned.

'We have to look after our streets. It doesn't hurt to put it in the bin.'

'Is he serious?' Shorty cut his eyes to K-Bar, who shrugged For a second, he grilled Lamont, then burst into laughter and went to get the bottle.

'You're a funny guy, L. People are becoming millionaires selling poison, and you're quibbling over a Lilt bottle.'

'Doesn't matter. It begins with us. We need to look out for our community,' Lamont replied.

'Whatever you say, *Malcolm-X*. Come on, let's go get a ball and play footy.'

———

Lamont had maths with Erica the next day, but she looked like she had been crying, and did her best to avoid him. It stung, but he expected it. Leon was everything to Erica, and the word was already out about the beating Shorty had given him.

Lamont had PE as the last lesson. When he exited the changing rooms, swinging his tattered sports bag, Erica waited.

'Afternoon.' Lamont knew she wouldn't speak first.

'That's all you have to say to me?'

'About what?'

'You and your psycho friends beat up Leon! You should see his face!'

'I won't talk to you if you're going to act like this,' Lamont said calmly, seeing his crush in a whole new light. The fact she had stuck by Leon after he verbally abused him had been a turning point. Their friendship would never be the same.

'How am I supposed to react? Was that really the best way to handle it?' She lowered her voice, but people walking by still glanced at the pair.

'We just wanted to talk. He wanted to act the big man in front of his boys and those girls.'

'One of your friends had a knife!' Erica hissed. Her brow furrowed. 'What girls?'

'That's for you two to discuss. He was a prick to me for no reason, so if you want to analyse anything, analyse that.'

'He's my boyfriend!'

'So what!' Lamont bellowed. 'So what if he's your boyfriend? Are you gonna be with him forever? No! It's a silly, schoolgirl relationship and you know it, so grow up.'

Erica gaped at Lamont. He seemed to radiate an aura, his

nostrils flaring, eyes piercing. It was unnerving to see the meek, quirky boy who walked her home, evolve before her eyes.

'He was asking for what he got. Hopefully, he'll watch his mouth now.'

'L, what happened to you? When did you stop being nice?' Erica asked softly.

'The second I realised that nice guys get crushed by pretty girls like you. I'll see you around.' With that, he strolled past Erica, leaving her openmouthed.

———

When Lamont arrived home, Marika sat on the sofa watching TV, devouring cereal like she hadn't eaten in days. He kissed her on the cheek, put his bags down and took his coat off.

'Where's Auntie?'

'Out. She said you'd make me dinner,' Marika said, with her mouth full of Coco Pops.

'Okay. I'll make it in about ten minutes.'

'I'm hungry now! Why do you think I'm eating cereal?' Marika shouted.

Lamont stood in front of the TV and looked at her. Marika opened her mouth to say something clever, but stopped herself. The fiery look in her brother's eyes scared her. His jaw was clenched tight, his gaze unflinching. Something was different about him, and Marika didn't want to make the wrong move.

CHAPTER FIVE

Friday 21 March 1997

LAMONT FOLLOWED Marcus as he knocked on Mia's door. She answered, giving Lamont a double take. His hair was trimmed, and he wore a new sports jacket with a pair of jeans and some trainers.

'Wow, you look different, L,' she said, her mouth open. Marcus nudged her.

'Let us in then. I've got liquor.' He held up the bottle of brandy. Mia led them into the living room. Rochelle again sat on the sofa, this time reading a book. She acknowledged Marcus and Lamont with a nod.

'Get some cups,' Marcus ordered Mia, who hurried to obey. 'Shelly, what's happening, darling?'

'Nothing, Marcus. Just chilling.'

'Cool. What you reading?'

Rochelle held up the book. It was *To Kill a Mockingbird* by Harper Lee; one of Lamont's favourites.

'Never read it. Any good? You know who else is a big reader?' Marcus didn't even wait for Rochelle to answer his first question.

'Who?'

Lamont's stomach lurched.

'My boy L here. He loves reading, I swear. His room at home is just full of books. Isn't it?' Marcus elbowed him.

Lamont wanted to strangle him. He knew that action wouldn't end well, so instead, he nodded.

'I've got a copy of that at home. I love it,' he mumbled.

'Really?' Rochelle sounded sceptical.

'Yeah. When I was younger, I . . .' Lamont broke off. He had been about to launch into a story about his parents.

'Spit it out then,' Marcus said, not realising.

'Leave him, Marcus.' Rochelle met Lamont's eyes for a moment, then Mia entered with three glasses.

'What are you doing?' Marcus's voice rose.

'What do you mean?'

'There's four of us. Go get another fucking glass.'

'Marcus, you need to watch the way you talk to my sister,' Rochelle said.

Marcus scowled. 'What are you on about?'

'You know what I'm on about. Talk to her properly.'

'Why don't you chill out and go back to your fucking book? This is nothing to do with you.'

'You're in our house, so I think you'll find it has a lot to do with me. Talk to her properly, or leave.'

Mia's timely arrival stopped Marcus from retorting again.

'Come on baby, let's go upstairs. We'll take the drinks with us.'

Marcus glared, vibrating with rage, but allowed himself to be led upstairs.

'You need some better friends,' Rochelle remarked when the door closed. She picked up her book.

'Marcus is family.'

'Marcus is a fool. He has good qualities, but he's got no manners. He talks to my sister like shit, and I won't accept that.'

'That's fair enough. Marcus is family though, like I said, and I don't want you badmouthing him around me.'

Rochelle raised an eyebrow.

'Well, look who grew a backbone while they were away. Guess you got over that whole stuttering thing from last time.'

'Guess I did,' said Lamont, smirking.

'That's good. I like the confidence. Just remember one thing, Lamont.'

'I'm listening, *Shelly.*'

'Good. First, it takes more than some new clothes and a haircut to get me. Remember that. Don't call me Shelly either.'

'You let Marcus call you Shelly . . .'

'If I told Marcus to stop, he'd probably call me it more. That's his mentality. What I'm trying to work out is if it's yours too.' Rochelle looked at Lamont again. There was none of the hostility she had shown last time, and this spurred him on. He stared back, entranced by the way her long dark hair fell over her face; the pronounced curves of her body in the sweatpants and tank-top. Rochelle was extraordinary. It was more than looks. Something about her assertive attitude appealed to him.

'Marcus is Marcus. I'm me.'

'Yeah, but who are you?' challenged Rochelle.

'I told you; I'm me.'

'I need more than that. You and Marcus live together, right?' Rochelle began.

'Yeah.'

'Mia said you both live with some relative of yours. Is that true?'

'Yeah.'

'And you go to the same school?'

'Marcus dropped out last year.'

'I see.'

'I might join him.' It was the first time Lamont had admitted that to anyone.

'Why?' Rochelle shot him a sharp look.

'Why what?'

'Why would you want to drop out?'

'I need to make money,' Lamont said, as if it were the most obvious answer in the world.

'And you don't think that staying in school a few more months and completing your education will lead to a better job?'

'There's no guarantee of that.'

'Oh, so you want easy, street money then?'

'I didn't say that. I'll take whatever money I can,' Lamont corrected.

Rochelle shook her head. 'There was me thinking you had more principles.'

'You know nothing about my life, so don't you dare pass judgement on me for wanting something right now.' Lamont breathed hard, incensed at Rochelle's comment.

'Slow your roll. I'm not passing judgement on you. I'm entitled to my opinion, which is that you're an idiot if you even think about leaving school.'

'What are you doing that's so special?'

'I work in an office in town.'

'What are you working towards?'

'What do you mean?'

'Look at you; there's no way you're going to be just working in an office forever. So what is it? What are you working towards?'

Rochelle blinked, surprised by Lamont's perceptiveness.

'I want to be a teacher.'

'Makes sense, with that little speech you just gave me about education. Primary or high school?'

'Primary. I don't think I could handle teenagers.'

'If you can handle Marcus, you can handle some cheeky teenagers,' Lamont joked. They both laughed, hers a melodic throaty sound that made him think of serene nights, laid on the grass, staring at the stars in the sky. It was so easy talking to Rochelle; no more nerve-wracking than talking to Erica.

Rochelle was older and more assured, but she was still a girl. Lamont no longer felt daunted.

'Thanks. I guess. Can I ask you something?' Rochelle started.

'Go for it.'

'You were going to say something earlier about this book.' She pointed at *To Kill a Mockingbird*. Lamont's stomach lurched again.

'Yeah. I was.'

'What were you going to say?'

'I used to read it with my mum and dad,' he admitted.

'What happened to them?'

'They died. In a car crash.' Lamont's words were hollow. He remembered the screech of tyres, then the darkness. Lamont had woken to a pain that never dissipated. He rubbed his chin, feeling the familiar scar.

'Oh my God. I'm so sorry to hear that.' Rochelle's hand went to her mouth.

'When I was younger, my parents were always trying to get me to read, but I couldn't concentrate. One day, my mum put that same book in front of me and offered me a pound if I read the first three chapters.'

'Did you?'

'By the time I got to chapter three, I'd forgotten to ask for the money. That story made me love reading. I've never looked back.'

Rochelle beamed. 'That's sweet. I feel sorry for people that don't read. Music and books are two of God's greatest inventions.'

'You're not wrong.'

'Lamont?'

'Yeah?'

'Don't leave school. Okay?'

Lamont said nothing. He was woefully inexperienced with girls, but even he was sharp enough to realise that with the story he had just told Rochelle, the dynamics of their conversation had changed.

'I know it's hard. But just promise me you won't. You're so close to the end. I hear what you're saying about the money, but education is important.'

'Okay, I promise,' Lamont said. They looked at each other for another long moment before he changed the subject.

'What part of the book are you up to?'

Rochelle smiled then and began describing to Lamont exactly what Scout Finch was doing. They discussed the merits of the book, the conversation fast-paced and passionate. By the time Mia and Marcus drunkenly lurched downstairs, the pair were closely sat, beaming.

'Aww, this is what I like to see. Don't they look sweet, babe?' said Marcus.

'Yeah, look at them giggling like some school kids,' Mia teased.

'Leave it alone, Mia,' Rochelle's was ice cold again, the smile vanishing. Lamont internally sighed, knowing that the night was over.

'Okay, okay, just saying, Shelle.'

'Yo, L, we need to jet. Ladies, it's been fun.' Marcus kissed Mia and waved at Rochelle. They were nearly at the door when Rochelle spoke.

'Lamont?'

'Yeah?'

'You can call me Shelly if you like,' Rochelle said quietly. Then she picked her book back up as if nothing had happened.

————

'You can call me Shelly . . .'

Lamont rubbed his eyes. Ever since they had left Mia's place, Marcus hadn't shut up.

'What was that about? While I was grinding, what were you two yapping about?'

'We weren't talking about anything in particular. We were just talking,' Lamont tried downplaying it.

'Whatever. I've never seen Rochelle smile like that before. I know when a man is talking smooth. You were running some serious game on her.'

'Just leave it.'

'Yo, I'm proud of you, man. That's a good place to start. Tell you what, if she's anything like her sis, then the grind will be amazing!' Marcus exclaimed. 'We need to go there again tomorrow, then you can vibe her and see what happens.'

'She's just a friend.'

'Don't gimme that nonsense, L. I know more about this stuff than you do. Rochelle is feeling you. You need to handle that.'

'Whatever you say.'

Marcus laughed. Loudly. A front door opened as they walked

past, and a man glared out at them. Marcus glared back, and the man hurriedly closed the door.

'This is a new start for you. Your balls are dropping. You punched up one kid at school, you're going on moves with me and making money! All you need now is to shag Shelly, and you're straight.'

'Focus on shagging Mia right and leave me to my business,' Lamont said jokingly.

'Oh, I see what this is . . . you get a pair of Nikes, and suddenly you're Superman? Let me see how quick you can run in them!' Marcus lunged at Lamont, who dodged him and scarpered up the road. Marcus followed, the pair of them laughing.

———

The next day, Lamont was at Levi's. His Nana was at some function, so they were at the kitchen table, studying a Morrison's carrier bag filled with weed.

'It stinks,' Lamont remarked, making a face and peering into the bag.

'That's good. Means it'll sell quicker.'

'What do we need to start then?'

'I don't know.' Levi scratched his head.

'Didn't Craig tell you?'

'Nah,' Levi laughed, rubbing the back of his neck, 'I made out like you knew what you were doing.'

'Why?'

'Because. He's my brother, man. You know how much shit he gives me. Wanted to show him I could be an asset.'

'We need to find someone who knows what they're doing with this.' Lamont motioned to the bag.

'I know a couple' dudes, but they're like Craig's age. They'll never entertain us.'

Lamont racked his brains, trying to think of someone they could go to. He thought of Marcus, but that was a last resort. Like that, the perfect person popped into his head.

'I know who we can go to.'

———

'L, what's cracking?' Shorty slapped hands with him and Levi.

'You busy? Kinda need to talk to you.'

'Nah, y'all come in. Kick those shoes off though. The carpet's new.'

Shorty had a small flat on Harehills Avenue, off Chapeltown Road, with a nondescript white door. Lamont didn't know who he'd made decorate, but they knew their colours. It had all the latest entertainment devices, similar to Marcus's and Levi's rooms.

Shorty directed the pair to sit on the leather sofa. He picked up his spliff from an ashtray on the coffee table, and lit it. Taking two burns, he offered it to Lamont, who declined. Levi eagerly took it, coughing loudly as the weed hit his lungs.

'Don't hit it so hard. Take time,' said Shorty, laughing. 'What's up, anyway?'

Lamont glanced at Levi for a second.

'We've got some weed. We want your help to sell it.'

Shorty doubled over laughing, almost burning himself with the joint. They watched as his laughter grew louder and more animated. After several minutes, he calmed down.

'Seriously. What's up?' he repeated.

'We've got an ounce of weed, but we don't really know where to start with it. We hoped you could give us some pointers.'

Shorty wiped his eyes. 'L . . . you know what I do, don't you?'

Lamont did. Shorty had been selling weed for a few years. He and K-Bar had started off small, but were growing in reputation.

'Yeah. You can help us.'

'L, y'all are competition. That's gonna mess with my money. What if you pinch my customers? I can't allow that.'

'I feel what you're saying,' Lamont started. 'We're boys though. I'm just asking for some help.'

'This is business. I can't fuck with you,' Shorty said firmly.

'Are you serious?' Levi sneered. 'We're supposed to be boys. Why are you going on dodgy?'

Shorty's expression hardened. '*Going on dodgy?* You lot turn up on my doorstep like the *Chuckle Brothers*, saying you've got weed to sell, but not knowing what to do with it? This is my life. I'm on this shit, twenty-four-seven, get me? I'm not fucking about going to school like you lot. Your brother hustles. Talk to him.'

'Shorty,' Lamont interjected before Levi could retort, 'we can all help each other here. You know my situation, and you know what I'm like. How desperate must I be to turn up here, talking to you like this?'

'That's true.' Shorty folded his arms.

'Nothing happens for free. You said yourself, Craig's doing big things. Come on board with us. Help us get started, and Craig will give us a better price. That means more money for you.'

'What?' Levi spluttered. Lamont impaled him with a look. Shorty leant forward, more interested now.

'You sure you can speak for Craig?'

'Course. Work with us and you'll make more money,' repeated Lamont. Shorty thought it over.

'Deal.'

———

'Lamont, what are you playing at?'

They were headed back to Levi's. He had kept quiet while Lamont and Shorty spoke, but now he wore an ugly expression.

'We needed Shorty's help,' Lamont said.

'What about that crap about a better price?'

'You need to talk to your brother. Make him see sense.'

'Are you serious? Craig will kill me.' Levi's eyes widened.

'No, he won't. This is about money. Tell him you've found someone with a solid client base, meaning he gets a better return. He'll be happy with the extra business,' Lamont assured him. Levi took a deep breath and nodded.

'I hope you're right, bro. I'm gonna get the weed bags and the scales. I'll get back at you when I've spoken to Craig again.'

———

The next few days passed without incident. Levi bought the equipment. He spoke to his brother who agreed to the proposal, just as Lamont suspected. Craig wanted to speak to them directly, summoning them to meet him.

Craig Parker could usually be found on Chapeltown Road, around Landport Street. He sat on a step outside a house, surrounded by an entourage which comprised two large goons, and a smattering of female admirers. Craig had the dark good looks Levi was developing. He dressed the part, usually sporting fresh designer clothes that no one else on the street had. He burned a hole through Lamont as they approached. Lamont met his gaze, knowing instinctively that movements were critical at this point.

'So, you're slanging now?'

It seemed an innocent question, but he sensed Craig wanted more. The street life was cold. Everyone suspected the others' motives. Craig was wilful, always willing to get what he wanted rather than sitting around. He was a Ghetto Prince, gaining momentum as he surged through the drugs game. He'd done well for himself. Better than most people expected.

'Yeah,' Lamont kept his response simple, wanting to lure Craig in. It worked.

'Why?'

'Because I'm broke.'

'So? Get a paper round.'

Craig's entourage burst into peals of laughter as if he had said the funniest thing in the world.

'Like you did?'

Lamont's comeback silenced everyone in the vicinity. Even Levi gaped, wondering how he had the gall to make such a fresh remark.

Craig surveyed Lamont, trying to compare the hustler confidently staring him down, to the scared kid his little brother used to bring to their house. He seemed prepared, and another bonus for Craig was that he was working with Levi. Craig didn't have the patience to teach his little brother about the hustle. If they flopped, it wouldn't backfire.

'I went out and got it. That's the difference. You kids want it all handed to you nowadays.'

'I'm ready to work. We all are.'

'You're speaking for Shorty?'

Lamont nodded.

'He's a little maniac. Can you control him?'

'It's not about control. It's about working with him. Shorty's my friend.'

'And Marcus? He your *friend* too?'

'Marcus is my brother.'

Craig nodded slowly, sharing a look with one of his guys, a giant in a grey hooded top. Whatever passed between them, Lamont didn't understand.

'Your brother robbed some of my people, did you know that?' Craig's jovial tone didn't fool Lamont. He needed to be careful. Craig could be referring to the robbery he had taken part in. Playing dumb was his best defence.

'No, I didn't.'

'What if I told you that to work for me, you had to give up your brother? Would you do it?'

Lamont's reply was immediate.

'No, I wouldn't.'

Craig smirked.

'As long as you keep them away from my people, I will give you a shot.'

Lamont beamed, his hands tingling. 'You won't regret this.'

The smile slipped from Craig's face. 'If I regret it, your whole team will too. Understand?'

'I understand, Craig.'

'I'm gonna hook you up on trust. I want my money every Friday. I don't care if you sell out or not. Understand?'

Lamont nodded.

'The money goes through Levi. If you run out, let him know and he'll let me know. Don't send any of your other people to meet me. Understand?'

Lamont nodded again.

'If you get into a beef, handle it. If it gets out of hand, I'll step in, but don't be ringing me because a sale slapped you and stole your draws. Understand?'

'Yes, Craig. I understand.'

'Good. Now, get out of here.'

CHAPTER SIX

Wednesday 26 March 1997

'L, man? Where did that come from?' Levi exclaimed when they were halfway down Chapeltown road. He'd expected Craig to bully Lamont and make him look stupid, but he'd dominated him. He wondered what Lamont was truly capable of. He seemed so harmless most of the time, but then sometimes . . .

'I had to show him it was beneficial to work together. Can you speak to him about supply? We need to know the weed will be available when we need it.'

Levi scratched his head. 'I'll speak to him later. He'll diss me in front of his boys if I press him now.'

'He seemed interested in Shorty and Marcus,' mused Lamont.

'They're crazy. People know you roll with them. Marcus, man . . . he's dark. Scares the crap out of me. Dunno how you can just chat to him normally. When I speak to him, I feel like I need my guard up.'

'They're family. With family, sometimes you only see the good parts.' Lamont quickened his pace, forcing Levi to hurry to keep up.

With their supply secure, Lamont and Levi arranged a meeting at Levi's place. They camped in the kitchen around a chipped wooden table while his Nana watched her programmes in the living room, the TV volume at a deafening level.

Levi closed the door and faced the gang. Lamont was at the far side, with K-Bar and Shorty at either end.

'It's all sorted, Shorty. We spoke to my bro. He'll hook us up with a cheaper rate,' said Levi

Shorty grinned. 'Deal's a deal then. Let's talk business.'

They ironed out the details, deciding they would start tomorrow, with the work being kept at Shorty's. He and K-Bar had their own spot so no one would find out what they were doing. As they spoke, Lamont felt Levi giving him funny looks. He waited until the others left before speaking to him about it.

'What's wrong?'

Levi shrugged, scraping his index finger along the table. 'I'm not sure I like how this is going.'

'What do you mean?'

Levi stewed a moment, chewing on his lip.

'I brought you in, and now you're taking over. You're talking with Craig even though he's my brother. You brought your own people into the plan without even speaking to me about it. Seems you're trying to push me out.'

Lamont saw the anger on his friend's face. He needed to handle this. He was committed, and would do what he needed to make money. If that meant making Levi happy, he'd do it.

'This is on you, Levi. It's your thing. If you think I'm making too many decisions, tell me to step off. Shorty and K-Bar have the links to sell quickly, and people won't trouble them. If you wanna do something different, tell me. Craig's your brother. This whole thing falls apart without you.'

Lamont held his breath. Levi and Shorty had a thing about respect. If he placated them, the operation would run smoothly.

Levi tried hiding his delight at his words.

'Okay. You're right. We'll get started tomorrow like we agreed.

Meet me at Shorty's. We'll bag up the drugs there, and sort out who deals where.'

Lamont nodded.

'Sounds good, Levi. Great plan, bro.'

––––––

Things escalated. They bagged the weed and using Shorty's network of buyers, sold out in no time. After repeating this several times, Craig began to take them seriously. He gave them two kilos of weed on credit to see if the crew could handle it. They could.

Word of their good product spread in the right places. The school crowd was an untapped goldmine. Lamont often found himself besieged by classmates wanting to buy, but only dealt with them off the school grounds.

In no time, they had the chain of command down to a T. Levi made sure Craig received his return, and would pick up the drugs and drop them on Shorty. Shorty and K-Bar would weigh and bag all the weed, then they would all slang it.

Being the strongest with numbers, Lamont oversaw the money side, making sure everyone was paid equally and promptly. Every-thing ran like clockwork, and that was down to Lamont. He tailored the strategy he'd used with Levi, using it on Shorty too. He allowed both to think they were dictating things and because of that, there was no strife in the ranks.

––––––

Lamont strolled down Chapeltown Road with Levi one night. They had just gone to meet some clients near Reginald Terrace, and he wanted to see if anyone was at the park to play football. They were almost there when a car pulled up alongside them.

'Lamont, can I have a word?' Nigel Worthington rolled the window down. Lamont sighed. He had avoided Nigel since the man's admission about wanting to become his agent. The last thing he needed was another adult trying to manipulate him.

'Yeah. What's up?'

Nigel cut his eyes to Levi. 'I'd prefer to talk alone.'

'I'll be at the park, L.' Levi glanced at Nigel and strolled away.

'Are you getting in?' Nigel asked. Lamont hesitated. Not wanting to press it, he parked and climbed out. He wore the navy tracksuit and worn Reebok trainers he normally wore for coaching, giving Lamont a once-over.

'New clothes?'

Lamont shrugged.

'Did your Auntie give you some money?'

He just stared. Nigel knew where the money had come from.

'Is this what you want to do, Lamont? I'm giving you an opportunity to be a superstar. I have people in place and you can ascend. I can help you. Why would you throw it all away?'

'That's your thing. Not mine,' Lamont finally spoke.

'And this is your thing, is it? You want to hustle, like all the other idiots on the street? You wanna go prison? Do you want to die?'

'I'm tired of the way I'm living. I wouldn't expect you to understand,' Lamont snapped, forgetting he was talking to a grown man.

'Do you really think you're the only person who has had it hard? There are many people out there who have struggled! I know you've been through a lot of crap with your Auntie. I sympathise, but you have a chip on your shoulder. Is this what your parents would have wanted?'

'Don't talk about my parents,' Lamont's voice had an innate chill. Nigel was aware he was going too far. Wisely, he backed down.

'I'm sorry, Lamont. I just don't want to see you waste your talent. You are capable of so much more. When you're on that field, you're composed; in the moment. I'd even venture to say you're happy. Don't throw that all away over a street dream.'

Lamont measured Nigel with a hard stare. 'You want the truth? Football's the street dream. It's all a game, and If I'm gonna play, I might as well get paid for it. Right now. Not years down the line.'

Nigel took a deep breath, picking his words carefully. Deep down, he knew it was futile. He had lost him. It was written in the boy's eyes. He tried again anyway.

'Okay, come and play for fun. We can take it from there.'

'There's nothing to take. I'm sick and tired of being treated like shit and manipulated.'

'I've never treated you like shit. I've treated you the same as the other boys, but I knew that you could go further. I still do. You're closer than you know to hitting the next level with football.'

'How many other kids are you giving that speech to? Let me guess, I follow you all the way and then I become just another player? Lost in the shuffle, probably end up dropped after a few games? No, I'll take my chances with what I'm doing.' His words had an adult's finality, which Nigel recognised and respected.

'I'm sorry to hear you talking like this. If you come to your senses, you know where to find me.'

Nigel drove away. Lamont watched after him for a second, wondering briefly if he had made the right decision. He turned on his heel and walked towards the park.

———

One night, the gang drove to a meeting. Their exploits had reached the ears of a shark named Blair. Blair had a distribution network of his own and was always looking for new links. He had reached out to Levi, and they agreed a price for an entire kilo of weed.

'Blair is the business,' Levi said from the passenger seat. 'I've asked around about him. He's definitely paid. If we deal with him, we're gonna make loads.'

'I've seen him about in town. He likes rocking chains and shit. He's a flashy guy,' added Shorty.

'Nothing wrong with being flashy,' said Levi, grinning. To emphasise his point, he wore a large gold chain which rested easily on his chest. Lamont hated it, thinking it made Levi look like a target. He couldn't tell him what to do though. Levi was fragile and he had to go to great pains not to undermine him. He'd disagreed with this meeting. Blair was established. There was no reason for him to be buying such a large amount of weed from some up and comers. He had been outvoted. If they shifted the entire kilo, they could reload quicker and restart the process. The team was hungry for more success. More accolades. More profit.

'We're nearly there anyway.' Shorty said, masterfully steered the car through the streets. He'd borrowed it from an associate, and wouldn't hear the end of it if he damaged the ride.

They parked down the road from the house where Blair waited. K-Bar and Shorty were at the back as Lamont and Levi led the way towards the house. Lamont scanned in all directions, looking for anything suspicious. Something wasn't right. His instincts screamed it, but he couldn't gauge the cause.

'Glad you could all make it,' a man Lamont assumed was Blair said, opening the door. 'Come right through.'

Blair closed the door behind them. Lamont looked around the room. It was basic. There was an old TV, peeling walls and wooden floorboards. He thought he heard a creak in the adjacent room, but then there was nothing. Blair clapped his hands together, getting their attention. He was older — Lamont assumed late twenties. His hair was neatly tapered, and the chain around his neck made Levi's look invisible. He wore a fresh red tracksuit and a gold watch on his right wrist. His hands were adorned with large rings and he rubbed his hands together, odiously smiling.

'You got the stuff then?'

'Yeah. We've got it. Where's the money?' Shorty replied.

'It's upstairs. I'll go get it.' Blair left the room and headed upstairs.

'Why didn't he have the money down here?' Lamont spoke.

'What are you on about?' Shorty frowned.

'We arranged this. Why wouldn't he have the money?'

'Just chill. I've got this,' said Levi. Before he could say another word, the doors on either side of the room burst open and two masked guys rushed at them. Lamont froze.

'Get on the floor!' One of them growled, wielding what looked like a pipe. The second the doors opened, Shorty was in motion. Whipping a gun from his waistband, he pointed it at the two would-be robbers.

'No. You lot get on the floor.'

'Wait . . . Shorty?' The man with the pipe said. Recognising his voice and build, Lamont stepped forward.

'Marcus?'

'L? What are you doing here?' Marcus pulled the mask off his face. Victor did the same.

'Doing a buy. What are you doing?'

'A buy? You're dealing now?'

Lamont nodded.

'We got a call earlier. Blair promised us half the take if we rushed some kids. Didn't know it was you lot, though. Oi,' Marcus turned to Victor, 'go grab that snake.'

Victor hurried to do his bidding.

'I can't believe this.' Marcus rubbed his face, breathing heavily. Lamont knew the signs. When Marcus got worked up, it never ended well for the perpetrator.

The sounds of a scuffle attracted everyone's attention. Victor dragged Blair into the room, the man digging his feet into the floor. Shorty smacked him in the mouth with the gun. There was a crunch and Blair sagged, allowing Victor to throw him to the floor.

'You little weasel. You thought you could send me after family?' Marcus spat at him.

'It's not like that! I didn't know he was your family! I swear,' he moaned through bloodied lips.

'Well, you've had it now. Vic, go back upstairs and search for the stash. I know it's here somewhere. In the meantime, you can take off those jewels. I'm taxing them for my pain and suffering.'

'Marcus, man, please—' Blair started, silenced by a kick to the ribs.

'If I have to do, I swear I'm gonna break every finger on your hands. Take them off. Now.'

Shaking with fear, Blair took off his watch, his rings and his chain. Marcus pocketed them. Victor came back downstairs with a brick-sized wad of money, which he handed to Marcus. He thumbed through the notes, nodding his approval.

'This'll do. You ever try anything like this again, and I'll kill you.' Marcus gave the beaten man one more kick, then they all left.

'Well, that was a result. Simple bit of work. I almost got shot, but still. Here,' Marcus split the brick of money and handed half to Lamont. 'For you and your little team.'

Lamont held the money, his heart beating. Selling weed had been easy, but tonight had been a stark lesson that anything could happen. He nodded at Marcus, willing himself to calm down.

'Anyway, we're gonna bounce. We're gonna lick another move. We were relying on robbing you lot, but luckily we had it as a backup.'

'What's the job?' Shorty asked, ever the opportunist.

'Like this one, only with better planning. Half a kilo. Maybe more. You in? We could use that gun.'

'I'm in. K is too. What about y'all?' he looked at Lamont and Levi.

'I'm going home. I'm tired,' Lamont said.

'Me too. Just drop us off on the way,' Levi added. Marcus and Victor climbed in their ride. When Lamont and the others were in their own car, they all drove off.

CHAPTER SEVEN

Wednesday 16 April 1997

LAMONT CHILLED at Shorty's after school, watching television. Shorty had cut him a key, so most of the time he would hang out. Shorty didn't care, usually out scheming or having sex. He was about to make a drink, when Levi bounded in.

'Yo, L!' he called out.

'I'm here, man. No need to shout.' Lamont appeared in the doorway.

'Well c'mon. We need to go.'

'Where to?'

'Craig wants to see us.'

Lamont put his shoes on and followed Levi. A taxi waited. Levi gave the driver directions, and the driver drove off. It seemed pointless. Craig was within walking distance. Levi was spending money for the sake of it.

As predicted, they were out of the car less than a minute later. Levi paid the fare, and they headed towards Craig. He slouched on a wall, kissing a girl Lamont had never seen before. She had large, dark eyes, skin the shade of cooking chocolate, and a body that poked out in all the right places. Lamont avoided staring, but Levi looked the girl up and down, almost licking his lips. Eventually Craig stopped kissing the girl and faced them.

'Everything good?'

Both boys nodded.

'I'm asking because I heard about last night.'

'Just a misunderstanding, bro,' Levi started. 'We were dealing with someone and he tried snaking us. We handled it.'

'You handled it, or Marcus did?' Craig smiled at the look of surprise that appeared on Levi's face. 'C'mon, baby bro. I know everything that happens on these streets. Why do you think I called you here? Blair's a punk. If you'd told me you were dealing with him, I would have told y'all not to.'

'He wanted to buy a keg,' Levi said. 'It was easy money.'

'Easy money had you getting stuck up. Don't be stupid chasing quick money. Grind for it. Stop smoking and shagging little girls and keep track of what's happening. If you'd bothered to check, you would have realised that me and Blair had beef.'

'Beef? Over what?'

'Over this fine girl I've got my arms around,' Craig palmed the girl for emphasis. 'See, Kierra here, she had a spell with Blair. When she realised what a bitch he was, she wanted me. He didn't like it, but he can't do anything. We used to run together.'

'What happened?' Lamont spoke for the first time.

'He was skimming. We were partners, splitting all the money down the middle. He was doing deals on the side and didn't want to cut me in, so I kicked his arse out of the squad.'

'Do we need to worry about him?' Lamont needed to establish what they were dealing with. This was why he hadn't wanted to do the deal. You just never knew what another person was bringing to the table, drama-wise.

'Blair's already shouting his mouth off about getting set up. He's not putting it on you lot directly, because you're nobodies. What he's doing is telling people I did it. He's harmless, but since I kicked him out, he's running with some crazy Yardies. Those are the ones you need to watch out for.'

'Understood,' Lamont said. Annoyed at being cut out of the conversation, Levi spoke up.

'If he comes for us, I'll cut him and anyone he wants to bring along,' he exclaimed. Craig and Lamont stared at him, unmoved by his posturing.

'Shut up. I don't wanna hear about you running your mouth, trying to impress me. Sort your head out, think about the money. Understand?'

Levi stared his brother down. Craig's eyes narrowed.

'I said, do you understand?'

'Yeah, bro.'

'Get out of here. I've got stuff to handle.'

———

'Who does he think he is?'

They were almost back at Shorty's place. Since leaving Craig, Levi had ranted non stop.

'He's just worried. We can't make money if we're watching our backs waiting for Blair.'

'Are you scared? I'm not scared. That motherfucker set us up.'

'It worked out for us. Marcus robbed him. We made money from an impossible situation,' Lamont replied.

'Why are you talking like you're in charge? Craig is my brother, so stop sucking up to him and support me. I brought you in!' Levi shouted. Lamont's body tensed, anger flaring. He took a deep breath. Levi had shown his petulance. He wouldn't lower himself to that level. It was about the money, nothing more.

'Okay, bro. Whatever you say. Like you said, you brought me in,' he replied.

It was Levi's turn to take a deep breath.

'L, I'm sorry, man. You're my bro. It's just Craig. He thought we would flop, and now that we're making money, he wants to play boss. He should have told us about Blair beforehand, then we would have known not to deal with him. He was probably in on it from the beginning.'

Lamont let him vent as they walked up the stairs to Shorty's flat. K-Bar was back from his excursions. He watched the pair enter as he smoked a cigarette.

'What's up?' He asked.

'More drama,' Lamont surmised Craig's warning.

'That's a bad situation. Blair got humiliated, so we need to be careful,' K-Bar said when Lamont finished.

'Forget Blair. We put him in his place,' Levi snapped, heading to the kitchen, returning with a bottle of Courvoisier and a clean glass.

'Shorty's not gonna like you touching his liquor,' K-Bar pointed out.

'Fuck Shorty. He's not gonna say anything if I buy him a bottle back, is he?'

K-Bar's eyes narrowed. Levi poured himself a glass, drank it and poured another, which he downed. He began coughing loudly, then poured himself another glass.

'Take it easy,' Lamont said.

'Fuck taking it easy,' Levi slurred, the brandy already touching him. 'Remember whose team you're on. I'm out.' Slamming the glass on the table, he tottered from the house.

'He's out of control,' K-Bar said as soon as the front door closed.

'Don't worry about it. He knows not to go too far.'

'Shorty might see it differently if he keeps running his mouth.'

'Levi's just angry. He wants Craig to think he's an asset. He doesn't realise that this isn't about Craig. We're just workers. We need to keep profiting and stay above water.'

'Did Craig say anything about who these Yardies were?'

Lamont shook his head. 'Just said they were crazy.'

K-Bar stroked his chin. 'I'll find out, so we know what we're up against. I'll let you speak to Shorty. Calm Levi down too; he's moving too fast, too quickly.'

The gang took it easy after that. They did their business, but didn't arrange any deals with anyone they didn't know.

Lamont passed on Craig's warning. Only Levi remained belligerent. Lately, he drank more, smoking more weed, bringing random girls to Shorty's place, nearly causing a fight. Levi thought Craig would protect him, but he wasn't taking Shorty seriously. There were rumours about the things Shorty had done, some even involving murder. Lamont believed the tales. He recalled how easily Shorty pulled the gun when he thought they were in danger. Shorty was ruthless and there was nothing to gain by Levi provoking him.

Still, he kept out of it. Lamont's prime focus was getting paid, and he did that. He had money hidden all over his room and there was no danger of Auntie finding it. Lately, she was spending more time out of the house, which he took to mean that she was hunting for a new sponsor. Lamont passed through and made sure Marika was okay, did his chores, then left again. The less he was in the house, the less chance there was he would argue with Auntie.

He also hung around Marcus more, which mostly meant standing around outside different houses. Marcus had heard the rumours about Blair, but wasn't taking them seriously. He was cool with the Yardies backing Blair, stating that as long as Craig kept himself to himself, there would be no problem.

———

Lamont arrived home one night. Auntie was in the living room with Marika. She looked up when he entered.

'Where have you been?'

'Out.'

'Don't get cheeky, boy. Where were you?'

'I was chilling in the park,' Lamont lied. Auntie glared.

'You don't have time to chill in the park. You have work to do.'

'I know that. I'll do it now.'

'What did I just say about getting cheeky?' Auntie shouted. Marika immediately looked at her, lip trembling. Noticing her niece's reaction, Auntie visibly calmed down.

'Get a dustpan and brush and sweep these floors. They're filthy.'
Lamont flashed a smile.

'No problem, Auntie. I'll do it now.' Without another word, he
practically skipped from the room.

———

Life went on for the team. For a while, they were paranoid over a
potential beef with the Yardies Craig and Marcus had mentioned. It
seemed Lamont was seeing crews and gangs everywhere, and he
believed he would be the target of a retaliatory attack.

'I keep telling you,' Marcus said one day, as they lifted weights at
a gym in Harehills, 'there's no problem. It's been ages, so leave it
alone. You still getting money?'

Lamont nodded.

'Focus on that then,' Marcus laughed. 'Still can't believe you're
slanging. If you wanted to make money so bad, you should have just
kept working with me.'

Lamont didn't reply until he'd completed his set on the bench.
They'd been in the gym over forty minutes, and his body ached.

'You saw how I was that one time. I'm not cut out for it.' He
recalled the disastrous robbery he'd been part of.

'It was your first go, L. No one's a master criminal their first
time. You did as you were told and kept your nerve mostly,' Marcus
shrugged. 'You're doing well, so it doesn't matter I guess. I'm
hearing you're about it. Proper natural leader.'

'Who said that?' The back of Lamont's neck tingled. No one
had said anything to him. Marcus refused to continue the conversation until the session was complete.

They were home eating tinned tuna and pasta in the kitchen
before Marcus revisited the subject.

'So, yeah, I'm hearing you've got skills. You're on point with the
money, and you're good at keeping things flowing. Keep it up, and
you're gonna see real money, bro.'

'Who told you this, though?'

'I work with your people, L. I know Shorty and them lot too, you know. Your name comes up. Him and K can't say enough good things about you.'

'I'm glad they think so highly of me.' Lamont noticed Levi's name hadn't come up. 'It's funny; they didn't even want to work with me at first.'

'Course not. They thought you'd fuck up their hustle. You proved them wrong, and now you're all benefitting.'

Lamont finished his food, taking Marcus at his word. He'd never thought of himself as a leader. Levi had a more forceful personality, which was why he clashed with Shorty so much. Lamont just steered the ship. He focused on the bottom line, which was money.

'What's happening with Shelly?'

Lamont rolled his eyes.

'C'mon, Marcus, not this again.'

'Not what? Do you like her?'

'You know I do.'

'So, what's stopping you?'

'We're just friends.' Lamont's reply sounded weak, even to him.

'Well, I was there the other night, and she was asking about you.'

'Nothing wrong with asking about a friend,' said Lamont, though his chest tightened at those words.

'Whatever you say, L. Step up and get it done.'

————

A few days later, Lamont fought to control his nerves as he approached Rochelle's. He looked down at his outfit, having settled for a white t-shirt, denim jeans and a high-top trainers. He felt the warmth of the sun on his arms, glad he'd left his coat at home. Forcing himself to stand with confidence, he knocked at the door, holding a carrier bag.

'Easy, L, you okay?' Mia's eyes widened, and she touched her throat. He blinked, startled by her reaction.

'I'm fine. Is Rochelle in?'

'She's out.'

Lamont's stomach dropped.

'Oh, okay. Could you give her this?' He held out the bag.

'What's in it?' Mia didn't move.

'A book and a CD I thought she might like.'

Mia studied him a moment.

'Come in.'

'What?'

'She went food shopping, so she won't be long. You can stay for dinner.'

'I . . . Is that alright?'

'Course it is. Come on.'

Not arguing, Lamont entered the house, heading straight for the living room. He felt Mia's eyes on him, hoping it wouldn't become uncomfortable with Marcus's girl.

'Have you been going gym?' She asked.

'Me and Marcus go a few times a week.'

'You can tell. Your back looks proper broad.'

'Thanks,' Lamont said, keeping his voice light. Her eyes surveyed him again, looking him up and down.

'You're scrawny compared to my man, though.'

Just like that, they laughed, and it lifted the tension.

'So, you like my sister then?'

'We're friends.'

Mia raised an eyebrow. 'Do you buy books for all your friends?'

'If they like to read,' Lamont shot back.

'Fine. If that's the story you wanna go with, I won't argue. Do you want something to drink?'

Later, Lamont sat with a glass of apple juice, when the front door opened.

'Mia, I'm back. I swear, I need to get my licence. The taxi driver was a right pervert. Listen, they didn't have any Red Leicester, so I—' Rochelle froze when she saw Lamont in the living room. 'L?'

'Hey, Shelly.'

'What are you doing here?' She stood in the doorway, holding the shopping bags. She wore a black jacket over some jeans and riding boots. Lamont rose to his feet more gracefully than he felt, taking the shopping bags from her.

'Let me help you with those.'

'Okay, but then you can answer my question.' She led him to the kitchen. When they'd put the shopping away, Rochelle shot him a glance.

'So . . .'

He raised his hands. 'So what?'

'Why are you here?'

'I was hungry. Heard you scrubbed up a good dinner.'

'L . . .'

Lamont grinned, jamming his hands in his pockets out of nervousness.

'Fine. I bought something for you today. Tried leaving it with your sister, but she made me stay.'

Rochelle processed this. 'Do you want to stay for dinner then?'

'Yeah.'

'When we finish, I want to see what you brought.'

———

Lamont helped Rochelle cook, using his vast experience from feeding Auntie. When they finished, Mia left the room, giving the pair privacy. Lamont had relaxed from earlier, but some awkwardness lingered. It often seemed he was one step away from messing up whatever he had with Rochelle, and it was confusing. He wanted to be comfortable in her presence, but not too comfortable, in case he did something stupid. He'd never gone to her house without Marcus before, and was half expecting to hear his friends booming laugh and see him bounding into the living room, but he didn't. There was no one to take the attention from Lamont.

'Can I see this mysterious gift now?'

He steadied himself and handed the bag to Rochelle.

'*Anita Baker.*' Her eyes were a question as she looked up at him, holding the CD. He resisted the urge to put his hands in his pockets.

'You said once that music and books were two of the greatest

75

inventions. I wanted to add to your collection. Anita Baker has a strong, distinctive voice. Reminds me of yours.'

'And the book? Why *The Colour Purple*?'

He wasn't sure if she liked his gifts or not, but she was putting him on the spot.

'I just thought you you'd enjoy it.'

Rochelle beamed, surprising him.

'I'm sure I will. And thank you. It's sweet of you.'

Relieved that she liked the gift, he grinned.

'It's fine.'

They spoke for a while longer, then watched TV. He became distracted when Rochelle started to lean on him. His heart hammered against his chest, but he tried to look cool. She smelt like cherries and some jasmine aroma. Lamont liked it a lot. He liked everything about just sitting with Rochelle, almost like they were a couple.

'You're finishing school soon, aren't you?'

'Couple of weeks left and then I'm done. My exams are in June.'

Rochelle shifted against him. 'Are you revising?'

'A bit.' Lamont had gone through old notes and school books, but he needed to make money. He spent more time with Shorty and Marcus than he did revising.

'L, exams are important. Promise me you'll take them seriously.'

Lamont nodded. 'I promise that I will. When they're done though, let me take you out for dinner, okay?'

Rochelle glanced at him, her smile so sweet it threatened to overwhelm him.

'Okay.'

Lamont's chest felt warm. The evening had been one of the best he could remember. All of his drama, all the pressures of the street had evaporated in Rochelle's presence, and he loved it. He needed to leave, though, and with great regret, extricated himself from her touch.

'I've gotta go.'

If Rochelle was disappointed, she hid it well as she walked him to the front door.

'Thanks again for the presents, L. I'm going to put the album on now and start reading.'

'Good. Let me know what you think.'

'I will.'

They glanced at one another, not knowing what to do next. Lamont took her in his arms, hugging her against him. She stiffened, then hugged him back. Acting on instinct, he kissed her on the forehead as he let her go.

'Night, Shelly.'

'Night, L.'

CHAPTER EIGHT
Tuesday 20 May 1997

LAMONT HAD books spread across his desk. He'd listened to Rochelle and started revising for his exams, which began next week. He had officially left school, turned in all coursework, and he was ready. There was no fear over completing his exams. He had always been a dutiful student and his personal circumstances hadn't impacted his desire to learn. Scribbling notes as he pored through his year eleven maths textbook, Auntie's shrill voice cut through the quiet.

'Lamont! Door!'

Mumbling under his breath, he hurried down the stairs. Levi waited in the garden, his movements jittery.

'L, I need you,' he started, looking up and down the street.

'For what? What's going on?'

'I got into a situation and I need you, man. We need to go find Marcus, or—'

'Levi, are you gonna tell me what's happened?' Lamont cut across his friend. Levi made a noise of dissent, his eyes wide with fear.

'Look, people are coming for me. Are you gonna help me find Marcus or what?'

Lamont wanted to leave Levi to it, but they were friends, and he couldn't abandon him. Hurrying upstairs, he put on a hooded top, squeezed his feet into some black trainers, and made his way back to the front door. He heard Auntie call out, but he had already closed the door.

'What's this situation then?'

'I was dealing on the side,' Levi hung his head. 'Gave some weed to someone I thought was harmless. It had loads of seeds and shit, practically unsellable. He's connected to a bigger guy. Now, they're after me. They nearly caught me near my house, but I ran and escaped them. They're probably still there.'

Lamont put out a hand to stop his friend.

'Why were you dealing on the side?' he asked, trying not to let his anger show.

'Why do you think? I needed money.'

'We all need money,' Lamont snapped. 'I look after that side of our thing though, so how did you do it?'

'. . . When I reloaded with Craig, I got some extra for myself.'

Lamont couldn't believe it. Levi needed money less than any of them. Craig made sure he wanted for nothing. He regretted getting caught up in his drama, but it was too late now.

'It wasn't the first time, was it?' He already knew the answer. Levi couldn't look him in the eye, focusing instead on the ground. Lamont sighed, shaking his head. He couldn't bring himself to shout at his friend. Like it or not, Levi was the link to their supply.

'Let's just deal with this mess.' He stalked towards Levi's place without even waiting for him.

———

Lamont stewed later, his mind alight. The guys Levi ripped off had been out for his blood, and it took him offering Levi's chain as collateral to call them off.

More often, Lamont wondered about the drugs game. It was easy to get caught up in the hustle. He sold weed to people who wanted to smoke, and on the surface that seemed fine, but it was still an offence, and he couldn't afford to get caught.

Absentmindedly, he played with the pieces of a battered chess-board. It had belonged to his father. He remembered the nights spent listening to his dad explaining the significance of each piece, teaching him the intricacies of taking his time with each move. They would play and his dad would always win at first, but before his death, Lamont could beat him. He wondered to himself now if his dad had let him win.

Lamont had a few friends he could play with, but he hadn't seen them much since he had started dealing drugs. It was time-consuming. He enjoyed the money, but there was a lot of running around involved. It was a distraction, though, and a distraction was what he needed right now.

Lamont thought about Rochelle. He'd been to the house once or twice since the dinner. The awkwardness lingered, but there was none of the initial ice and scorn. Now they talked easily about TV shows, literature, but never about anything too deep. Maybe that was the problem.

Lamont was sure that Rochelle liked him the way he liked her. Marcus teased him, saying that they acted more like a couple than he and Mia did, and he would play along, *but how the hell was he supposed to know?*

His experience with the opposite sex was minimal. He could talk to girls because they didn't take him seriously. He was a friend to them, just like he had been to Erica, but it differed with Rochelle. There was something more there, but he had nothing to compare it to. And that was the problem.

If they were just friends, then he wouldn't feel how he did. He wouldn't be moping around, confused, not knowing if he was imagining anything between them. Blinking, Lamont looked down, realising, he was fingering the black queen piece. He glanced down at it, his eyes blurring for a moment, then he decided.

———

'L? What are you doing here?'

He could have kicked himself for his impulsiveness. Rochelle looked out at him. She wore a tight sleeveless top with big gold buttons. Two of the buttons were undone, leaving a tantalising trail to her cleavage, her thick thighs encased in a skirt. She was bare-footed, minstrel brown polish on her toenails. He stared, thinking how dumb it had been to turn up on her doorstep.

'L?' She spoke again, louder this time. Lamont met her eyes. He wondered if she knew the sexual vibe she put out. He didn't think she did. There was no way she could know the full effect she had on him.

'I wanted to see you,' he mumbled. The way the scenario had played out in his head and the reality couldn't have been more different. For a fleeting second he was tempted to run. Instead, he again met her eyes.

'Why?' she asked.

'Because I like you.'

'I like you too, L. I think you're a great guy.'

'Good. If we both like each other, that's all it should take, right?'

Rochelle shook her head. 'It's not that simple. I have baggage; complications in my life I can't explain. I'm the last person you want to get involved with.'

'You're wrong. When I'm around you . . . I can be myself. I don't have to put on an act or blend in. You make me feel secure. If I have someone like that, I should keep them close, right?' Lamont fought to keep his words even, to stop his voice from shaking, heart madly pounding. He had never put himself out there like this before. The words were out now. He was being a man, telling Rochelle how he really felt, hoping to hell she wouldn't shoot him down.

The insecurities whipped at him like an abusive partner. *How could she want him? What the hell did he have to offer her?*

Lamont's eyes watered, unblinking. He wanted to break his gaze. He couldn't; he had to show her. This was more important than he knew.

'L, please listen to me . . . you can't get involved with me. Please, just go home and let's forget about this.' Rochelle's voice had lost its usual assertiveness. Her eyes glistened with tears. Lamont didn't know why they were there. Only that she was weakening. She liked him. That was all he had needed to hear. If she liked him, then he was in control.

'No,' he replied, her fledging resistance strengthening his resolve.

'You don't have a choice. I can't do this with you. I *won't* do this with you.' Rochelle tried to close the door but he jammed it with his trainer. Pain shot through his foot but he didn't care.

'I'm not going anywhere. I'm tired of shying away from things, too scared to stick a toe in the pool and risk getting wet. I like you. I'm not missing this opportunity to make you understand how much.'

'Lamo—' Rochelle didn't get his name out. He moved forward, capturing her lips, hands grazing her hips. She resisted only for a moment before kissing him back. He savoured her mouth, hungrily massaging her lips with his own, trying to avoid worrying if he was kissing her right. He seemed to be doing okay. She moaned in his mouth, grinding her hot body against his. His erection tented in his tracksuit bottoms now, pressing into Rochelle. There was no way she couldn't know it was there. Lamont's embarrassment immediately evaporated when she rubbed against it.

They were in the house now, stumbling upstairs, lips glued to one another. Rochelle threw him on the bed, slowly undoing the buttons on her shirt. Raising her eyebrows, she paused. Lamont took the hint, quickly stripping. He lay on the bed fully naked, feeling foolish, yet more turned on than ever before. She watched him wordlessly, clad in a black bra and thong. Then, they were gone.

Lamont's breath caught in his chest. He had never seen a naked woman in the flesh before, so he had nothing to compare it to, but she was a vision. Her opulent breasts hung freely, complimenting proportioned hips and thighs. Her caramel skin glowed in the street-light's ambience outside the window.

'Do you have a condom?' Rochelle whispered.

Lamont nodded, rummaging through his trouser pockets for his wallet. He had two condoms in there that he'd started carrying around. He opened one with trembling hands, hoping he was putting it on the right way. When it was secure, Rochelle started kissing his body, knowing precisely where to strike. Everywhere she touched left a warm tingling feeling that he relished. His breathing shallow, He tried to stay calm; to avoid finishing before he'd even started. Rochelle slowly stroked him, her grazing grip sending bolts of pleasure down his shaft. He groaned out loud, unable to hold back, then reached out and probed her with one finger. Rochelle shuddered and threw her head back. Lamont stopped.

'Sorry! Did I hurt you?' he spluttered. Rochelle gripped his jaw.

'Don't stop. Do that again,' she ordered. He obliged, amazed at how wet she was. She moaned his name softly, and he revelled in the power of giving her pleasure.

'That's enough.' Rochelle moved his hand and climbed on top, lowering herself onto him. Lamont closed his eyes and braced himself. This was it. He was finally losing his virginity. And it was like nothing else he had ever experienced. As enjoyable as every-thing else had been until this point, the feel of Rochelle cancelled everything out. Putting her hands on his chest, her hips bucked, slowly rotating in circles. He closed his eyes, trying to stave off how good it felt. He couldn't finish now. He had to go the distance. Rochelle moaned, rocking faster, eyes closed, mouth parted. Lamont grabbed her breasts. Raising his body off the bed, he began sucking as if they were the most succulent fruit he had ever tasted.

Rochelle's moans spurred him on more. He pushed up his, wanting to increase her pleasure as much as his own. Both moved at a clumsy pace, but it was an enjoyable clumsiness. Rochelle tried to dictate the pace, but in his inexperience, Lamont didn't realise. He greedily grabbed at her body, unable to keep his hands to himself.

'Let me do it,' Rochelle whispered, the softness of her voice sounding like the song of angels. She began bucking her hips crazily, Lamont unable to keep up. His teeth gritted together, his toes wiggling, a twinge in his midsection. What she was doing felt too good and before he could stop himself, he exploded. His body jerked a few times as he filled the condom, and then he was still.

Lamont breathed heavily, Rochelle too. She placed both her

hands on his chest, digging her nails in. It hurt, but he wasn't going to tell her to stop. He was semi erect, and it didn't feel comfortable. Sensing this, Rochelle climbed from him, hurrying to the bathroom, leaving him to tidy up.

A few minutes later, Rochelle came out of the bathroom. She smiled, but it flickered, never showing in her eyes.

'What's wrong?' He asked, praying she wasn't disappointed with his performance.

'I'm just mad.'

'Mad at me?'

Rochelle's expression was rueful.

'Madder at myself. I told you nothing could happen, and then I slept with you . . . I can't believe I was so stupid!'

'Rochelle, I wanted this. I've never wanted anything more in my life. I mean that.' Lamont openly stared at her magnificent body, wanting to file away every inch for future reference, scared he was dreaming. Reaching out to touch her, he froze when she recoiled.

'I think you should go. Please, just leave.'

Lamont watched in dejected bewilderment as Rochelle burst into tears. Respecting her wishes, he dressed himself. As he was putting on his t-shirt, he couldn't help it. He tried to hug her, but she pushed him away.

'Don't touch me! Don't ever touch me again!'

Lamont backed away. He opened his mouth, then closed it. Tugging his hooded top over his head, he mumbled an apology and hurried down the stairs at the same time Mia walked in. They stared at one another. Mia gaped at him like he was a ghost.

'L? What are you doing here?' she asked, noting his rumpled appearance. His hair was tousled, and he had what looked like teeth marks embedded in his jawline and neck.

'Gotta go.' Lamont darted past her, out of the front door and was halfway up the street before her mouth closed. He needed the safety of his bedroom. One thing was for sure, Lamont thought sadly as he turned the corner: He would never have another shot with Rochelle again.

CHAPTER NINE

Tuesday 20 May 1997

MARCUS CAME into Lamont's room later that night. He stared into space as Marcus closed the bedroom door behind him, not even looking.

'You cool, L?' Marcus loomed near the wall. It was funny how different Lamont's room was to his own. In his room, you could tell it was his. Lamont's could have belonged to anyone. Apart from the books and writing notepads, it was practically empty. There was a battered wardrobe for his clothes, some shoeboxes and an old cassette player. Apart from that, there was nothing. Nothing to show he belonged.

Marcus wondered if that was the reason Lamont acted as he did sometimes; because he didn't believe he had a home.

'I'm fine,' Lamont's voice was hoarse. Awkwardly, Marcus wondered if he'd been crying.

'I spoke to Mia.' Marcus rubbed the back of his neck. 'She said she saw you at the house.'

Lamont didn't speak. Marcus continued.

'Said you left in a hurry, and that Shelly was quiet. Didn't even come down from her room. What's up with that?'

'What do you want me to say, Marcus?' Lamont finally glanced at him. Marcus's face broke into a wide grin.

'You know what I want you to say. Tell me you handled your business,' he said gleefully. Lamont looked at him but didn't reply. He hesitated a moment too long, and that was all the inclination his friend needed.

'Yes! That's my fucking boy! I knew you had it in you!' Marcus clapped Lamont on the back.

'Chill. It's not a big deal.'

'Course it's a big deal! You finally lost your v, and more importantly, you lost it with a thoroughbred. Rochelle is all that man. I bet it was good. Be honest, was it good?'

Lamont grinned at Marcus's enthusiasm. 'How would I know? I have nothing to compare it to. Enjoyed it, though.'

'Did she?'

'She looked like it . . . during, anyway.'

Lamont told him Marcus what happened after they'd finished. Marcus made a face.

'That is strange. Shelly's quiet, though. Never know what she's thinking. She's like you. Why do you think I said you needed to grind her? You're a lucky dude, man. Wait till I tell people. You're gonna be the man around here.'

'Don't tell anyone.' Lamont's voice hardened.

'Why? L, this is a good thing. This is what you need. Finally, people are gonna see what I see. You're stone cold, but within, I dunno. Hard to say, but there's like . . . an aura,' Marcus said. Lamont stared at him.

'An aura?'

'Yeah, man. Listen, you know I'm shite with words, but you're quiet. Lot of people, they see that and it makes them think you're weak. But I know different. Always have. You're a force. You just need to let people see it.'

Lamont's mouth fell open, his eyes widening. He had never heard Marcus speak with as much conviction as he was now. He didn't know if he was drunk or high, but he immediately dismissed his words.

'Don't tell anyone. I want you to give me your word that you'll keep it to yourself.'

'L, man, c'mon.' Marcus kissed his teeth.

'Please. This is important to me.'

'Fine. You wanna keep quiet on the best piece of news you've ever had, then fine. I'll make Mia keep her big mouth shut too.'

Lamont smiled again. 'Thanks, bro.'

———

Lamont finished his History exam earlier, and was walking down to the shop when he heard a voice calling him. Turning, he saw Shorty. They touched fists.

'How's it going, Shorty?'

'It's all good. Just went to go meet someone,' Shorty replied, his eyes flashing excitedly. 'Did you hear about Craig?'

Lamont hadn't, but lately, Craig seemed more stressed than normal. The last time Lamont saw him, he'd worn the same hooded top and trousers he had worn the time before that. As he and Levi weren't seeing eye to eye, he didn't know what was happening, but suspected it concerned Blair and the Yardies. Lamont couldn't help but recall the incident where Marcus had beaten up Blair. He wondered if that was the right way to handle the situation.

'What happened?'

Shorty laughed. 'Him and two of his boys stomped out Leader on Francis Street. It was wicked!'

'Which *Leader*? Who's that?' Lamont asked. Shorty snorted.

'You need to stop reading them books and hit the streets. Leader runs one of them little Yardie groups. He's the psycho Blair ran to for protection.'

'So, why would Craig attack him?'

'Because he's an idiot. Everyone knows about Leader. This ain't gonna be the end; I guarantee that.'

Lamont didn't understand why there needed to be a war. There was enough money for everyone to get rich. There was no profit from the violence.

'What's the point?' He finally said.

'What?' Shorty frowned.

'Craig's supposed to be about making money. Why would he allow himself to get caught up?'

'Hype, nothing more. Craig's snorting, running with pure fools who just wanna see him in trouble while they steal his money. I'm telling you, when he flops, they'll move on to the next guy.'

'Craig's on drugs?' Lamont blinked rapidly, taking a step back.

'Yeah. Has been for a while. Why do you think he's entertaining this stupidness? He's taking coke, trying to keep hold of that slut he stole from Blair. That's what all this shit is over. He's fronting like he's got a real piece, when really she's always been available to dudes. Even I shagged Kierra.'

Lamont's mouth hung open. 'When?'

'Ages ago. Met her at a party. Linked her afterwards and banged her in an alleyway.' Shorty laughed at the expression on Lamont's face.

'Why would you do that? What about Craig?'

'What about him? He's got a couple guys he chills with that slap people around, but he's got no heart. He was just in the right place when Delroy was looking for people and he got put on. He's nothing.'

Lamont didn't reply. Delroy Williams was known for importing and supplying drugs all over Yorkshire. Lamont hadn't known he was Craig's supplier, but it made perfect sense. Craig had access to weed whenever he wanted it. There weren't many suppliers who could accommodate. Shorty sighed, his expression changing.

'Listen, you need to learn the streets if you wanna survive. Craig's running around on that powder thinking he's invincible. If he thinks Delroy will back him in this war, he's a dickhead. Delroy likes it quiet.'

'So what's gonna happen?'

Before Shorty could reply, they heard gunshots.

'L! Down!' Shorty hit the deck. Lamont mirrored his actions, his heart pounding with fear. There was no way to tell where the gunshots were coming from.

'C'mon, we're alright. The gunshots were round the corner. Let's go see who it was.' Shorty hurried down the street. Lamont followed, not knowing what he was getting into. They were running now. Lamont's nose dripped. He hastily wiped it, noting that it was snot rather than blood. He'd hit the pavement hard, but he was okay.

A crowd gathered a few streets down, whispering about what transpired. A woman in tears ran past Lamont and Shorty. He wondered if she would call an ambulance. They moved in closer, pushing their way through the crowds.

Two guys were stretched out on the pavement. They were so still it appeared they were sleeping, but the blood seeping from their bodies was a sign that they wouldn't be waking up. They were face-down, so it was impossible to tell who they were, but Lamont recognised the hooded top one of them wore. He hoped he was wrong, but the nauseous feeling in his stomach told him otherwise.

Finally, an ambulance turned up, two flashing police cars behind it. The police began pushing people back and trying to establish order. The local youths didn't take kindly to the pushing, and there was a stand-off, resolved when the police threatened to call for backup.

When Lamont finally got a good look at the clothing, his heart leapt in his throat.

'C'mon, L, we need to leave. Now.' Shorty was already stomping up the road.

'Shorty, that was Craig!' Lamont hissed, hurrying after him.

'I know it was Craig. He's dead and standing around won't do anything. We need to find Levi.'

'We need to go back; find out who did it.'

'We know who did it. Leader's guys. Craig thought he could beat him up and get away with it.'

'So, now what? Do we get him?'

Shorty stopped in his tracks. 'You wanna go after Leader? Do that, you're dead. Simple as that.'

'Yeah, but—'

'But nothing. Craig did something stupid. I'm not letting you do the same thing. Now, cut that suicide talk and let's find Levi. He needs to hear from us, not someone else.'

———

Hours later, they gathered in Levi's kitchen. His Nana was upstairs, but every once in a while they would hear a wail. Lamont didn't know why Levi wasn't comforting her, but kept it to himself. Shorty had bought brandy. They'd each had a glass out of respect, but Levi had drunk three more. With each glass he became more animated, before finally standing, tears streaming down his face.

'They're all dead. I'm gonna wipe the lot of them out.' Draining the last dregs of the glass, he threw it against the wall.

'Levi, calm down,' Lamont said. Shorty stared at the floor. K-Bar dolefully watched Levi's tirade.

'How am I supposed to calm down? They killed my fucking brother, L. Murdered him on the streets and you want me to just let it go?'

'I'm just saying; think rationally. There's no use getting mad. It won't solve anything. We need to plan our next move.'

'I know exactly what my next move is. Shorty, get me a strap and I'll dead every one of them!'

Shorty finally looked up. He met Lamont's eye before he replied to Levi.

'I'm not getting you a strap. You wanna go prison over your brother's beef?'

'You got away with murder; why shouldn't I?'

'Shut it. Don't talk about things you don't understand,' Shorty snapped.

'I'll talk about anything I want.'

'Lay off that brandy, because you can't handle it. Your bro knew what he was getting into. He rolled with a crew. Fall back and let them handle it.'

'If you don't gimme a strap, then Marcus will,' Levi said matter-of-factly.

'No, he won't. We're not gonna let you go shooting up the streets over this. Calm down, sleep off the liquor and comfort your Nana. Listen to her, man. She needs you to be there for her.'

'Shut up! I run this team. I brought you all in. If it wasn't for me, then—'

'Are you still harping on about that?' Shorty kissed his teeth. 'Levi, get real. I was doing this long before you. You ain't the boss of nothing. L kept this in line. Don't go thinking you're Nicky Barnes because your brother supplied us. Chill out and stay in your lane.'

Levi stormed over to Shorty. 'Get up.'

'Why?' Shorty sniggered.

'We're gonna fight.'

Shorty grinned. 'Are we?'

'Yeah, we are.' Levi's voice shook.

'This won't get us anywhere,' Lamont interjected. They ignored him.

'C'mon. Get up,' Levi urged.

Shorty shook with laughter. 'What did I just say about staying in your lane?'

'What did I just say about getting up?'

'You wanna hear the truth? If I get up, they might end up burying you next to your brother.'

That was the last straw. Levi caught Shorty in the side of the head with a good shot. The blow stunned him enough for Levi to pull him to the ground, but that was where the advantage ended. Levi was drunk. Even if he was sober, he wouldn't have been a match for Shorty, who quickly overpowered him, punching him twice in the mouth before K-Bar and Lamont pulled him off.

'Get off me,' Shorty roared, trying to break free. Levi crawled into a sitting position, his mouth bleeding. He glared at Shorty, but didn't make another move.

'Shorty, chill! His brother just died,' Lamont tried reasoning with him.

'Fuck him and his brother.'

'No, fuck you, Shorty,' Levi screamed. 'I'll deal with it myself.' stumbling to his feet, he hurried upstairs, leaving the trio in his kitchen.

———

They didn't see much of Levi after that. Every time Lamont called for him, his Nana said he was out. Lamont hoped this meant he'd calmed down, but knowing Levi he doubted it.

In the meantime, the streets buzzed with different stories about Craig's murder. Even his crew were swapping tales rather than doing anything. Just as Shorty predicted, the second Craig died, they moved on. Their lack of loyalty disgusted Lamont, but he couldn't do anything about it.

Supply-wise, they were stuck. Craig had been the only connection to Delroy, and now he was dead, they were in the cold. Shorty was forced to link up with his old supplier. He hadn't forgiven Shorty for ditching him, and hiked up the price, knowing they were powerless to do anything about it. People were put off by the decline in quality and it showed in their profits.

Lamont had to continue, though. He dealt with more people outside of Chapeltown, sweet-talking them into taking the substandard drugs. He didn't convince everyone, but made the most of a bad situation.

Marcus and Shorty, who always had their ears to the streets, reported back on what was going down in the Hood. Leader and a few of his guys had been questioned about the murders, but without evidence, they were forced to let the killers go.

After finishing his exams one day, Lamont slumped on Shorty's sofa, half asleep, when Shorty charged into the living room.

'Get up!' He yelled, his face panicked.

'What the hell, Shorty? Why are you shouting?' Lamont yawned, rubbing his eyes.

'Levi got arrested.'

Lamont sat up. 'What for?'

'He went after Leader. Stabbed him on the street in front of witnesses and then ran off. Police snatched him from his Nana's. He's in custody now.'

'What about Leader? Is he alive?'

'One of his boys shouted a warning when Levi ran up. Sliced his chest a little, and there was loads of blood. He's all right, though. Already out of hospital.'

Lamont shook his head, his mind alight with the nonsense of it all. He should have tried harder to get in contact with Levi. He had known exactly what he was capable of, and had just dismissed it. Now, Levi was facing prison time.

'I can't believe it . . .'

'Well, you need to. He's got no sense. Craig shoulda schooled him better on the game. He's done summat dumb and now he's going away for it.'

'Levi's our boy. Don't talk about him like that.'

'He's a dickhead. Him and his brother never used their heads and now look at them. Dead and in jail.' Shorty rubbed his forehead. 'I'm not getting into an argument, anyway. I'm off to get some food. You want summat?'

Lamont shook his head again. Shorty left. Deep down, he knew he was right to be annoyed. Levi had acted rashly and would pay the penalty for it. The situation caused Lamont to consider his own future. *Was this really what he wanted? Pitching on the streets, dodging overzealous drug squads and rival dealers?* He needed to think about his next move.

———

They'd had a good run.

That was all Lamont thought in the following days. With the drama surrounding Craig's murder, and Levi being locked up, things were turbulent. Shorty and K-Bar were out in town getting drunk, doing drugs and waiting for things to fix themselves. Lamont didn't see how they could without a decent supplier.

He had visited Levi's devastated Nana, and told her he would look out for her, but she insisted she didn't need it. Craig had always been generous, and she had money saved. Still, she loved her grandchildren and the fact that everything was so fractured had wounded her.

Lamont tried finding Levi's mum, but she was in the wind. The streets had a way of hiding people who didn't want to be found, and he didn't have the resources to track her down.

Life at the moment was a lot of reading and soul-searching. Exams were finished, so he gave more thought to the future. He was confident he had done well on the exams, and could use that to secure something more worthwhile. The jig seemed to be up. He felt awake from the dream of spending drug money on new trainers and clothes. Even as he sat on the bed, he saw the Nike shoe boxes piled against the battered chest of drawers Auntie scrounged for him when he went to live with her. He had his Walkman at full blast, listening to *Life After Death* by *The Notorious B.I.G.*, absorbing every word.

As he tried reading a *Stephen King* novel, he thought about the promise he'd made to himself. After shuffling from Rochelle's, he vowed he wouldn't contact her until he knew where they stood. She had Auntie's number. She could call at anytime to explain what had happened, what he had done wrong.

In the heat of the act, it seemed he was doing okay. She'd making all the right noises, and seemed as connected as he was. The aftermath made him wonder. Every time he thought back to the night they had shared, he remembered the aftermath more than anything. He hated replaying the way she had recoiled afterwards when he tried to touch her. He wanted her to feel what he had felt. He wanted to tell her she had made him feel whole for the first time since he was ten-years-old.

And that was when Lamont decided to break his promise. He would go to Rochelle. Tell her he would get a job; that he wanted them to be normal together. He was smart. He knew how to get the best out of people. *Surely there was something out there for him on the job front?*

Baring his soul had worked well last time, and it would work again. Hitting the stop button on his Walkman, he hurried to get ready.

———

Lamont hurried along the streets, Rochelle's house soon looming in front of him. The bedroom light was on but the downstairs lights were off. He knocked, laying out the game plan. When the door opened, his rehearsed words vanished.

'Yeah?' A man looked out at him. He appeared older and more unnervingly, he was half dressed, his defined upper body on show. His shaggy afro was unkempt, and he had a five o'clock shadow across the underside of his face. There were marks all over his body, along with a scar that went through the middle of his right eyebrow down to his eyelid.

Lamont stared, not knowing what to say. He felt like he had seen the man somewhere, but couldn't think where.

'Oi? What do you want?' The man said, louder this time. Lamont heard footsteps and Rochelle appeared next to the man. Her mouth fell open at the sight of Lamont.

'L?'

'This is that little kid you were grinding?' The man looked him up and down.

'Ricky, let me handle this,' Rochelle said. He ignored her.

'Yo, piss off. You got a little shag, and that's the end. This is mine,' Ricky taunted, putting his arm around Rochelle. Instinctively, Lamont's hands balled into fists. Ricky noticed.

'Oh? You wanna go? C'mon then!'

'Ricky. Go back upstairs. Please, let me handle this,' Rochelle repeated. Ricky gave Lamont a scathing look.

'Guess I'll warm the bed back up.'

An awkward silence lingered in Ricky's departure. Lamont's heart hammered as he gazed at Rochelle. He hadn't noticed she wore nothing but a bed sheet. Once he saw it, something in him seemed to shift, his insides turning to lead. He wanted to fall to the ground. He realised then, at that horrid moment, that he was in love.

Lamont wanted to cry. He wanted to hit Rochelle. He wanted to hit Ricky. He wanted to keep attacking them both. Most of all, he wanted to hold her, and he wanted her to hold him back. To be there for him. He wanted to call her names. He couldn't though. He couldn't speak.

'I'm sorry.'

Rochelle's simple words cut through him like a knife. He forced himself to maintain her gaze, eyes filling with tears that he quickly blinked away.

'Is he the baggage?' His words came out as a croaking sound. She hesitated, then slowly nodded.

'So, what happens now?' he asked, his voice thick. She didn't hesitate.

'Now, you go home and forget all about me.'

With that, Rochelle closed the door on both Lamont and his broken heart.

TEFLON

CHAPTER TEN

Thursday 23 April 1998

'WE NEED A PLAN.'

Lamont didn't immediately reply to Shorty's words. They stood outside a local shop in the Hood, enjoying the warm evening, well-received after two weeks of wet weather. He knew his friend was right. They needed something solid.

Lamont had finished his education the previous year, scoring highly in all of his exams. Upon picking up his results, his teachers tried talking to him about his future goals, only to be coldly rebuffed.

Lamont, Shorty and K-Bar had continued to sell weed, but the profits they enjoyed with Craig were long gone, and Lamont had to dip into his savings more often.

Auntie knew he had money and turned up the pressure on him, first by demanding he pay board, to which Lamont agreed, then by badgering him about what he was doing. He was storing more things in Marcus's room. Marcus didn't mind. He had all but moved out, spending his time in the streets.

Lamont hung with Shorty most of the time, and with Shorty anything could happen. A trip to the shop to buy milk one day, escalated into Shorty shaking down a sale for twenty pounds and repeatedly stomping on him. Why he had done it, Lamont couldn't say.

'I know,' he finally replied.

'We can't keep going like this. I still think robberies are where it's at. Marcus is making grands.'

Lamont shook his head. 'You can, but I'm not getting into that.'

'What then? What's the big plan? Trevor doesn't give a damn how much money we're bringing. He's never gonna give us a break.' Shorty referred to their weed supplier.

Lamont half-listened, his attention on a black Mercedes Benz ghosting down the road. Loud rap music blared from the speakers. When the driver looked out of his window, His stomach lurched. He was now fully clothed, but it was the man Rochelle had been with that night.

Ricky slowed the car down, staring at him over the top of expensive sunglasses. The exchange only lasted a second before he was down the road and out of sight.

'Yo, how do you know Ricky?' Shorty frowned at Lamont.

'What?' Lamont stared after the car.

'Ricky. Ricky Reagan. He works for Delroy, man.'

'I've seen him around,' Lamont lied. He didn't need Shorty to tell him about Delroy. Delroy Williams was the biggest criminal in Leeds, and had been so for decades, heavily involved in drugs and other forms of crime.

'Ricky's the guy Craig wanted to be. Delroy has him running most of his street teams. I heard he bought that Benz brand new. Cash.'

'That's impressive,' Lamont replied through gritted teeth. He couldn't help but remember Ricky's arrogance that night as he'd stared down Lamont. It occurred almost a year ago, yet he remained equally affected. Shorty babbled, oblivious to the change of mood.

'There's pure money in those hard drugs. I know a couple guys selling coke small-time. They're making loads off them white people in town,' said Shorty, laughing. Lamont's brow furrowed.

'Let's do that,' he said.

'Do what?'

'Sell coke.'

Shorty sniggered. 'You wanna sell coke? *You?*'

Shorty's laughter grew. His shoulders shook, tears of mirth streaming from his eyes. Lamont didn't say a word. He stared down his friend in a way he never had before, and when Shorty noticed, he immediately straightened.

Lamont's face was placid, but his nostrils flared, eyes like ice. Shorty froze, stumped by the transformation.

'Do you want money?' Lamont said, when he was sure he had Shorty's full attention.

'Course I want money. We're dying out here, L, for basically nothing. We make enough to do what we're doing, but where's the profit?'

'This is the chance to get ahead. We can do it. We only need one thing.'

'Yeah. Cash. Packages cost money, bro. Drugs aren't cheap. I doubt that even between you, me and K, we could come up with enough. Unless you wanna rip off Trevor and not give him his cut?'

Lamont gazed into the distance again, his mind on Mercedes Benzes' and women he couldn't have.

'If we were to sell, do you think you could find us a customer base?'

Shorty needed only a second to think.

'Yeah, I know people. They'd buy from us.'

Lamont smiled, the icy look in his eyes fading.

'We'll need to get someone to give us credit then.'

'No one's gonna front us for some coke. Everyone's out for themselves. No one's trying to bring anyone else in. It's not that kinda game.'

'Get us a meeting and I will do the rest,' Lamont said.

Shorty stared at him in wonder. Lamont quietly went about his business, ruffled no feathers and kept it moving. At times, though, he was a different person, driven, radiating some inner power that demanded you take him seriously.

Shorty first noticed when they were selling drugs with Levi. Levi would act like he was the boss but when in crunch time, Lamont made the crucial decisions. It confused him, but also filled him with a sense of reassurance. He didn't quite know what was going on with Lamont, but he was calculated and intelligent. Shorty was in.

'Cool, L. I'll see what I can do.'

———

'Lamont? Why haven't you swept the kitchen floor yet?'

Lamont slumped over the table, eating cereal and listening to *Mobb Deep* on his Walkman. He heard Auntie shouting, but she didn't need to know that. The Walkman and cassette tapes were proving a worthwhile investment. Realising he wasn't listening, Auntie snatched the earphones from his ears.

'Do you hear me?' She screamed. Lamont glanced at her.

'Yes, I hear you. I'll sweep when I'm finished.'

'No, you'll do it now.'

He swallowed another mouthful of cornflakes and looked at his Aunt.

'No, I won't.'

Auntie's eyes bulged at Lamont's defiance. 'I'm not sure where you think you are, but this is my house and you'll do as I say.'

'I don't think you heard me the first time.' Lamont put the spoon in the bowl without taking his eyes from his Aunt. 'No. I. Won't.'

Auntie shook her head. 'You think you can take me on?'

Lamont smiled, viewing Auntie as if for the first time. He no longer feared her. He wasn't a child anymore, and she was beneath him.

'*Take you on?* What is it you think is going on here? I'm a grown man and my days of being bossed around by you are over.'

'Oh really?' Auntie's sunken cheekbones quivered, her mouth opening and closing as she tried to gather her words. He didn't give her a chance.

'Yes, really. I pay you rent. Why should I even do chores?'

'I'll tell you why, because—'

'The question was rhetorical,' Lamont interjected. 'I'm not doing chores anymore. So either you do them, or get Rika to.'

Auntie gasped at his words. Before she could retort, there was a knock at the door. Lamont smiled sweetly and stood. 'I'll get that shall I?' Leaving Auntie in stunned silence, he left the kitchen.

'We need to talk,' Shorty said when Lamont opened the door. It had been a week since Lamont had given Shorty his task. They'd chilled since, but Shorty hadn't mentioned it, and he hadn't pushed the issue. Lamont stepped outside, closing the door behind him.

'I've been all over the place, L. No one wants to deal with us.'

'What?'

'People turned me down left right and centre. A couple' people said they'd sell to us for a price, but no one's trying to give anything for free. Not to me anyway.' Shorty's brow furrowed. Lamont read between the lines: Shorty had done robberies in the past, making it hard for people to trust him.

'No one would deal with you?'

Shorty nodded. 'One guy said he would. He's a loser, though.'

'What do you mean?'

'This dude called Louie. Lives near Bankside. He said he'll meet us.'

'So, let's deal with him.' Lamont didn't understand.

'He's a drunk, L. Got a few kids running for him and even they rip him off. He's no good for us.'

'We have to start somewhere, Shorty. Set the meeting up.'

Shorty shrugged. 'Fine. If this fucks up, it's on you.'

———

Days later, Shorty and Lamont stood outside Louie's place. The house itself was unforgettable. It was a ramshackle terraced spot with shutters over the windows and a brown front door with the paint peeling from it. Leading the way, Shorty knocked. After a few moments, they heard movement and what sounded like cursing. Soon an old man glared out.

'Shorty? What do you want now?' Louie had a prominent gut,

fleshy face and a copious amount of grizzled facial hair. He wore a pair of greying tracksuit bottoms and a rumpled sweater.

'I'm here to do business, unless you want to do it out here?'

'Who's he?' Louie looked at Lamont, who met his gaze.

'He's my boy. I told you about him. He's with me in this thing.'

'What's his name?'

'Lamont.'

'Surname?' Louie all but shouted.

'Jones. His surname is Jones,' Shorty muttered.

'Jones . . . *Carmen Jones?*' Louie's eyes were wistful. Lamont didn't have to ask how he knew the name.

'She's my Auntie,' he spoke for the first time.

'Come in. Quickly.'

The living room looked even worse than the outside of the house. Cleaning evidently wasn't one of Louie's talents. There were plates of food on the coffee table, everything covered in a fine layer of dust.

'Take a seat.' Louie collapsed in a dilapidated armchair. The pair remained standing. 'Fine. Suit yourselves. What do you want?'

Lamont started to speak, but Shorty beat him to it.

'We want an ounce of coke. You'll get your fee back, plus interest, when we move it.'

Louie took a second to reply, loudly sucking his teeth. Both boys ignored the disgusting sound.

'I give you that, I'm shorting myself. It's bad enough I've got little kids out there making me look dumb trying to rip me off. People think I don't know, but I do.' Louie met Lamont's eyes, then Shorty's.

'That's between you and your people. We're looking to get our feet in the door. Furthermore, we already talked about this, so why are you messing around?' Shorty's voice rose.

'Because, I've already got one set of people ripping me off. You lot might make it two sets, and then I'm losing out even more. I dunno if it's worth it. Not without summat up front.' Louie picked his words carefully. Shorty's hands balled into fists, a prominent vein throbbing from his neck.

'You're taking the piss.'

'I'm not trying to—'

'I don't care what little pricks you've got juggling for you on the streets. You're messing us around.'

Louie nodded, swallowing hard. 'I'm not trying to mess you around, but I have to do what I think is right.'

'What are you talking about? This is business. You said we were getting an ounce, so we're not leaving without one.'

'Now you're threatening me?' Louie shouted. Lamont saw his hand slip into his pocket. In his rage Shorty missed the movement.

'Does anyone want a drink?'

Lamont's words had the desired effect. Louie and Shorty stopped shouting.

'You what?' Louie had taken little notice of the quiet Jones boy. He wore a black crewneck sweater and jeans, and had an air of healthy confidence about him.

'I'm thirsty. I'd like a drink. Does anyone else want one?' Lamont replied.

'I wouldn't mind a beer,' Louie said slowly, unsure of what was going on.

'Shorty, can you get Louie a beer please while I speak to him?'

Shorty glared at Lamont but rather than argue, he stomped to the kitchen. There was another moment of silence when he left.

'So, you know my Auntie,' Lamont finally spoke. Louie assessed the words before he replied.

'I know a few members of your family. I knew your mother too.' He looked Lamont in the eyes. 'You look a lot like her.'

Lamont felt a jolt in his stomach at the mention of his mother. Louie wasn't the first to say this. People had been saying it to him all his life, and every time they did, he had the same feeling.

'So I've heard. You and my Auntie . . . was it serious?'

'Why?' Louie narrowed his eyes and crossed his arms. Lamont maintained the eye contact. He stood by the window, the light from outside the dirty windows illuminating his profile, making him appear more dominant, bathed in the brightness.

'She raised me after my parents died. I guess I just don't understand what men saw in her.'

'You don't?' Louie raised his bushy eyebrows. Lamont laughed, conceding the point. He was old enough to understand the sexual effect women had on men.

'Okay, maybe I don't want to see it from that angle.'

'Your Auntie, she was something special. Even now, people still talk about her in her heyday,' Louie paused, checking if Lamont seemed offended before he went on. 'She had this wild energy. Pure passion. She could go in a room and get any guy she wanted. Any guy!' Louie's voice rose. Lamont gave him a moment before he spoke.

'And she wanted you.' It wasn't a question. The answer was already clear.

'You probably see me as some grubby old man, but back then, I had the wardrobe, the jewellery, a big car. People waited around for me. We started spending time together.' Louie's eyes darkened. 'She used me. Got what she wanted . . . money, powder, everything, and then she just switched. Didn't avoid me or anything; she just changed. When a woman as passionate as your Auntie turns cold on you, you feel horrible. That was how I felt. Ill.' Louie's words were tinged with a sadness that Lamont understood.

What Rochelle had taken from him was far worse than any money, or clothes or jewellery. She had taken his heart.

Lamont had spoken to no one about it, not even Marcus. At times, he felt he was over his feelings, and then they would intensify, returning more powerful than ever. He needed to convince Louie, because he had no intention of ending up like him.

'I understand, Louie. Really, I do.'

Louie seemed surprised at Lamont's sincerity for a moment, and then his eyes narrowed.

'I wanna ask you summat now.'

Lamont nodded.

'Why do you wanna sell drugs?'

'Why not?' Lamont quickly replied, before he'd even considered the question. Louie shook his head.

'Seriously. Be straight up.'

'You weren't the only one who got bled by my Auntie. Any money my parents might have left, I never saw. I remember the wild parties she held that I had to clean up after, though. As a kid,' Lamont shook away the memories, focusing, determined to make the older man understand. 'I need to build something and this is the best way to do it.'

'You're different. I can see that. You can fit in out there, in that normal world. You don't need to stay in the darkness.'

'The other reason I need to do this,' Lamont went on as if he hadn't heard Louie, 'is because I had someone I cared about too, and she screwed me over. The *normal* life is what I might have had with her, but that's done. I always listen to my instincts, and when my instincts tell me to do something, I do it. More importantly, I make sure I do it better than anyone else.'

Neither spoke now, knowing a level of understanding connected them. Shorty re-entered the room. He gave Lamont a funny look and handed the beer to Louie.

'What's the deal then?' he said, voice still thick with anger. Louie rose with a grunt and went upstairs. He returned and handed a carrier bag to Lamont.

'There's two ounces in there. Shorty knows the price. Come back when you have my end, plus ten percent.'

CHAPTER ELEVEN

Monday 4 May 1998

NEITHER LAMONT nor Shorty spoke after leaving Louie. Lamont glanced around as they walked, his earlier confidence buried. Chapeltown was full of predators, and the police were always around in some form. The last thing they needed was to get caught with drugs.

The fear propelled him forward, his step quickening. Shorty moved more assuredly next to him. He didn't look daunted about walking with drugs. Instead, he looked thoughtful.

'I heard what you said to Louie.' He finally broke the silence. Lamont didn't respond, though by the look in his eyes, it was obvious he'd heard him. 'Who did you catch feelings over?'

Lamont stopped, turning toward Shorty. He was taken aback by the seriousness etched into every line of Lamont's face.

'I don't want to talk about it. Not now. Not ever. Okay?' Lamont's tone was chilling, and he nodded.

'Fine,' Shorty changed the subject. 'I'm gonna link up with K-Bar. We'll cut and bag these ounces. He's getting hold of the equipment for us, so I'll get at you when it's done. There's this crackhead named Chalky. He'll let us use his place.'

'Sounds like a plan.'

When Lamont entered his home, the noise from the TV was deafening. Auntie sat in the living room, watching her evening soaps with a cup of coffee. She glanced at him standing in the doorway. A frown appeared on her face but she didn't say a word. Instead, she turned her attention back to the TV.

Lamont headed upstairs, smiling at the reaction. Auntie had grown comfortable with him giving her money. It was why she hadn't pushed back after their argument. As much as she disliked him, he knew Auntie would do anything to make sure the cash continued coming in.

Upstairs, Lamont tried reading a book, but found himself restless. He made some food in the kitchen, washing the tasteless microwave meal down with a glass of water, thinking about the venture they were undertaking.

Convincing Louie to give him a package was only the first step. Selling weed was relatively safe. They dealt mostly with people he knew and there was no real danger. Cocaine, crack and heroin were different ball-games. The stakes were larger and people were willing to maim to keep what was theirs. Lamont needed to be tough, but more importantly, he would have to use his brain like he never had before. It was vital that he succeed.

Lamont thought again to the Mercedes Benz; the cool assuredness of the man driving it. The way Shorty had spoken about him. Ricky had it all. A flash car, money, a reputation . . . Rochelle.

Putting his plate in the sink, he quickly washed and dried it then left the house, needing some air.

Lamont moved along the streets with his head down, fighting the urge to yawn. He was tired after the day but he knew if he laid down, he wouldn't sleep. His brain refused to shut down, to stop thinking about Rochelle. Lamont hated himself for the weakness. He wanted to be more like Marcus and Shorty. They could effortlessly detach from whatever girls they were seeing. They were ruthless, and that was what he wanted to be. Callous. Cold.

He couldn't help but yearn for Rochelle, though. He only had to close his eyes to remember the feel of her body against his, the parting of her mouth as she moaned. So many months had gone by, but he could still see it all, and it killed him. He had messed around with other girls since, but she'd burrowed under his skin.

Lamont's feet took him to Chapeltown Road. He stood outside Warsaw Stores, one shop amongst a row, staring straight ahead. Street lights threw the row into prominence. He wasn't the only one hanging around, but the older men gave him his space, talking in loud tones.

His thought went from Rochelle, to prison. The thoughts of failing almost overwhelmed him. He closed his eyes. He needed to succeed.

'Lamont?'

He almost didn't hear the soft voice calling him, but looked up instinctively as a girl ambled towards him. It took a second before he realised they'd gone to the same school. She wore a black jacket, fitted denim jeans and flat shoes, carrying a leather portfolio and a handbag. Her skin was a butterscotch shade that gleamed under the streetlights. His depressive thoughts dissipated slightly.

'Layla, how are you doing?' He found his tongue.

'Good. Just coming back from college. How are you? I haven't seen you since school ended. Didn't you go to the end-of-year party?'

Lamont shook his head. He'd heard that Erica and some of her friends were organising a party, but he had given it a miss.

'I couldn't make it. So, how's college? Are you still wanting to be a solicitor?' Lamont remembered Layla's passion from school. Her eyes widened slightly, and he could tell she was surprised at him remembering.

'Yeah, that's right. I'm loving college. It's good to be around new people and the classes I'm taking are enjoyable. What are you doing with your days?'

Lamont shrugged. 'Would you believe me if I said I was still trying to find myself?'

Layla grinned, looking at his expensive tracksuit and trainers. It didn't take a genius to work out what he was into, and it was made obvious by his vague answer. She had spotted him from the bus, and the sorrow in his eyes intrigued her enough to get off a few stops early to speak to him. They had only spoken a few times in school, but this somehow felt different.

'What's wrong with you? You don't have to tell me if you don't want, but talking about whatever it is might help.'

'I've just got things on my mind. It's not even worth putting into words.'

'That means women.'

Lamont grinned, but didn't deny it. Traffic whizzed along behind them. A kid and his friend dribbled a football down the road, passing it between them and keeping it from the edge of the pavement. For a moment, Lamont remembered doing the same thing as a kid. He watched them harder than he should have. Layla entered Warsaw Stores whilst he was distracted and bought herself a bottle of water.

'Well . . . It was nice running into you, L, but I'm gonna go. I got off the bus to speak to you, but I have an early start tomorrow.'

'Where are you walking to?'

'St Martin's.'

'Can I walk with you?'

Layla nodded, and they walked up Chapeltown Road. Lamont warmed to Layla as the conversation flowed. She told funny stories about college and they shared memories from school. He ambled along, feeling freer than he had in a long while.

Layla was surprised at Lamont. She remembered him chasing after Erica in school and stuttering around women. Now, he seemed more confident and direct. He smiled easily, but she couldn't help but notice that his eyes, a beautiful rosewood shade, were hard, none of the supposed joy reaching them. It was thought provoking. By the time they reached Layla's, their pace had slowed, trying to make the talk last.

'Well, here we are,' Layla said, motioning to her house. 'It was nice running into you, L.'

'You too. I'm glad you're doing well. I'd like to stay in touch if it's cool with you? Feels weird to reconnect and then forget about each other again.'

Layla smiled, reaching into her portfolio and writing her number on some paper. She handed it to Lamont.

'Ring me and we'll hang out sometime.'

Lamont grinned and hugged her, enjoying the feel of her slim curves against his body. He inhaled a vanilla scent and pulled away.

'I'll speak to you soon.'

———

The next morning, Auntie stormed into Lamont's room at the crack of dawn. He snored gently, his head burrowed into a simple white pillow.

'Lamont! Wake up!'

'What do you want?' He yawned, not even opening his eyes.

'I want some money. Do you know how much things cost around here?'

Kissing his teeth, he clambered from the bed.

'Get out of my room. I'll bring it down to you.'

Auntie gaped at him, fury resonating in her eyes.

'Who the hell are you talking to?'

Lamont met her eyes.

'If you want your money, leave.'

Glaring at her nephew for a long moment, Auntie turned on her heel and flounced from the room. When he heard her stomping back down the stairs, he smiled, happy to have won another verbal spar. He washed and dressed, sauntering downstairs with four ten-pound notes. Laying them on the kitchen table, he was about to walk back out when Auntie called after him.

'What's this?' Her lip curled.

'You wanted money. There's your money.'

'This isn't enough. I need more.'

'Tough. You'll get the rest on Friday. Until then, make it last.'

Without waiting for a reply, Lamont walked out of the house, realising with a jolt that he was thinking of Layla, and not Rochelle.

———

112

Lamont was in his room reading when the call came through. K-Bar met him outside Auntie's, and they drove to Chalky's. He lived near Bankside, close to Lamont's home. He took a deep breath, trying to calm his nerves. When they entered, Shorty stood in the kitchen, the drugs haphazardly wrapped. There was cocaine residue on numerous surfaces, but Chalky was nowhere to be seen.

'We're good to go, L. We've got everything cooked and bagged. Chalky's putting the word out that we've got some strong shit, and I've let my people know, so it's time to get cracking.'

Despite the fear gnawing at Lamont, he felt uplifted to hear Shorty state they were ready. Ever since he'd spoken to Louie, he had flip-flopped so many times between wanting to sell drugs and wanting to get out and get a real job before it was too late. When he sat down and gave the subject some thought, he realised there was nothing else he wanted to do.

———

Lamont stood near Spencer Place in the Hood, doing his best to remain inconspicuous. He rubbed his hands on his trousers, glancing around, his heart racing. Every time he saw someone he recognised, he would keep his head down, praying they wouldn't guess what he was doing. Every person who looked at him from a passing car was an undercover officer, determined to lock him up.

Lamont kept his hands in his pockets, the wraps stored there burning a hole in his palm. He had refused to store the drugs in his mouth the way the others did. He couldn't believe people did this every day. Selling weed had been easy by comparison. Lamont dealt with people he knew, and everything was lovely. Crack was a whole different game. It presented much more risk. His stomach twisted nervously the longer he stood there.

After a while, a dusty-looking man shuffled towards him, dirty faced and limping. As he drew closer, Lamont scanned his face, trying to gauge if he the man was legit, or an undercover officer.

'Have you got owt?' the man mumbled. His heart pounding, Lamont remembered Shorty's teachings, and signalled for the man to walk down a nearby alley. With a quick glance around, he followed.

'What are you after?' His voice shook. Clearing his throat, he tried getting it under control. 'What do you want?'

The sale watched him intently. Lamont met the look, the beating of his heart more frenzied. He willed himself not to look away first. Finally, the sale began coughing profusely, 'Gimme three please.' He scratched his neck.

'Got you.' Lamont scrambled in his pockets for the wraps. The sale took them with sweaty fingers, gave Lamont the money, then hurried away as fast as his limp would allow. Letting out a deep breath, Lamont stuck the money in his sock, glanced around again, then slowly walked back out to Spencer Place.

———

After the initial selling of his first wraps, it took almost a week for Lamont, Shorty and K-Bar to move both ounces. For a few days, they clipped sales — addicts — where they could, before deciding to try working shifts. Lamont worked the day, K-Bar the evening, and Shorty overnight. After they sold out, Shorty brought Louie his profit, and took another two ounces.

Some days were slower, but they slowly built up a rhythm. Shorty helped when he went to town one day and purchased some pay-as-you-go mobile phones. These phones were cumbersome, but would help the trio build up their drug line, and become more known.

———

A few weeks later, Lamont was at Shorty's eating when the mobile phone rang. Hastily swallowing his food, Lamont answered.

'Yeah?'

'You got owt? I need eight,' A scratchy voice said. Lamont grinned. The morning had been dry so far. If this sale was serious, Lamont would be closer to selling out for the day.

'Meet me at Spencer's. Two minutes.' Lamont waited for the sale to confirm, then hung up. Wolfing down the rest of the sandwich, he guzzled a glass of water and hit the roads.

The sale waited in the alleyway by Spencer Place. He looked shifty, but that was normal. What struck him as strange was that he didn't recognise the sale. Assuming he had got the number from another customer, he approached.

'You got that?' He asked, referring to the money. The sale didn't move. Lamont was about to repeat himself when he heard scuffling from behind. He had no time to react before he was barrelled to the floor, a flurry of feet repeatedly kicking him.

There were three men, stinking and tattered. Surging to his feet, he hit one man, sending him reeling. The other attackers dragged him back to the floor, desperation lending them strength as they rained hits on him. When Lamont stopped moving, one of them rummaged through his jacket pocket, relieving him of his wraps.

'Check his pockets! Get his money!'

Luckily, he'd left the rest of his money at Shorty's. Hitting him twice more, the trio scampered away, leaving him moaning on the ground in pain.

———

'L! What the fuck happened?' Shorty leapt to his feet when Lamont staggered inside. His jacket was torn, his mouth bleeding.

'Got jumped by some fiends.' Lamont collapsed into a chair and massaged his ribs.

'Did they get anything?'

'Eight shots,' Lamont moaned.

'Motherfuckers!' Shorty growled. 'What did they look like?'

Lamont gave the best description he could, but everything had been a blur. Shouting for K-Bar, who was resting upstairs, they hit the roads to look for the thieves. Once the door slammed, Lamont closed his eyes, shaking.

———

Shorty and K-Bar searched all over for the thieves, but they had gone to ground. Eventually, they had to take the loss, and let it go.

Lamont spent the next few days in deep thought. Being attacked by people he believed to be the lowest of the low was degrading. It made him wonder if he had the heart to be a drug dealer. Everyone in the game was out to win. Lamont played out in his mind all the different ways the situation could have gone. If the fiends had knives, he might be dead. The thought of Marika being alone scared him as much as being shot or stabbed.

He was nearly eighteen; smart enough to get a legitimate job if he put his mind to it. When it came down to it, he refused to fail. He had goals, and a group of decaying smack-heads would not determine his destiny.

———

Lamont's robbery was glossed over fairly quickly, and he decided he would not be a victim. He stepped up his training, sparring with Marcus and Shorty, ensuring he was in peak physical condition and ready for any conflict.

The goal for the team was to make as much money as possible, and Lamont made sure they did that. They pitched around the Hood, serving as many fiends as possible and making sure Louie got his return. In no time, they were his best customers, and though Shorty and K-Bar would drop off the money and collect the drugs, Lamont made sure they treated him right, forever grateful to the man for giving him his start.

They hit the streets with a vengeance, working hard, letting the crack heads know who they were and where to find them. When they disagreed with other teams, Shorty and K-Bar handled it, and their reputations were enough to keep people at bay.

The money improved, but not quickly enough for Lamont's liking. One day, he sat down with Shorty. They were at his spot, Lamont pacing the boxy living room while Shorty relaxed with a beer.

'Why are you so worried, L? We're smashing it.'

Lamont paused, scratching his chin, weighing up his words and debating what to say.

'I want more.'

'We all want more, but we need to keep moving carefully. Isn't that what you're always saying?'

'I am, and we are, but we also need to step our game up, or we'll be like everyone else, hustling every day to stay ahead. We need people working for us.'

Shorty nodded. 'I feel you on that. I've got a couple dudes that would work for us if the money was right. We need to keep making links, though, plus we need to move on from Louie, bro. He's dead weight. His own people rip him off, for fuck's sake.'

'That's them. For now, Louie's supply will do. When we've grown, we'll look to other suppliers. I want you to reach out to any who you think can work with us. Speak to K-Bar, make sure we're all in agreement.'

'K-Bar will be down with whatever makes us more money, L. I'll speak to him, but he's cool.'

Lamont agreed. K-Bar didn't like to weigh in on many of the big decisions. He was an asset, though, and like Shorty, had a vibe that warned against messing with him.

'We need to trim the fat too.'

'What the hell does that mean?' Shorty frowned.

'It means there are a lot of dealers in similar positions to us. We need to be above them, and we need them working for us, so that we grow. We're seen as the bottom of the barrel, and I don't like that.'

Shorty yawned. 'I get what you're saying, but like you said, we're at the bottom, so there's no reason for any of them to come and work with us.'

Lamont grinned, but there was no joy in it. It was bloodless, full of menace, and made Shorty feel uneasy.

'This is where we get creative. We need to meet Marcus, and I'll fill you both in on the plan.'

Days later, Lamont was on the streets, wanting to get inside so he could eat and chill. He had a few wraps left to sell, but he wasn't seeing as many fiends around, and no one was calling the phone boxes he hung around, nor were they calling the mobile phone he carried.

He was exhausted after a long night and day, but he had a rule about finishing his shift with product on his person, so he would stay outside until he'd sold out. The longer he stayed, the more risk of running into police or stick-up dudes who preyed on dealers.

Dipping down a side-street with his hands jammed into his pockets, Lamont noticed a prostitute he'd sold drugs to in the past. She tottered along, trying to light a cigarette.

'Daisy, how are you doing?' He asked, startling the woman. She was shorter than he was, with bedraggled blonde hair, pale blue eyes and truckloads of makeup. Once upon a time she'd been a looker, but life and drugs had worn her down. She was good-natured, though, and he didn't avoid her.

'I'm knackered, L,' she said, finally lighting her cigarette. She offered Lamont one from the battered pack, but he declined.

'I know how you feel. I'm looking to get inside and get some food.' He reached into his pockets for the wraps, showing them to her. 'I'll sell you these three for forty quid.'

Daisy sighed, shaking her head.

'I've barely made anything, L. My man will kill me if I go home with no money.'

Lamont would have walked away, but could tell by the gleam in Daisy's eyes that she was interested.

'Daisy, baby. We both know it's only a matter of time until you get scooped up and paid. When the punters come cruising, you'll be the first port of call. I'd have a go myself, if I thought I could keep up.' He smirked, watching Daisy grin.

'I'm sure you'd do fine, L. You can have a go for half-price,' she offered, leering. He resisted the urge to shudder, forcing the grin to remain on his face.

'Maybe next time. Gimme thirty five and they're yours. You

know no one else will do you a better deal, and you can go home and get merry.'

Daisy considered it for all of two seconds before she fumbled in her pockets and gave him his money. He gave her the wraps, then watched her totter back down the alley. Deep down, Lamont knew she'd likely not make anymore money, which would infuriate her pimp, but couldn't find it within him to care. Turning on his heel, he hurried away, keeping his eyes open for any activity.

CHAPTER TWELVE

Monday 15 June 1998

LAMONT LEFT THE PARK, beaming. He'd gone to hang with some old football friends. Since he stopped training with Nigel, he'd seen little of them. They'd had an impromptu football game. He held his own, scoring multiple times against his skilled friends. It was a boost to his confidence and even as he walked home covered in sweat, he couldn't stop smiling. For nearly a year he'd allowed the darkness to overwhelm his thoughts. Now, he was thinking clearly. He hoped.

As Lamont approached Auntie's, thinking about where to watch the Germany vs USA World Cup match that night, he noticed Marcus waiting, leaning against a car smoking a joint. He eyed Lamont carefully, touching his fist.

'Where are you coming from all sweaty like that? Hope it's a woman.'

'I was kicking ball with some friends. What you doing round here?'

'Come to see you, obviously.'

'How's independent life?' Lamont hadn't seen much of Marcus since he moved out. The times they had spoken were mainly in passing, so he was surprised that he was waiting for him.

'You know me, I've always been independent. Forget that for now.' Marcus motioned to the ride. 'Let's go for a drive.'

'Have I got time to get a shower?'

Marcus raised an eyebrow. 'We're not going on a date, blood. You don't need to freshen up.'

'I've been playing football for hours, bro. Gimme twenty minutes.'

Lamont hurried inside, quickly showering and dressing in a sweater and jeans. He shrugged his feet into some black trainers and headed out the door, grabbing his wallet and keys. Marcus waited in the car. When Lamont climbed in, he drove away.

'How's things?' Marcus asked after they'd been driving for a while.

'Can't complain. Just trying to make things happen.'

'Drugs?'

Lamont wondered who had been talking. He immediately ruled out Louie, as he couldn't imagine Marcus making time with the small-fry.

'Shorty tell you?'

Marcus nodded. 'Said you secured a connect so you can start slanging Class A.'

'What else did he tell you?'

'He said you spoke to Louie, and that you were sharing stories. Said you caught feelings.'

'Did he also say that I told him I never wanted to discuss it?' Lamont's voice was cold. If Marcus noticed, he didn't comment.

'Maybe you didn't wanna discuss it with him, but I know who you were talking about. Explains a few things.'

Lamont tried to control his breathing, his heartbeat pounding. He had tried for so long to put his feelings behind him where Rochelle was concerned. What she had done to him had shattered his core, and the hardest thing at the time had been to go on as if nothing was wrong.

The pressure had nearly broken him, and he never wanted to go through anything like it again. Marcus wouldn't listen, though, he knew that. He had sought him out for a reason, and nothing would prevent them from having the conversation.

'Are you hungry?' Marcus asked after a while. He shook his head, but was betrayed by his rumbling stomach. Marcus laughed.

They stopped at a West Indian spot near Roundhay Road. Marcus practically ordered the whole menu, whereas Lamont settled for oxtail with rice and stewed peas. They sat inside the crowded restaurant to eat. Marcus nodded and greeted a few people, some of whom Lamont was familiar with. They ate in silence for a while and then Marcus began talking again.

'She was fucked up, you know.'

Lamont wanted to pretend he didn't know who he was talking about, but it wasn't worth it.

'I tried asking about it. Mia did too. She wouldn't speak, though. It was obvious she was hurting. Just like you.'

'How do you know something happened if she didn't speak on it?'

Marcus paused. 'I saw Ricky.'

Lamont's fingers tightened around the fork he was holding. Everything about Ricky Reagan made him want to kill the man, and that was a dangerous mindset to have. If Lamont wanted to survive the drugs game, he needed to keep his emotions in check.

'What did he say?'

'He wanted to know about you. Said you came by the place, and that he'd heard about you sexing Rochelle. He wanted it to stop.'

'Did you know about him?' Lamont looked his friend in the eye. Some of his anger must have slipped out, because Marcus looked startled for a minute.

'Yeah.'

Lamont grit his teeth, his body tensing.

'Why didn't you tell me?'

'Because . . .' Marcus blew out a breath.

'Because what?'

'Because I didn't know, okay?'

'Didn't know what? Stop skating around it and just answer me.'

Lamont's voice rose, and people glanced over. He took a deep breath.

'I didn't know how you felt for her.'

'What are you talking about? Course you kn—'

'I just thought you wanted to have sex with her. I didn't know you were caught up. Whatever happened, it fucked her up. She hasn't been the same since.'

Lamont wasn't sure how he even felt about that. He didn't want Rochelle to hurt but, couldn't deny feeling a certain relish that her decision had affected her that day. They ate again without speaking, but he enjoyed the comfort. He knew Marcus had his best interests at heart, as annoying as it was that he'd held information from him.

'So, you're stepping your game up then?'

Lamont looked up, wiping his mouth with a napkin as he finished his food.

'Do you think I should?'

Marcus shrugged. 'You'll have thought it all through. The streets are rough, but I know what you're like, and I definitely know what Shorty's like. You'll be stacking in no time, no doubt.'

Lamont scratched his chin, warmth spreading throughout his chest.

'Did he say anything about the other thing?'

Marcus frowned. 'What other thing?'

'I need your help with something. I'll pay well.'

———

Marcus stopped his car down the road from an unkempt terraced house. Pulling on a pair of leather gloves, he tugged his hood tighter over his head, and climbed from the car, keeping his head down.

In front of the dirty house, a group of guys were laughing and cracking jokes, one talking on a mobile phone almost the size of his head. Marcus didn't hesitate. Assessing the biggest man first, he caught him flush with a blow, sending him sailing through the air. Two of the others turned and ran, the last man frozen on the spot.

Marcus grabbed him around the throat, lifting him off the ground like he weighed nothing.

'Get off this strip, you little punk. You're not man enough to be out here. Look how quickly your people dusted and left you?'

Marcus flung him to the floor and kicked him in the ribs. Looking around, he took his money and drugs, then walked away.

———

Marcus and Victor repeated the same tactic on half a dozen different independent dealers over the next few weeks, beating them senseless, and robbing their product. After a while, Shorty or K-Bar would pass through, feigning concern and promising safety if they started buying directly from Lamont.

The plan was a success, and every affected person began indirectly working for Lamont. Marcus received five thousand pounds and was impressed with Lamont's cunning in manipulating a situation to get paid. With his help, he devised a similar strategy, and waded into the protection market, quickly swelling his profits.

'You're a crafty guy, L,' Shorty later remarked, as the pair sipped drinks in a club in town. 'How did you know that would work?'

'I took a shot,' said Lamont shrugging and lifting the drink to his lips.

———

In August, Lamont and Layla left the cinema, both grinning as they navigated through the city centre. They had been to see *The Negotiator*.

'Do you want to go for food, or do you fancy something to drink?' Lamont asked, looking around him as they walked. It was early evening, and still warm enough for Lamont to be in a white t-shirt, and Layla to be wearing a blouse and skirt. They were an attractive couple, and men and women alike checked out the pair as they strolled.

'Let's go for food. I don't need to be getting drunk around you,' said Layla, grinning.

'What do you mean by that?' Lamont laughed. Layla refused to answer until they'd settled down for food at a Chinese restaurant near the market. After they placed their orders, she spoke.

'You knew exactly what I meant; I don't even know why you asked.'

She was right. As always. Ever since running into Layla on Chapeltown Road, Lamont had spent a lot of time with her. She was fun and easy to talk to. Rochelle had damaged him, though, and he was fully aware of that fact. As much as he enjoyed spending time with Layla, he often backed away at crucial moments. If Layla realised, she'd never commented on it.

'You think I need you to be drunk to take advantage of you?'

Layla shrugged, tucking into her food when it arrived.

'Maybe you would. I don't know; as long as I've been spending time with you, you've been nothing but a perfect gentleman.'

'I thought that would be seen as a good thing.'

'It's strange. I mean, you're a good-looking guy. You're smart and you dress nice; the dirty looks I was receiving from other women are proof of that. I guess I just don't know what your game is.'

Lamont mulled that one over, deciding exactly to answer.

'When we were in high school, I started juggling weed, as you know.'

Layla nodded, eating her food as he spoke. Lamont took a bite of his chow mein before he continued.

'I met a girl. You saw me in school; a complete loser, spending all my time chasing after a girl who wasn't worthy. I met one who seemed to understand me, who had similar interests, who seemed to want the best for me.'

'I'm guessing it didn't turn out that way.' Layla met his eyes.

'We grew closer, I let her know how I felt, and we had sex.' His stomach churned, remembering seeing Reagan in the doorway, Rochelle's face as she closed the door on him. He willed the images away, taking a deep breath. 'She destroyed me.'

That was it. Lamont said no more. Layla reached over and squeezed his hand, then went back to her food. They spoke after that about regular topics, speaking about the movie, their plans for the rest of the year. They left town and Lamont ordered a taxi. Outside Layla's, he asked the driver to wait. They stood in the street for an awkward moment.

'I'm sorry if I ruined the mood. I don't want you to think I don't like you, because I do. The way I am, though; the life I'm in. I don't want to ruin you.'

Layla smiled, pulling him in for a hug and feeling him stiffen. She kissed him on the cheek and let him go.

'Thank you for being honest, L. I can tell it wasn't easy. When you want to spend more time together, call me.'

With that, she grinned and headed inside, Lamont watching her every step of the way.

———

Lamont, Shorty and K-Bar continued to plod along. They were becoming more known to the fiends and were making good money.

As months passed, Louie was finding it difficult to keep up with them. He was making more money than before but he still wasn't happy. When Shorty took Lamont with him to reload one day in September, he made his feelings clear.

'I'm glad you're here.' He jerked his thumb at Shorty. 'He never wants to listen to me.'

'Because you talk shit. I swear, the more money we make, the more you complain.'

'Oi, don't forget who got you started. You'd still be scratching your ass if it wasn't for me.'

'Guys, we don't need this,' Lamont interjected, when Shorty opened his mouth to reply. 'What's the problem, Louie?'

'The bloody problem is I'm too old to be running all over the place. I need to keep you lot happy, but now my other youngsters are complaining. They need product too.'

'Fuck them little pricks. We're getting through ten times as much as them. Cut them loose,' Shorty said.

Louie bristled. 'Hang on a—'

'—Guys,' there was more bite in Lamont's tone now. Both men heeded this. 'We're all working together, and we're all getting paid. There's a way around this.'

'What way's that?'

'Let us make the money for you.'

'I thought that was what I was doing now?'

'What I mean is, introduce us to your guy. We supply you, and you supply your regulars with no fuss.'

'So you wanna cut me out?'

'No, not cut you out. Make it easier for you.'

'Sounds like you're trying to cut me out.'

Shorty narrowed his eyes at Louie's petulant tone. Lamont smiled, like he'd expected this response.

'Cutting you out makes little sense, and it's not productive. We want to continue making money but our demand is higher, Lou. If you have a better suggestion, let's hear it.'

Shorty and Louie both stared, mouths agape. Lamont could be so quiet and unassuming that it was easy to overlook the dominance he showed. Shorty coughed, Louie shifting slightly in his seat.

'Look, take a quarter for now. Gimme time to have a think.'

———

'That motherfucker is getting too cheeky for his own good,' Shorty grumbled as they left.

'Louie's grouchy, but he's just used to being ripped off.'

'Why you always taking his side?' Shorty stopped and glared at Lamont.

'It's not about taking sides. If we keep Louie comfortable, he'll be easy to control. He's on the way out; he just doesn't wanna admit it.'

'You think?'

'Louie's lazy. The game has left him behind and he doesn't want to chase after it. We need his supplier so we can keep growing.'

'Okay. I get you.' Shorty understood. Lamont nudged him.

'Let's turn up the pressure and get rich, Shortstuff.'

Grinning, Shorty slapped hands with him. He didn't know who Lamont had caught feelings over, but he'd never seen his friend looking so focused. He liked it.

———

Lamont slouched over the kitchen table at Auntie's. Nowadays, he spent most of his time chilling at Shorty's or out and about, meeting links and selling.

The life had hold of him, and he was obsessed with making money. His team was growing, and his portion at the end of each week was increasing. It wasn't enough. The streets were wide open, and Lamont wanted to be one of the established cliques making big money. It was possible, but he needed to keep pushing and continue watching the angles.

Raising his tea to his lips, his eyes narrowed as Auntie hovered next to him. He forced himself to meet her eyes, lowering his cup.

'Yes?'

'I need more money.'

'I gave you your money yesterday.'

'I need more. You definitely have it.'

Lamont gave her another look. He'd done his best to keep the peace. They argued, but he never crossed the line, comfortable having a place to stay near Marika.

'Where does your money go?'

The reaction was immediate. Auntie stepped back, her mouth wide open, but no words coming out. Calmly, Lamont waited.

'What do you mean? I've never had any money because I spent half my life looking after you and your little sister. Don't you remember any of that?'

'Are you serious?' Lamont's eyebrows rose. He shouldn't have been shocked at Auntie's complete white-washing of the facts, but he was.

'You lot never wanted for anything. I fed and clothed you, made sure you were both looked after, and you've never been grateful for any of it. Marika always was. You never were.'

Lamont laughed in her face, the sound chillingly devoid of mirth.

'You profited from my parent's death. You received a live-in slave, and never once did you show me anything that resembled love. You loved Marika, but taught her nothing but your disgusting bad habits. For you to stand there and talk about us being looked after is nothing but a joke.'

'You're nothing but a little lia—'

'What happened to my parent's money?'

Auntie visibly paled, running a hand through her hair.

'What do you mean?'

Lamont rose to his feet, noting that he towered over Auntie. After her years of bullying, it was indescribable to see her on the back foot, unable to hit him or think of a decent comeback. The years of fear were over.

'My parents worked all their lives. They paid off the house we lived in when they were still alive, which everyone in our family knows. Where did the money from the sale of that same house go?'

'Are you crazy! Do you know how expensive it was to take care of everything? That money was eaten up by legal costs, inheritance fees, all of that stuff. I took care of you lot out of my pocket, with no help from family, and no gratitude. You'd have gone to a home if it wasn't for me.'

'I'd have preferred that to growing up around you,' retorted Lamont, his words calm despite his boiling blood. 'Do you think I'm stupid? I was ten years old when I came to live with you. I remember the drink and drugs, and your little parties, the expensive clothing. I know about you falsifying details to become a foster mother, even though you were claiming benefits and living off my dead parents blood and sweat. You have no idea of what it means to struggle. You're nothing but a bitter, out-of-touch lush who never wanted to earn any money for herself. No wonder everyone hates you.'

'That's it!' Auntie screamed. 'Get out of my house. I've put up with you and your ways long enough. I want you out!'

Lamont smiled, shocked at how free he felt.

'I'm leaving, don't worry. I won't spend another night in this house.'

'Good! You drug dealing piece of shit. I should call the police and let them know what you're doing.'

'I'd rather be a dealer than a user,' Lamont tilted his head, staring at the vile woman. 'A question; how did you keep paying for all of those drugs after your money ran out?' Not even waiting for her to answer, he made a face. 'On second thoughts, I don't want to know.'

'You piece of shi—' Auntie went to strike Lamont, but he grabbed her wrist, overpowering her with ease.

'You'll never lay a hand on me again,' he said, enunciating each word as she struggled against his grip. 'You have no power anymore. I'm leaving, and you get nothing from me. Not a single penny. Any money I give Rika from now on is hers. If I hear you've taken any of it, or you've mistreated her, you'll regret it. That I can promise you. If you know I'm dealing, you know what I can do to you. Do not push me.'

Shoving her to the side, Lamont finished his drink and left the room, Auntie cowed into silence behind him. He went to his room and packed his belongings, then left without another word.

CHAPTER THIRTEEN

Wednesday 10 February 1999

FINANCIALLY, Lamont was doing well. After abruptly leaving Auntie's, he'd stayed with Shorty and K-Bar for a few weeks, before getting his own place nearby on Cowper Street.

The streets remained steady, and their crew continued to hold its own against others. Everything hummed. The cash came in fast and everyone did as instructed. Lamont ran a tight ship and Shorty was on hand to ensure discipline was maintained. He managed Shorty correctly, allowing him to do what he needed, keeping him sharp, knowing he would then do the same for the guys below. Lamont had hit a snag now, though: He had too much money.

At first, he'd saved his money in shoe boxes like a lot of guys he knew. He gave money to his sister, put some in the bank, and had even started hiding money outside, wrapping it well.

It wasn't sustainable. Lamont was wary of the police. He needed to set himself up. Just because things were going well, didn't mean they would continue.

He made a black coffee, staring into space and holding the piping porcelain mug in his hands. He thought about investing the money and buying more drugs, but that would just lead to more cash lying around.

As Lamont thought about what he could do, an idea came to him. With a grin he reached for his phone and dialled a number.

'It's L. We need to talk.'

———

Lamont took a taxi into town, heading for a pub near the university. Outside, scores of drunk, boisterous students ran around making noise. He made his way through the masses. Inside, the pub was stuffy and full almost to capacity. Pushing his way to the bar, he ordered a pint and scanned the room, finally spotting him in the corner, whispering in the ear of a giggling girl. Making his way over, Lamont plopped on the seat opposite them.

'How's it going, Xiyu?'

'L! What the hell man, where have you been?' Xiyu Manderson's eyes twinkled. The pair were old friends and had spent a lot of time together before Lamont started selling weed. Xiyu was fair skinned, with straight jet black hair and piercing almond eyes that he'd received from his Chinese mother.

'Busy working. Same as you.' Lamont smiled at the girl Xiyu was entertaining. She smiled back.

'Uni man . . . It's crazy. You should start going. You'd love it.'

'Maybe I will. I need to talk to you. It's urgent.'

Xiyu nodded, rubbing his hands through his hair.

'Babe, go sit with the others. I'll come and get you after.'

The girl didn't like it, she forced a smile on her face and moved.

'What's the drill then? How can I help?' Xiyu asked.

'You're studying business at Uni aren't you?'

'You already know I am.' Xiyu rolled his eyes.

'I want to invest some money.'

'Into what?' Xiyu sipped his drink. Lamont didn't know what it was, but it smelt fruity.

'Something legitimate. I was hoping you could help.'

Xiyu scratched his chest. He was dressed like the other guys in the pub; white t-shirt, jeans and canvas shoes. His clothes appeared in better condition, though which didn't surprise Lamont. Xiyu had always been finicky about his outfits. Lamont assumed it came from growing up poor; trying to look your best when you didn't have the resources to do it.

As they sat, people kept approaching Xiyu, slapping him on the back, offering to get him another drink. It surprised Lamont just how popular he was.

'I work in an office to pay for Uni, mate. Barely earning above minimum wage. I dunno what I could tell you,' Xiyu said a few minutes later, after his fan club dispersed.

'You know business though. I want to know it too. Money isn't an issue. I'll pay you for the information.'

Xiyu shook his head. 'I don't need you to pay me. You're my friend and I want to help you. I'm just . . .' he trailed off, staring intently at the table. Lamont didn't interrupt. He had seen Xiyu's thinking face before, distracting himself by scanning the bar.

A couple of scantily clad girls glanced glancing in his direction. He smiled, but didn't make a move. He was on the clock tonight. Pleasure would have to wait. He wondered how many of the students in the pub had lectures first thing, and if they would even show up. Lamont's phone rang, but he ignored it. He needed to get this sorted.

'There's a guy I know. Martin. He's older and works in the same building as me. Trust fund kid who got cut off by his parents. He's doing well for himself, and he's always looking for investors. I could speak to him.'

Lamont beamed. 'That would be great. While you're ringing him, I'll go to the bar. What are you drinking?'

Lamont returned with Xiyu's drink, annoyed to see that his lady-friend from before draped all over him again. He had a seedy smile on his face as she whispered something into his ear that made him glance around to see if anyone overheard. Approaching, Lamont gave him his drink and sat down with a glass of water. If he had another pint, he'd end staying all night.

'Martin's busy this week, but said to give you his number. You can have a meeting on Tuesday. Ring him for the details.'

'Thanks, Xiyu. Means a lot.' Lamont took out his phone,

ignoring the missed calls and texts. Xiyu relayed Martin's number and he stored it in his phone.

'I'm gonna be off then.'

'Finish your drink at least, pal,' Xiyu insisted, pointing at the water that Lamont hadn't touched. Lamont did as bidden. 'Can I ask you a question, L?'

'Go for it.'

'How much are we talking about here?'

'In terms of?'

'How much are you wanting to invest? I mean, Martin's small-time, but he's not gonna want an investment of like five hundred quid or summat. He's a serious guy.'

'So am I.'

'How much then?'

Lamont drained his water and stood.

'Don't worry about that,' he reached into his pocket and handed Xiyu a fifty pound note. 'Buy yourself a few drinks on me. Thanks for the introduction.' Nodding at his girl and shaking Xiyu's hand, he made his way out of the pub, phone already to his ear to call a taxi.

———

Lamont sat in the reception of an office building in town, reading a magazine and trying his best to relax. He'd spoken to Martin over the phone and they arranged a sit down to get a feel for one another.

Lamont felt out of his element. Everyone around him seemed immaculate in their neat business attire. They carried briefcases, fancy bags and containers of coffee. They seemed busy, sure-footed, never hanging around to chat, always moving from point A to B. Even the receptionists were demure and professional. For Lamont it was a brand new environment, but he was determined to navigate it.

The reception was spacious, with marble flooring and mahogany desks, neutral walls covered with various paintings and certificates announcing the authenticity of the company. He was definitely sold. He wasn't sure if that was a good or a bad thing yet.

As Lamont waited for Martin, he realised he didn't even know what the man looked like. He was about to ring Xiyu and ask for a description when he heard a small voice call his name. He turned, watching as a red-faced, lumpy man hurried towards him. The man held out his hand and as he did so, the folder he carried fell to the floor, papers going everywhere. If possible, the man's face turned an even brighter shade of red. Several workers passed, openly sniggering.

'You must be Martin.' Lamont bent down to help him pick up the paperwork.

'Yes, I'm Martin Fisher. It's good to meet you. And thank you.' Martin gestured to the papers. He forced them together in a haphazard pile, then shook Lamont's hand with his clammier one. They went into the lift and took it to the second floor. Lamont was led into the work area, dozens of others dressed like Martin talking loudly on phones. The smell of sweat, sickly sweet aftershave and coffee were prominent.

He took everything in on his way to Martin's shabby cubicle. It was boxy, the wooden desk too small for the assortment of paper-work covering it. There were two dirty coffee mugs that needed cleaning and a copy of a broadsheet newspaper that Lamont saw that was three days old. He sat opposite Martin and waited for him to begin.

'I'm sorry about the mess. I haven't had much time to do a clean.'

'Don't worry about it.'

'Can I get you something to drink?'

'No thank you.'

'Did Martha downstairs offer you something?'

'She did.'

'And you're sure you don't want anything?'

Lamont nodded. Martin copied the movement, frenziedly nodding his head like an idiot. He stopped, taking a deep breath. With shaking hands, he reached for the prospectus folder he had dropped in reception and opened it. His eyes scanned the first page quickly. Cursing under his breath, he moved it to the side.

'Really sorry about this. I had them all in order, and now . . .' He ruffled his floppy black hair, breathing hard. 'I'm just going to get a drink. You sure I can't bring you one back?'

'I'm fine.' Lamont's words had a slight edge now, that Martin recognised. Shuffling from his chair, he tottered to the kitchen at the far end of the office. He came back a minute later, drinking from what looked like a canister of water. Wiping his mouth with his hand, he reached for the papers again.

'So . . . Xiyu says that you were interested in investing some money? Depending on the figures, I think I can help.'

'In what way?' Lamont asked. Xiyu had given little insight into what Martin actually did.

'I mainly deal in property. Buying into houses, doing them up, renting or selling them. In terms of business, I know of quite a few companies looking for investments. One of these companies is a letting agency. I think it could be a good fit for you in terms of what you're wanting to invest.'

Lamont mulled that over, not wanting to speak before he understood what he was saying.

'If I'm interested, what happens then?'

'I put you in play, introduce you to the others, and you can decide, sign the contracts, whatever.' Martin seemed more relaxed now, more confident talking figures.

'Can I take the prospectus away with me?'

'Of course. You're in control here. This doesn't move forward without you being fully committed,' said Martin.

'If you don't mind me asking, what do you get out of this?'

'A simple middleman fee. A percentage from you and a percentage from whoever you work with.'

'So, you don't invest in any of these companies yourself?'

'I have a share in the letting agency.'

'Do you make money from it?'

Martin took another sip from his water.

'Yes. The aim of the game here is steady, consistent profit. Xiyu said you'd probably deal in mainly cash. What I will help you do is invest that cash into a portfolio so you're much more flexible in terms of capital. Cash is good, but also not good if you understand my meaning.'

'It's why I'm here.'

'That's good. I promise you that any of these companies you consider will do wonders for you in the long run. Take the prospectus away, consider your options and then get in touch with me. I'll have a meeting set up in no time.'

———

MONDAY 22 FEBRUARY 1999

'This is big for us, L.'

After several months, Louie had finally stopped dithering, allowing Lamont and Shorty to run his drugs line for him. He had made the initial introduction to his supplier, and they were on the way to meet him whilst K-Bar handled business.

'I know, Shorty.'

'If we can go away with a kilo, then we're up and running.' Shorty continued, driving to the Hyde Park meet. They had rented a vehicle using Louie's credit card.

'Shorty, I know,' Lamont repeated. Shorty glanced over but said nothing. Louie had said little about the supplier, other than saying they went way back.

They climbed out after reaching the spot, knocking at the door. A woman opened it. She looked to be in her forties, busty with bleached-blonde hair. She smiled at the pair, and they smiled back.

'You lads here to see Bill?' she asked. They nodded.

'Follow me. I'll take you to him.' She led them to the kitchen. Two men sat there, eating large meals and talking to one another in quick tones. They paused when they saw Lamont and Shorty.

'You lot must be Louie's lads,' one of them said. He was bald with a thick moustache and the makings of a beard. He stared at the pair through pale blue eyes as he shovelled food in his mouth.

'That's right,' said Lamont.

'Sit down then. We'll talk when I've munched this.' He gestured to the food. Shorty and Lamont took seats. The woman waited by the wall.

'Do you want a drink or owt?'

They shook their heads.

'Babe,' Bill turned to the woman, 'kick your feet up and watch TV. I'll be along soon.'

The other man continued staring at Lamont and Shorty.

'This is my bro, Jonny,' said Bill. Both men nodded at Jonny, who didn't respond. Lamont wondered if they should have brought Marcus.

'Right, let's talk.' Bill pushed his plate to the side and stifled a burp. 'Louie speaks bloody highly of you two. Says you're reliable and you've never tried fucking him over.' He nodded in approval to his own statement. 'Lou's a good guy. Used to help our old man a lot before he died.'

'He's been good to us too. We want to make him richer,' said Lamont. Bill laughed.

'And yourselves.'

'Definitely. No point doing this otherwise.'

'I normally give Lou half a kilo. He's gone over prices hasn't he?'

Lamont nodded. 'We want to step up. Order wise.'

Bill and Jonny shared a look.

'Step up to what?'

Lamont paused for a second, keeping his eyes on the brothers.

'A whole box of each.'

'Can you afford that?' Bill let out a low whistle.

'We can afford half up front. The rest plus five percent when we've shifted them.'

'Can you move it though?'

'Everything is in place,' said Lamont. 'We can move it with relatively little effort.'

Bill stared Lamont down again. Lamont matched his expression.

'I'm gonna give you lads a play. Mess about with my money

though . . .' Bill didn't need to finish. Shorty's eyes narrowed, but Lamont held out his hand. Bill shook.

'I'd expect nothing less, Bill.'

'I'm gonna shoot off now that's sorted. Jonny will sort the particulars. I want my end in two weeks. Toodle-oo gents.'

As Jonny turned to address them, Lamont felt a happy glow in his stomach.

———

After meeting with Bill and Jonny, Shorty and K-Bar broke the drugs down, ensuring Louie got a portion for his runners. They hit the streets with a vengeance, selling out quicker than any of them expected. Bill and Jonny were stunned when Shorty returned with their profit after less than a week, asking for more.

They spread far, establishing new links. Bit by bit, the gulf between Lamont's faction and others grew. Lamont wanted more though, and intended to get it.

CHAPTER FOURTEEN

Friday 30 April 1999

LAMONT AND MARIKA sat in a high-class restaurant in the city centre. Lamont wore a grey shirt, black trousers and shoes, with Marika wearing a ruffled shirt and tight denim jeans. It was difficult to see his little sister was growing up. She looked older than her years, with a fresh-faced beauty, intense eyes and dark hair tumbling over slender shoulders. Several patrons in the venue openly eyed her. Lamont shot each a vicious look, making them look away.

'Can I get some wine?' Marika asked.

'No. You're sixteen.'

'Why bother bringing me to this expensive restaurant then? May as well have bought me a takeaway.'

'Whatever. How's school?' Lamont ignored Marika's pouting.

'Boring.'

'Are you revising for your exams?'

'Yes. Every day.'

Lamont knew she was lying. Despite being bright, Marika spent more time trying to get out of school than applying herself.

'Take it seriously. Please. You can do whatever you want, with the right qualifications.'

'Is that why I barely see you anymore? Are you doing whatever you want?'

'I'm doing what I need to. You need to be better than me.' Lamont sipped his sparkling water. 'How are things at home?'

'L, don't go there.' Marika shook her head. The waiter approached them to take their orders. They both settled for a pasta, fish and salad combo.

'I'm just saying. If you wanted to move out, I'd help you rent somewhere. You wouldn't even have to pay rent until you found a job.'

'Look, you're my big bro and I love you, so I'm not gonna mention the blatant disrespect you've shown Auntie.'

'You don't know what you're talking about.'

'Auntie told me about you threatening her before you moved out. Tell me your side.'

'You've already decided, so what's the point?' Lamont folded his arms, nostrils flaring.

'Cool.' Marika shrugged, and they sat in silence. When their food arrived, they kept their eyes down. Once they were finished, Lamont paid the bill, and they left the restaurant, walking through the city centre, particularly beautiful tonight, the moon shimmering amid the dark backdrop of the sky. People glanced at the striking pair as they ambled by.

'I don't want to argue,' Lamont finally said, breaking the tension.

'Me neither. Let's agree not to talk about home life.'

'I like that.' Lamont had a wide grin on his face now. He saw a movement out of the corner of his eye as a couple walked towards him. He was on edge until he recognised the man.

'Hello, Lamont,' said Nigel Worthington, his old coach. His eyes fell on Marika. 'You've grown up since I last saw you, girl.'

Marika beamed.

'How are you doing?' Lamont asked Nigel. He smiled at the woman by Nigel's side and she returned the gesture.

'I'm fantastic. This is my wife, Paulina. Paulina, this is a young man I used to train, Lamont, and his pretty little sister Marika.'

Marika's face lit up when Nigel introduced her. She made small-talk with Nigel's wife while the men moved a short distance away.

'How's it all going then?' Nigel asked.

'I'm living.'

'Looks like it. That's a very expensive looking outfit you're wearing.' Nigel gave him a once-over.

'Look the part, be the part, right?'

Nigel nodded. 'That makes sense.' He glanced over at the women. 'I'm glad I ran into you. I always hated how we fell out. I was never trying to preach to you. I just wanted you to know.'

'I appreciate that.'

Nigel coughed, taking a deep breath.

'I walked your path. Long time ago, I was in those same streets, shotting poison because I thought it was all I could do. I saw the light after a while,' Nigel paused again, his dark eyes boring into Lamont's. 'I'm not trying to lecture you, L. Just think about what you really want,' he finished, heading back to the women. Lamont stared into space for a moment, shocked at his confession. It explained a lot. With another glance at the deep night sky, he followed Nigel.

―――――

When Auntie's home loomed into view, Lamont tensed, but maintained his composure.

'You're not coming in are you?' said Marika, her voice quiet. Lamont reached into his pocket and gave her some money.

'Buy yourself something nice, sis.' He held her tightly.

'Can I see you again soon?' Marika said into his chest.

'Anytime you need me, I'll be there. I promise you that.' Letting his younger sister go, Lamont watched as she went inside, then turned to walk home, buoyed. He was almost at the corner of Hamilton Avenue when a black car pulled up next to him. The passenger window wound down.

'Are you Lamont?' A bald man said in a deep voice.

'Who's asking?'

'Get in the back. Someone wants to talk to you.'

'Who?' Lamont's eyes narrowed.

'If we wanted to hurt you, you'd be hurt. Don't be awkward.'

Weighing this up, he climbed in the car.

———

The journey to the unknown destination proceeded in silence. Lamont had no idea who had summoned him. The driver and passenger looked solid. Lamont wondered if it was Marcus or Shorty's idea of a joke but when the car stopped at the iron gates of a mansion, he knew this was bigger.

After the driver spoke into a mouthpiece on the side of the gate, the gates opened and the car cruised in, pulling to a stop at the top of a long driveway.

'Get out.'

Lamont complied. The driver stayed in the car as Lamont and the lackey walked towards the front door and entered the house. The hallway was adorned with paintings. Knocking on a mahogany door, the lackey instructed him to sit, closing the door behind him.

A few minutes later the door opened again, another man ambling in, his large frame filling the doorway. He stared Lamont down, then took a seat opposite him in a regal leather armchair.

'You know who I am.' It was a statement, not a question. Lamont nodded. He'd recognised the man straight away.

'Who am I then?' The man barely spoke above a whisper. Lamont still caught every word.

'Delroy Williams.'

'Do you know what I do?'

'Whatever you need to.'

Delroy Williams controlled much of the local drug trade. He was a powerful man who had ordered people killed, even occasionally pulling the trigger himself. He'd moved to Britain from the West Indies, cutting a bloody swath through the streets as soon as he stepped off the boat. He was large and dreadlocked, with beady, piercing eyes, a bulbous nose and huge hands. He wore a polo shirt that stretched over a massive gut.

'*Whatever I need to*. I like that.' Delroy rose, heading to a drinks cabinet in the corner. He poured two glasses of brandy, handing one to Lamont.

'You wondering why you're here yet?' He asked. Again Lamont nodded. 'You don't talk much do you?'

'Only when necessary.'

'Why?'

'You learn more when you listen,' replied Lamont. Delroy's eyebrows rose.

'I like that. I like that a lot,' he said, swirling his brandy around in the glass before taking a liberal gulp. 'I hear good things about you. I knew your people.'

Lamont's stomach jolted as it always did at the mention of his parents.

'You look like your mother,' Delroy continued. He dumbly nodded.

'I don't make it a habit to bring strangers to my home. I've checked you out, though. You run that little team of yours to perfection.'

'I do my best.'

'Your best is brilliant. With the right coaching, you could be a big deal. What are you after?'

'What do you mean?'

'You went from selling ten pound draws to moving kilo's in what? A year? Two years?'

'Something like that.'

'I'm asking how far you want to go. You're a smart kid, I can tell that right off. You can make money doing anything, so why play the game?'

'Because what I do is the easiest way to win.'

Delroy studied him carefully.

'I agree, and I wanna help you get there.'

He was supposed to ask how, but didn't take the bait. Delroy chuckled.

'Work for me and I'll make you rich. I'll show you the view from the top and by the end, you'll be richer and bigger than me.'

Lamont saw the satisfaction on Delroy's face. He wondered how many greedy youngsters had swallowed what he told them hook, line and sinker. He sensed the malice in the older man's eyes, easily making up his mind.

'I appreciate the offer. Meaning no disrespect, I'm happy with how things are going for me right now.'

The smug look hadn't left Delroy's face, but his eyes hardened. Lamont knew how dangerous the answer was, but had his principles. He wouldn't work for anyone else. *Even Reagan worked for someone else*, Lamont mused with a certain satisfaction.

'Maybe you need a little incentive.' Delroy stood in front of a painting. Moving it aside, he revealed a wall-safe and typed a combination on the keypad with his fat fingers. Removing a stack of money, he locked the safe again. 'Ten grand. Call it a signing-on fee.'

'It's generous,' Lamont admitted. 'I can't accept it, though.'

Delroy's eyes narrowed. 'Don't you like money?'

'I love money. I just love control more,' said Lamont. Delroy eyed him.

'Man to man, I have to respect your decision.' Delroy scratched the underside of his beard. 'Tell you what . . . I have something that I know you'll take. Wait here.' Delroy left the room again. He sauntered back in with a box and handed it to him. 'Open it.'

Lamont took the box. When he saw what rested there, he couldn't speak. Delroy watched him closely.

'Take it you recognise that?'

In the box was an old gold watch; more weathered than the last time Lamont had seen it. He nodded, feeling a lump in his throat.

'Me and your pops respected each other. I know he always wanted to give that to you.'

Lamont wanted to ask how Delroy had procured the watch but it didn't matter. When Lamont was younger, his father had promised he would give him the watch one day, but Auntie gave it to one of her boyfriends after his death.

'Thank you,' Lamont said, his voice more of a croak, eyes wet.

'Take it. Take the money too,' Delroy urged. Picking up the box containing the watch, he stood, facing Delroy and holding out his hand.

'Thank you.'

Delroy nodded, mirroring the seriousness.

'You're a good kid . . .' he hesitated. 'My man will drop you where you need to go.'

———

That night Lamont lay in bed fingering the watch. He didn't think the gesture had been made out of kindness but right now he didn't care. Slipping the watch onto his wrist, he smiled. He couldn't explain it, but it felt good. The watch was loose, but he would get it resized. He felt a deep euphoria within, as if he had crossed some mythical line. Drifting into an easy sleep, Lamont felt truly happy for the first time in years.

The next morning, Delroy's people knocked and delivered the ten thousand pounds he'd turned down. He hadn't shown them where he lived.

CHAPTER FIFTEEN

Thursday 17 June 1999

LAMONT PAID for a brandy and coke, navigating his way across the room to Xiyu.

'What's up then?' He asked. Xiyu had called, asking Lamont to meet him at the pub again. Like last time, it was packed, and he was already wondering if it was worth investing in a pub in the city centre. He resolved to speak with Martin.

Xiyu was by himself, no women in sight. He was slightly hunched, and seemed to be avoiding the crowds. It was a direct contrast to their last meeting.

'Is business going well?'

'Business?' Lamont frowned. Xiyu scooted closer.

'I know what you do, L.'

Without warning, he gripped Chink's shirt.

'What's your game? Are you grassing?'

'Course not.' Xiyu jerked away. 'Look, people talk. You're the man, and Martin's been dressing better. Obviously, he's making good money.'

Lamont nodded.

'Sorry. Go on.'

'I want to borrow some money.'

'Are you in trouble?'

Xiyu shook his head.

'I'm not, L. Honestly.'

Lamont sipped his drink.

'How much?'

'Five thousand pounds.'

Lamont didn't immediately respond, watching Xiyu's fingers tighten around his pint. He admired his friends composure. If he knew what he did, it was likely he knew about Shorty, K-Bar and the others too.

'That's a lot of textbooks.'

'I'm sure it is, but that's not what I want the money for.'

'Are you going to tell me what you do want the money for, or would you like me to guess?'

'I want to invest in some nightlife.' Xiyu didn't go into detail, but it intrigued Lamont.

'You'll have to be more specific.'

'I've been doing some experimentation in the clubs, and I believe I've found an easy resource that can be tapped to make us both money.'

'What kind of explanation is that?' said Lamont with a laugh. Xiyu grinned.

'I wouldn't ever mess with your money, L, but I can do this. There's money to be made on the club scene and I'm the man to make it.'

'When did you start hustling?'

Xiyu shook his head. 'I'm just someone who knows what he wants in life and is willing to take multiple pathways to get there. If you lend me the money, you'll get it back plus an extra ten percent.'

'When would I get it back?'

'Within a month.'

'And if you can't do what you think you can do?'

Xiyu met Lamont's eyes. 'I can do it.'

Lamont weighed it over. Five thousand pounds wouldn't leave him in any debt, and something in Xiyu's manner made Lamont confident. If there was another easy outlet for profit, he needed to risk it.

'When do you need the money?'

'Whenever you can get it to me.'

'Take my address. Come tomorrow after seven. I'll have the money. I hope that this hunch of yours pays off,' Lamont said, studying Xiyu. The meaning was clear.

'I wouldn't ask if I wasn't positive,' said Xiyu, smiling widely again. 'Let's get another drink, and I can tell you more about it.'

SUNDAY 4 JULY 1999

Lamont stifled a yawn as the black cab pulled up outside his home. When he'd paid the driver and retrieved his luggage, he headed inside. Deciding to take care of unpacking later, he went to the kitchen and made a cup of tea. He drank it standing at the counter, reaching for his mobile to call Shorty.

'I'm back,' he said as his friend answered.

'Good to hear from you, blood. Pass through to my place anytime. I'm not going nowhere.'

Finishing his drink, Lamont made a quick meal, and had a shower. He dressed in a tracksuit, then drove over to Shorty's. The smell of weed stung his nostrils as he walked into the living room. Shorty slouched in front of the TV, staring at the screen as he puffed on a spliff. He had his feet on the coffee table next to a selection of mobile phones. He slapped Lamont's hand in greeting.

'Yes, L! What was it saying over there? How did you get back from the Airport?'

'Greece is all right, actually. I met some good people over there. You should head out for a trip sometime. I just got a taxi home from the airport. Forgot to arrange transport.'

Shorty shook his head. 'I would have got one of the youths to pick you up if you'd let me know. Those black cabs are expensive.'

'Don't worry about it. I'm here now, so it's cool. How are

149

things?' Lamont had left Shorty in charge for the week while he went to Greece. It was his first time leaving the country, and he'd enjoyed the experience. Shorty shrugged.

'Dead really. There was drama, but none of our people were involved.'

'What sort of drama are we talking about here?'

'Reagan killed someone. Out in public too. Blew this guys head off because he owed a chunk of money and apparently made it clear he wasn't paying. Police picked up Reagan and everything, but he had an alibi.'

Lamont's mouth tightened. His hatred for Ricky Reagan had never abated, and he doubted it ever would. Even the thought of him brought back memories of his half-naked body pressed against Rochelle's in the doorway, and his parting words of disrespect. It had been over two years, but those feelings lingered.

'Weren't there any witnesses?'

'Course. None of them were gonna testify though. Delroy would kill their whole families.'

'Business still strong?' Lamont changed the subject.

Shorty grinned. 'We're selling out everywhere. People can't take our product quick enough. K-Bar's got some new links out near Halton Moor, and they're begging him to get more product.'

Lamont was pleased, but concerned by Shorty's words. Their explosion had come out of nowhere. At one point they were growing in stature and gaining more clientele, then suddenly they had exploded into one of the largest teams on the streets.

They'd ramped up, with Shorty building up an army of runners and lieutenants, meaning less moving around for them. He oversaw the streets and Lamont oversaw him and K-Bar. The pressure rose at the same time, and their growth was putting a spotlight on the team; a spotlight that led to increased police activity, among other potential threats.

'Make sure he's taking it easy. Make sure everyone is actually. Things are going well. We don't want to mess that up.'

'L, don't worry, bro. Things are cool. Now, take a seat, stop

being a baby and tell me about Greece. I know you got laid over
there!'

———

Days after Lamont's return from Greece. He, Shorty and K-Bar
went for food. They spoke as they ate, discussing the streets. People
were still buzzed from Reagan's arrest, and the summer had
everyone out to prove a point.

'Next reload is coming in on Thursday. Make sure you give
more to Shane's lot. They moved loads last week. Think they've got
some crews buying wholesale, so we'll take advantage of that.'

'Cool.'

Shorty wiped his mouth after finishing his food.

'What about Blanka? He's making a lot of noise.'

Blanka was named after the *Street Fighter* character. He was
erratic, but had solid connections and a good supply. Lamont had
heard his name before, hearing he treated his team badly and kept
most of the profits for himself. Because of his reputation however,
people gave him a wide berth.

'Blanka is a machine,' said K-Bar. 'Remember when Bali tried to
take him out last year? He's been on the run ever since.'

'Bali was a dickhead, K. He had sloppy people trying to do the
job. That whole situation made Blanka look better than he was. It
helped his rep. His whole team hates him, and he's been slapping
the wrong people around.'

'You want to take him out?' Lamont scratched the underside of
his jaw. He could see the merit, as removing Blanka would increase
their reputation and their market share. With Blanka's antics
however, he was almost definitely a police target, and if they linked
their team to his murder, it would mean more negative attention.

'Me and K could get the job done.'

'You could, but it's a big risk. Police are watching, waiting for us
to mess up.'

'Get Marcus to do it then. He's built up a team of wolves.
They'd do this easy.'

Lamont considered this. It wasn't a bad plan. Marcus was still involved in robberies, but he had diversified into other areas, and his team had adapted with him. He had several young killers who would do whatever he ordered without fail. Lamont mulled it over, feeling Shorty and K-Bar's eyes burning into him. After a few minutes of silence that he finally decided.

'Speak to Marcus. Treat it like a proper job, give him the right instructions and get it done. Reach out quietly to Blanka's number two guy and offer him money to sell out Blanka. If he says no . . .' Lamont let the words hang, but the meaning was clear to both Shorty and K-Bar, and they wore matching grins.

'Blood, it's already done. We'll sort all of this, don't worry.'

After the meal, Lamont headed home. The life was hotting up, and he needed to make sure he was ready to move. Shorty and K-Bar were out to make waves, and he would need to keep them in line.

———

THURSDAY 7 JULY 1999

Lamont was slouched in front of the TV when his phone buzzed on the coffee table. Lazily picking it up without even checking who it was, he answered.

'L, are you at home?' Xiyu sounded breathless.

'Yeah. Is something wrong?' Lamont sat up now.

'I need to come and see you. Is that cool?'

'Course it is. I'll leave the door open.'

Less than ten minutes later, Xiyu bounded into the house, carrying his rucksack and two containers of coffee. He offered one to Lamont and greedily sipped at the other one. Lamont watched, disgusted.

'You could at least let it cool down.'

'I don't want it to cool down. Strike while the iron's hot. Drink while the coffee's hot. The two together . . .'

'Whatever, *Sun Tzu*. What was so urgent? You sounded like you were getting a blow job on the phone.'

'You might want to give me one when you find out what I've got for you.' Xiyu bounced on the soles of his feet. He wore a light-weight black jacket, jeans and shoes. Lamont wondered if he was going out tonight. Or, if he had been out already.

'Nothing you say could push me to those levels.' Lamont shook his head. 'What's up?'

Xiyu opened his bag and handed him a brown envelope. Lamont sifted through, surprised to see a bundle of neat twenty and fifty-pound notes. He fingered a few, tickled to see that all the queens heads were facing the same way.

'How much is here?'

'Six grand. I paid extra on top of the agreed amount.'

'I only gave you the money the other week. What the hell did you do?'

'I invested it like I said I would. Put some product out in the clubs. The money helped pay off a few of the little bouncer firms; the rest took care of itself.'

Lamont gazed from the money, to Xiyu. The club scene wasn't easy. He had made a few feelers after he started dealing with Bill, but no one seemed able to handle it.

'How solid is your team?'

'Watertight. Everyone knows their role. I've been cultivating people for a while now. All that was missing was the money. Even after paying everybody off, I've cleared nearly ten thousand pounds. I'm going to flip that now.'

'What are you moving?' Lamont was wary talking drugs in his house, but enthusiasm won over.

'Everything I can. I have reliable clientele in the clubs. Not like the lagging crackheads on the streets. These are working guys; they're dependable, with good jobs. They don't want the aggro. They just wanna do business. Isn't that what it's about?'

Lamont nodded, looking down at the money again, doing calculations in his head.

'Xiyu, I think we need to have a talk . . .'

CHAPTER SIXTEEN

Saturday 10 July 1999

'I DON'T LIKE IT.'

'What's not to like?'

Shorty and Lamont were driving from a meeting, waiting in traffic. He'd mentioned Xiyu, and the money he'd made for them. The discussion had continued ever since. The car they were driving, a tidy grey Alfa Romeo, had been rented specifically for the trip. Neither wanted the police getting too familiar with their cars.

'Chink is legit. He's not dirty like us.' Shorty turned up the *Jay-Z* track pumping through the speaker. Lamont turned it back down.

'Why do you call him *Chink*?'

'Because. He's Chinese.'

'So if he called you *nigger*, you'd be okay with that?'

The lights changed to green. Shorty beeped at the Vauxhall in front of them to hurry.

'I'd smack his face off. Fact is, I don't like it.'

'He made us six grand. In a few weeks. Think of the return if we gave him more money.'

'Why are you talking about *we* like you haven't already decided?' Shorty scowled.

'I haven't decided anything. I'm talking it over with you.'

'You don't need to. Do what you wanna do.'

'I want to know why you have a problem with it.'

'I have a problem with Chink. Like I said, he's not dirty like us,' Shorty repeated.

'What the hell does that mean? Is that a race thing again?'

Shorty shook his head as he swerved into the next lane, cutting off the driver behind him. It was a tactic he undertook now and then to ensure he wasn't being followed.

'We're grinders. We came up hard and that's why we're doing this. Chink is a little Uni punk. He's not built for this life.'

'Yet, he made six grand for us. Six grand in a few weeks, with no extra help. Why can't you see the potential in that?'

Shorty made a face. 'It's only six bags. Big deal. We make more than that daily. Much more.'

'Yes, but now we have another source of income, one that we don't have to do any groundwork for, because Xiyu did it for us. The club scene isn't easy. He's navigating it and that means a whole different type of customer. A more reliable, clean cut type.'

Shorty sucked his teeth but didn't reply.

'Shorty, this is a good move. At least consider it. If it doesn't work out, we don't lose much.'

'We lose money if he flops. When he flops.'

'Like you said, though; we make more than that already,' Lamont reminded him, laughing. Shorty didn't reciprocate.

'I don't trust him.'

'Trust me. I've never steered you wrong yet, and I have a good feeling about this. It could take us to the next level.'

Shorty shrugged. They were approaching the city centre now. The music volume had increased again, but he didn't mind. If it helped placate Shorty, he was fine with it.

Lamont wondered what he'd missed with Xiyu and Shorty. He'd hung out with both, but time spent with Shorty normally involved running around the streets, playing football. Lamont's time with Xiyu consisted of playing chess and practising maths for fun. It had been a weird balance but seemed to have worked out. He wondered if simple jealousy was affecting Shorty's decision.

'Do you want me to arrange a meeting so he can explain the plan to you?'

'Nah, if you wanna deal with him, then do it. I'm down with you but I ain't gotta like that Chinky motherfucker and I don't. First time he messes up, he can fuck off back to those little puffs he goes Uni with.'

Lamont laughed again. Shorty was hilarious when he was grumpy.

'Let's get you some food and put a smile on your face. I'm buying.'

———

Lamont parked his car on Chapeltown Road, smoothing the folds of his jacket and walking towards the barber shop. The sign gleamed, but the windows were stained with compensation. He hadn't been in a while, but it still reeked of sheen, hair grease, and a lingering fast food smell. There were three ripped barber seats, unkempt and barely held together. The wooden seating area looked uncomfortable, and there wasn't a customer in sight.

'Lamont Jones, is that you?' Trinidad Tommy came from the back, limping toward Lamont. The pair shook hands. Trinidad didn't look like he'd aged in the few years it had been since Lamont had seen him. He was balding, but his skin shone and he looked healthier than some younger people Lamont knew. His grip was like rock. The strength never left some people.

'Nice to see you, Trinidad.'

'You too, you too. I haven't seen you in a long time, but you've grown up good. You favour your mother.'

Lamont swallowed a lump in his throat at the mention of his mother.

'Thank you.'

'Are you wanting a trim?' Trinidad half-heartedly gestured to one of the barber chairs. He slid into the seat, instructing Trinidad to shape him up.

'How are you doing then?' Trinidad asked, combing Lamont's hair before he shaved it.

'I'm doing well. In fact, when you're finished, I want to talk with you. Cool?'

Trinidad frowned, but nodded. When he'd finished, they went into the kitchen area. Trinidad sat down, Lamont remained standing.

'What's the problem?'

'I've heard about your money troubles,' Lamont said. Trinidad scowled.

'People shouldn't be telling tales. My problems are my own, and I'll sort them myself.'

'What do you need?'

'I don't need anything, Lamont. I've never needed anything. I've worked hard, looked after myself my whole life. I'll make it through this.'

'Trinidad,' Lamont looked at the wizened barber, holding his stare until the man looked away. Trinidad had known Lamont Jones since he was a child, and he'd never known him to exhibit such a quiet intensity.

Trinidad had heard rumours about what Lamont was into, and that he was doing very well. Looking at him now, it wasn't a surprise. 'I want to help you. I understand you're proud, but I'm asking you what you need, and I want an answer.'

Trinidad swallowed, sighing. 'I need ten thousand pounds to get the creditors off my back.'

Lamont scratched the scar on his chin, silently staring into space. Trinidad watched, not knowing what to do. Finally, Lamont smiled.

'I want to be partners with you.'

'Excuse me?'

'I'll give you twenty thousand pounds. Ten, you can use to pay what you owe. The other ten will be an investment. We'll breathe some life into your business and work together to grow.'

'Is this a joke?' Trinidad's eyes narrowed.

'I don't joke about money, Trinidad. We can draw up an official contract, but I'm deadly serious about this.'

Shaking his head, Trinidad smiled and shook his hand.

'I agree.'

————

'What's the plan here, L?'

Lamont and Shorty were at the barbers, sitting in his new office. In the background, they could hear the hammering and drilling as the contractors worked on renovating the premises. The office had been completed first at Lamont's request, and he was looking forward to filling the space with his own belongings.

'You'll need to be more specific,' replied Lamont, staring around the room, envisioning what he would put where.

'Why did you invest twenty bags in this piece-of-shit barbers?'

'Trinidad needed help for starters, and some businesses are important in Chapeltown. A barber shop is one of them. Another reason is the money factor.'

'What do you mean by that?'

'We're growing. Our crew is already one of the biggest in the streets. It's only a matter of time before people look at us, and we have to be able to justify the money. Investing in a cash-rich business like this place is smart. I've been working with that white dude Xiyu put me onto, and he's helping me move my money around. There's more to life than buying new chains and clothes and cars.'

'Fam, look how we grew up,' Shorty replied. 'We were broker than broke. Now that I've got money in my pocket, you better believe that I'm buying everything that I always wanted. That's the Hood dream, L.'

Lamont shrugged. 'My dream is a little bigger, Shorty. And I don't want any police officer or person of authority to take my dream away from me whenever they wished.'

With that, the old friends sat in silence, listening to the work of the builders.

———

'We're here.'

Lamont and K-Bar climbed from the ride, approaching the meeting spot. K-Bar was armed, and his confident demeanour emboldened Lamont. The door opened as they cleared the garden. A man shook both their hands, leading them into the living room.

A few others milled around, glaring at the pair. He held the eyes of everyone, K-Bar doing the same, until the men looked away.

'Clear the room,' Lamont said. They didn't work for him, yet didn't hesitate to listen, heading upstairs. The man they'd come to meet looked put-out, but said nothing.

'Is everything in place then?' Lamont asked Terry Worthy. Terry ran a hand through his slicked-back hair, making a sucking sound with his teeth.

'Blanka's proper paranoid. Doesn't know who he can trust. Spends most of his time snorting his own coke and snapping at people. His guys are looking to be led by someone else. A few are saying it should be me.' Terry puffed out his chest, smirking.

Lamont resisted the urge to laugh. Terry was a clown, but he was entertaining, and something often overlooked in this business of theirs. He was an independent dealer, but had links amongst Blanka's people and in wider circles. He'd been pushing to do business with Lamont for a while, and they'd fed him crumbs, slowing introducing him to the plan to take out Blanka. He'd proved instrumental, and Lamont was good at keeping his ego in check.

'Do you want to lead?'

Terry shrugged. 'Sometimes guys step up, don't they? I mean, look at you. You came out of nowhere, and now you're top guy. Why can't I do it too?'

Lamont could have easily named fifty reasons he couldn't do it, but smiled. Terry was easy to control, and they only needed him a while longer. In the meantime, he had other links that Lamont had already started to plunder. His bank balance was increasing at an alarming pace, and a lot of it was down to the extracurricular moves he was making. Terry had unwittingly been a massive help in that regard.

'I'm on board with you stepping up. Spencer's in place and ready to work with us for now?'

Terry nodded. 'Spencer is a good lad. He's loyal when you give him reason to be, and Blanka has been taking him for granted for a while now. By the end of this week, everything will be in place, and he'll be gone.'

––––––

When the pair left Terry's and climbed into K-Bar's car, Lamont turned to him before he started the engine.

'Put a man on Terry, follow him wherever he goes. Until Blanka is dead, I don't trust him.'

'You've got it, L,' said K-Bar, before driving away.

––––––

WEDNESDAY 21 JULY 1999

Blanka was ready.

Nothing would stop his takeover. He'd seen the gaps for a while; weaknesses in the Hood infrastructure. There were a few established kingpins at the top. To topple them would take a lot of firepower and resources, which he didn't have at present.

Blanka had shown great patience in biding his time, building links, bullying those he could, and amassing money. He planned on waging war on a few factions that were getting too big for their boots, namely an organisation led by Lamont Jones.

Blanka knew a little about Lamont; he was supposed to be some kind of genius who everyone raved about like he was *Lucky Luciano*. He too had built his crew from the ground up and had solid people under him. Blanka knew about Shorty and K-Bar. The pair had earned their deadly reputations, but so had he. He'd killed before too, and he'd do it again.

Blanka had told none of his people about the plan to take out Lamont Jones, unsure of whom to trust. He'd reveal it to them in time and put one of them in place to run the remains of the crew after he decimated them.

Snorting another line of coke and turning up the volume on the *Scarface* video cassette, he wiped his eyes and reached for a bottle of water, chugging it before stumbling to his feet. He lurched upstairs to use the toilet. As he was washing and drying his hands, Blanka heard a banging noise from downstairs.

'Oi, what's going on down there!' He'd ordered two kids to cook crack in the kitchen, but he hadn't told them to have a party while they did it. When he didn't receive an answer, his nostrils flared. He hurried to one of the bedrooms, rooting under the bed for his equaliser; a Mac-10 machine gun with an extended clip. Making sure it was loaded, he hurried downstairs, noting the front door had been left wide open.

Eyes darting around, Blanka heard another noise and decided enough was enough. He began firing, hands jerking to keep the gun steady as he sprayed rounds, hearing the cracking sounds of bullets hitting walls, the churning of metal on metal. He paused, taking cover next to the door, then fired again.

There was return fire this time, bullets thudding around him. Blanka didn't know who was coming for him, but they would regret it.

'You ain't taking me!' Blanka yelled as he pumped out rounds. 'Come take me head-on, you pussies! You think I'm scared?'

It was hard to see through the gun smoke and debris, but Blanka was sure he had more weaponry dotted around than whoever was out there. They were near the garden, but he had them pinned down. He was so focused on the men in front, that watching his back hadn't occurred to him.

Marcus strolled through the back entrance Blanka's workers had unlocked, smirking at the sight of him posturing like Pacino. He had all the time in the world to raise the gun clutched in his hand and fire.

Blanka screamed as the back of his leg seemed to explode. He lost his balance, and the gun tumbled from his grip. He didn't have time to see who was shooting as two more bullets thudded into his back, dropping him. The last thing he saw was a smiling Marcus aiming the gun at his face. There was a bang and a flash before everything went dark.

Standing over Blanka's prone frame, Marcus shot him twice more in the head, then disappeared through the back again. He climbed into the waiting car, and Victor drove away. In the destroyed living room, blood seeped from Blanka, as *Scarface* continued to play out in the background.

CHAPTER SEVENTEEN

Tuesday 16 May 2000

LAMONT LEFT HIS HOUSE. A grey Suzuki jeep idled by the curb, and he climbed in the back.

'Moneybags, how you doing?' Marcus pulled away, the engine purring.

'I'm fine. Wish I knew where I was going though,' replied Lamont. All Marcus had said was that they were going to see someone. With Marcus that could mean anything. He stayed quiet as Marcus turned up the track. He was heavily into his old school music, not that Lamont minded. It was easy to settle in and listen to *Rakim* blessing the tracks.

After a while, they arrived at a semi-detached home in Shadwell. Lamont glanced at the surrounding houses, wondering who Marcus knew in this area. He noted he'd turned the music down and was tapping his hands on the steering wheel. Lamont knew they weren't going to see women. Marcus had dragged him to see them in the past, and there was never so much fuss.

'Right, c'mon.' Marcus killed the engine and climbed from the ride. Lamont followed, eyeing his friend strangely. Marcus had his hands jammed in his pockets, and his face seemed tense. Lamont wondered if he was having problems with another crew. They knocked on the door which was answered a moment later.

'Marcus, good to see you.' A man smiled warmly at them. He was average height and build, with a lined face and salt and pepper hair. He led them to the sitting room. It was elaborately furnished, with thick carpeting and dark brown furniture.

'Drinks?'

Both men shook their heads. The older man fixed himself a glass of whiskey and sat in an armchair, his eyes on Lamont.

'Marcus has told me a lot about you. He wanted us to meet.'

'If you don't mind me asking, sir, who exactly are you? Marcus never said.' Lamont noticed Marcus tense up next to him, but the giant stayed silent. The old man seemed unaffected by Lamont's directness, smiling mildly.

'My name is Junior. I'm an old acquaintance of Marcus's.'

Lamont nodded. 'How did you make his acquaintance?'

'I import things. Marcus was introduced to me and we hit it off. He's mentioned you often. We figured it was time for us to meet.'

'What has Marcus told you?'

'He's told me you're the smartest person he knows. I have other sources too, and they tell me you're the future of our business.'

Lamont didn't respond straight away. He'd stepped up in the past few years, but he'd never met Junior, and was shocked Marcus knew someone he wasn't aware of.

'I see.'

Junior continued to smile. 'You're nervous. I understand. Your reputation precedes you, and I know you like things quiet. You have to realise that everything you do makes ripples. Blanka for example.'

Lamont leant forward, eyes fixed on Junior. Marcus had murdered Blanka for him nearly a year ago, and the streets had been hotter than ever. The police investigated and kept up the pressure on the streets. Blanka had a reputation for violence, so there were many rumours of how he'd met his demise, and every crew in the area was linked to the murder. The fact they found nearly a dozen weapons dotted around the safe house proved he knew his days were numbered.

Lamont had spun a story through the streets that Blanka owed some Dutch gangsters money and was murdered because of this. The story gained traction, but eventually, people just stopped talking about Blanka and moved on.

Lamont took over his territory, absorbed his customers, and put one of his old workers, Spencer, in charge. Spencer paid Lamont forty percent of his profits for the privilege and protection.

'Do you think it was handled badly?' He was interested in Junior's opinion.

'Blanka's death was always going to cause waves. He was a force, larger than life to some. There is no way to quietly murder such men. He was a mad dog and needed putting down. Have you made the most of the situation?'

Lamont nodded, cutting his eyes to Marcus. He remained slouched against the wall, his muscled arms folded.

'Be careful. You're known now; people will seek to take advantage, and the authorities will be watching. I won't ask about your financial situation, but I imagine you're doing well, so let me give you the following piece of advice; diversify and don't let them come after your money.'

Lamont considered that information, sitting back and allowing Marcus and Junior to hold a conversation. He was making more money than he could manage. Some of it was lent to people at extortionate rates that they had to pay back. Most was invested into buying more drugs. He'd bought a stake of the barbers, and funded a few smaller businesses, but he lived in fear that he would lose it all, a fact Junior had cottoned onto immediately. He resolved to speak with Martin and his solicitor, and ensure everything was watertight.

———

'What did you think then?'

Lamont and Marcus were in town drinking beers. They'd gone to get some food after leaving Junior's, then Marcus suggested hitting the city centre.

'He's shrewd.'

Marcus nodded. 'He came up alongside Karma, Delroy and Mitch. You needed to be ruthless back then to survive, but Junior played them all and stayed out of the crossfire.'

Lamont lifted his beer. 'How did you meet him?'

'Did a job. Took something from the wrong person. He reached out, and I sent his guy packing. Gave him a few slaps and told him I was keeping what I took.'

'What did Junior do?'

Marcus grinned. 'He reached out again through some guys I respected, and they set up a meeting. This was in like 97/98. We spoke, and I guess I realised he would benefit me. I never gave him the work back, but I did other jobs he put me onto, and paid him back ten times over. He's given me money in the past, and even saved money and invested it. He's a good guy to know, that's why I wanted you to meet him.'

Lamont scratched his chin, glancing around the bar. It was fairly quiet, unsurprising as it was a Monday night. A few people having after work drinks were milled around, but nothing major.

'Has he ever advised you to invest?'

'All the time.'

'And?'

'And nothing. I like my money where I can see it. I don't know nothing about stocks and investments and all that shit. If I don't have money, I just go out and make more.'

'Is that enough for you?'

Marcus surveyed him with a long look.

'Blood, I'm not you. I don't hoard money, because we're in the jungle, and I can always make more. Junior's been telling me about investments for the longest. He has loads of money but that's his thing. My thing is just to keep doing what I'm doing. When people step out of line, I show them. I enjoy spending money more than I enjoy saving it.'

The friends didn't speak much after that. Lamont understood his mindset. It was similar to other criminals he knew; they lived for today and barely considered tomorrow. Lamont had never been able to live that way, and he would not start now.

_____

FRIDAY 18 AUGUST 2000

Lamont stared out of the taxi window as it pulled to a stop outside a house on Francis Street in the Hood. As Shorty paid the driver, Lamont surveyed the house, noticing the loud music shaking the ground. He didn't know whose party it was. Shorty had called, told him to throw on some clothes, and they were off.

'Shorty, good to see you.' A svelte woman in a t-shirt and equally tight jeans opened the front door. She kissed Shorty on the cheek before turning her eyes on Lamont.

'You too, Tash. This is Teflon.'

Lamont noted Tash's eyes widening. _Teflon_ was a nickname Shorty and K-Bar had given him, mockingly proclaiming that nothing ever stuck to him, and that he was a wannabe Mob boss. He had stopped protesting, mostly because he knew they wouldn't listen. It surprised him that Tash seemed to know him, though.

'Nice to meet you, Teflon. C'mon in, babe, have a drink.'

They did the rounds. Shorty knew everyone, and couldn't move without people stopping him to speak. He introduced Lamont and everyone that heard his nickname had the same awed reaction, following up with attempts to hold a conversation. Shorty left him in a corner saying he'd be back soon.

Lamont sipped the brandy and coke Tash had fetched, listening to the music in silence, tuning out the buzzing noise of the party. He didn't know how to interact with the party-goers. They were from the same area with similar experiences, but life was different for Lamont. He was different. Appearance wise, he dressed the same as many of the guys in attendance; navy crew-necked t-shirt, jeans and Air Max trainers. His mindset set him apart, though, and his cold eyes. Not that he knew that.

A movement caught his eye and he noticed a girl dancing at the other side of the living room. His eyes were drawn to long legs that the tight jeans and boots only helped accentuate. Feeling his eyes on her, she danced a while longer, watching him the whole time. He held the stare, a mirthless smirk flitting over his features. She beckoned him over, but he didn't move, killing the instinctive part of him that wanted to go to her. She took the hint, moving to him, ignoring the three guys who tried speaking to her on the way. She stood in front of Lamont, taking in his frame.

'What you drinking?'

In response, he held out the plastic cup. She took a sip, wiping her mouth and giving it back. She'd missed some residue, the liquid hanging on her plump bottom lip. Lamont's eyes flickered to it.

'What's your name?'

'My friends call me L.' Lamont didn't ask her name. Part of him wanted to, but the past had him tethered, and he was different now.

'Okay, L. I'm Kim.'

Lamont smiled, but it didn't reach his eyes.

'Do you know Tash then?'

'We went to school together. Carr Manor. Where did you go?'

Lamont told her. He learned they had people in common and before long, an hour had passed. He'd finished three drinks and still couldn't see Shorty. Kim stayed by his side the whole night and even now she pressed against him, swaying to the music. Lamont blearily scanned the room, noting at least half a dozen guys glaring in his direction and grumbling to one another.

'Wanna come and have a drink at my place?'

Lamont needed less than a second to decide.

'Lead the way.'

———

Kim's place was a small, one-bedroomed spot near Roundhay Road. It appeared clean, with cream walls and bright furniture. Kim signalled for him to sit. She'd had more drink than Lamont, and this was evident in her movements. Without asking what he wanted, she came with half a bottle of brandy. She drank from the bottle, then handed it to him. She clutched him tightly on the sofa, gazing through lidded eyes.

Lamont put the bottle on the coffee table, tracing her jaw,

drawing her even closer. His mouth covered hers, the kiss deepening. She moaned in his mouth, practically sitting on his lap as he clutched her body. His brain was surprisingly coherent, recalling the moves that worked for him.

Kim's moans increased, and soon he peeled her out of her clothing, kissing her as she grinded on him. She tugged at his jeans and boxer shorts, devouring him with her warm mouth, causing him to let out a hiss of pleasure. Her motions increased, the suction her mouth provided causing Lamont's body to jerk. He collapsed onto the sofa, panting as Kim looked into his eyes, her mouth moist. Composing herself, she took his hand and led him upstairs.

———

Morning came, and Lamont's eyes slowly opened. He didn't recognise the room, but the previous nights actions quickly came back. Kim remained asleep, arm draped across his bare chest, her hair cascading over her face.

Lamont disentangled himself and quickly dressed, uninterested in a repeat performance. Without even looking back at the bed, he made his way downstairs, located Kim's key and left. It wasn't far to his flat, so he walked rather than call a taxi. He was glad he hadn't been steaming drunk. His mouth was dry but other than that, he seemed to have avoided a hangover. He couldn't help but wonder about people's reactions to him.

As soon as Shorty had dropped the name *Teflon* last night, people had treated him with a certain reverence. He planned on speaking to Shorty and clarifying exactly what his friend had said. Putting all thoughts out of his head, he quickened his step, looking forward to having a shower and going back to sleep.

CHAPTER EIGHTEEN

Saturday 2 September 2000

SHORTY AND LAMONT WERE INDOORS. A heatwave had recently hit Leeds with a vengeance, and Shorty lay on the sofa with his eyes closed. Lamont sat upright in his chair, apparently lost in thought.

'What time's the meet?' He said.

'K'll be there now. It better go as planned too, or I'm gonna smack up Terry.' Shorty didn't even open his eyes.

'Terry knows what he's doing. No reason it shouldn't go to plan,' replied Lamont. Privately, he was concerned. Terry had been cool for a while after they murdered Blanka, but now he was overly cocky, walking around the streets like he owned them.

'He's a flake. Always has been. Raider and them lot nearly killed him after he flirted with Keisha that time.'

'Terry tried it on with Raider's sister?'

Raider was a loud maniac, with a reputation similar to Marcus's.

'He's a clown. Watch he doesn't try that with Marika.'

'Rika would chew him up. You know what my sister's like,' said Lamont. Shorty laughed.

'Raider's sis isn't all that, anyway. I tapped it last year.'

'Jesus, you need testing.' Lamont shook his head.

'How do you know I didn't use a rubber?'

Lamont glanced at Shorty. He had a small smirk on his face, eyes still closed.

'Did you?'

'She didn't gimme a chance. Got myself checked after. Clean as a whistle.'

'For now.'

Shorty sat up. 'Fuck off. You need to get out there and start sampling these chicks.'

'Don't worry about me.'

'Are you sleeping with someone on the sly?' Shorty sounded interested now. Lamont just smirked, not bothering to reply. 'Tell me, man. I tell you about all of mine. Who are you screwing?'

Lamont was about to speak, when they heard a rush of quick footsteps. K-Bar bounded into the room, panting.

'What happened?' Lamont asked, letting him catch his breath.

'Got rushed at the meet. Police licked us,' K-Bar pulled off his damp hoody and slid into a weathered armchair. Several of his dreads stuck to his forehead. Impatiently, he brushed them away.

'Did you lose them before you came here?' Shorty demanded. K-Bar cut his eyes to him.

'I was careful. Had to drop the pack, though,'

'Where's Terry?' Shorty stood, bristling, his jaw tight.

'He ran. All of us did. Everyone went in different directions trying to throw them off.'

'We need to go find him. He planned this deal. He needs to make it right.'

————

'Boss, I didn't know it was gonna happen either.'

They were at Terry's place, a spot he'd rented in Chapel Allerton. It was a three-bedroom place, the living room hosting a gigantic flat-screen TV, along with a DVD player and the usual medley of action DVDs. Lamont glanced at a copy of the film *Commando*. Terry reclined on his cheap sofa, sipping a beer.

'We lost half a box, Terry. You organised the meet, and you were supposed to protect our interests,' said Lamont. K-Bar and Shorty brooded behind him, glaring at Terry.

'Half is nowt.' Terry waved his hand.

'We feel differently.' He kept his eyes glued to Terry, who sat up, rubbing his palms on his trousers.

'It's your damn fault, so you're taking the hit,' Shorty cut in, tired of the slow dance.

'You what?' Terry frowned.

'Don't pretend you didn't hear me. K said you rolled to the spot in a Porsche. How hot is that?'

'It was a *TVR*. What's the big deal? It's a rental.'

'It draws attention, Terry. What we do isn't supposed to draw attention,' Lamont added.

'I've been doing this longer than you lot. I know the game.'

'That means you should know what you can and can't do. What we need to decide is where to go from here.'

'If you've got a couple more boxes knocking around, we can do the deal now,' said Terry. Lamont shook his head.

'We don't walk around with stuff—'

'—Yo, you need to pay back what we lost before you talk about more business,' Shorty snapped, rubbing his face.

'It wasn't my bloody fault. Why should I have to pay for that?'

'Are you retarded, you forgetful prick? Didn't we just explain why?'

Terry turned to Lamont. 'Mate, call off your dog.'

Grabbing Terry by the throat, Shorty dragged him from the chair and punched him in the stomach. He folded from the blow, collapsing to his knees and dry-heaving.

'Shorty, that's enough.' Lamont pulled him back. Shakily, Terry staggered to his feet, pale and wincing. 'You want to do further business, Terry, you take the hit. Not us. You need to pay the difference, plus an extra two thousand, as a reminder not to mess up again,' said Lamont. Behind him, Shorty breathed hard, eyeing Terry. Terry swallowed, his upper lip trembling.

'Fine . . . only because I wanna do more business with you lot though,' he glanced towards the door. 'Wait here and I'll go get it.'

Lamont made a decision right then. He would finish the deal, then he would distance himself from Terry Worthy. His help with Blanka aside, the man was a magnet for trouble.

———

THURSDAY 21 SEPTEMBER 2000

Lamont fiddled with the zip on his black jacket, looking both ways as he crossed the road and entered the Italian restaurant. He was shown to a table.

'Would you like a drink, sir?'

'A gin and tonic, please,' Lamont replied to the waiter. He settled back, waiting for the man he'd come to meet, to speak.

'Thanks for coming, L,' the man finally said. He wrung his hands together and took furtive sips from a glass of water. He was sallow-skinned, with lank black hair and a wispy moustache. His eyes were a washed shade of blue, beset with reddish, crisscrossed veins.

'You didn't leave much choice,' Lamont's tone was mild. Colin Leary was a former heavyweight. Once upon a time he'd yielded power within the Leeds night scene, using money earned from cashing in on selling ecstasy to set up a nightclub. People flocked and money flowed. He made friends with up and coming young gangs, allowing them to sell discreetly for a fee within his club. Everything ran smoothly until recently, where it all exploded.

Colin looked around the room, nearly jumping from his seat when the staff returned with Lamont's drink.

'Calm down,' Lamont told him. Colin rubbed the back of his neck, wetting his dry lips.

'They're after me, L. They threatened to chop my kid's head off if I didn't give them eighty grand.'

'So, why don't you?'

'No! I-I haven't done anything wrong,' Colin's voice shook,

several tears tumbling down his pale cheeks. Lamont signalled for the staff to bring more water and handed Colin a tissue.

Colin had a point. All he had done was make friends with two rising hotheads, Parker and Blotto. The pair started out doing robberies, branching out to drugs, loans and whatever else they could get away with. Despite being reckless and temperamental, they made a cunning pair, skilled at staying out of trouble.

When a West Indian gang hailing from Tivoli Gardens in Kingston, demanded Parker and Blotto start paying a percentage of their drug money, the pair laughed it off.

A few weeks later, Blotto was leaving a restaurant with his girl-friend, when the pair were set upon by two men wielding knives. He fought them off, but was stabbed twice. He lost a lot of blood and was taken to hospital. Parker refused to back down and shot up the house of one of the suspected gangsters. Unfortunately, his crew picked the wrong house, narrowly missing the six-year-old son of another Yardie, this man a known shooter.

Since then, the war escalated, and Colin was forced into the conflict when his bouncers were shot at and jumped. He was also robbed and had his Porsche convertible set on fire. Parker assured Colin he would handle it, but he and Blotto were on the move, hiding underground and trying to plan a counter. In the meantime, Colin remained left in the open, easy prey for the Yardie gangsters. He'd reached out to Lamont in his panic, and here they were.

'That's the life we're in. Whether you've done anything wrong, you're involved. Guilty by association.'

Colin wiped his eyes. The waiters were hovering, but looked reluctant to approach. Lamont shook his head, and they dispersed.

'Can you help me?'

'How?' He leaned toward Colin, his eyes never leaving the man.

'Talk to them, get them to leave me alone. You've got friends in that camp. I heard you do.'

'You know what rumours are like.'

'So, you're saying you don't?' Colin demanded.

'I'm saying, you're asking me to get involved in a volatile situation that doesn't concern me. Why would I do that? Would you?'

Colin didn't reply. Lamont steepled his fingers, letting the silence manifest until Colin couldn't stand it.

'What if I pay you? All you need to do is talk to the other side on my behalf. You don't have to raise guns or anything like that. Just, let them know we're friendly and that you're watching my back. I'll pay you ten grand.'

Lamont hid the smile that threatened his face, steeling his features.

'I want a piece of your business, and I want the names of the main people you do business with, along with an introduction.'

Colin's face paled further, if possible.

'Are you daft? That's worth loads more.'

'Depends on how you look at it. You approached me. I'm not forcing you to be here.'

Colin audibly swallowed, dabbing at his shimmering face with the same tissue from earlier.

'If I do all that, are you promising they'll leave me alone?'

Lamont met Colin's eyes again. 'I can't promise that, but I will intercede on your behalf, and I'll talk with the right people to get this sorted. In the meantime, we're gonna meet my associate, and I will leave you two to talk.'

Lamont signalled for the bill, still holding the smile back. Colin's misfortune would do wonders for his bank balance. As he paid, he was already ringing Xiyu.

CHAPTER NINETEEN

Friday 30 June 2001

LAMONT HUNG around across the road from an office building, checking his watch to make sure he had the right time. He jammed his hands in his jacket pockets, hoping he didn't look as nervous as he felt. When he saw a familiar face walking from the building, he headed over.

'Hey, Layla.'

'L?' Layla Kane did a double-take, her eyes widening. She wore work gear; a simple blouse and trousers with a black coat. Her butterscotch skin emitted an aura, and he felt her presence. There was something special about her. It had taken him the longest time to realise it, but he was glad he'd reached out. Even if it had taken three years.

'How are you doing?'

'I'm . . . how did you know where I worked?'

Lamont winked, making Layla smile.

'I have my ways. I wanted to see you. Do you want to go for a drink?'

'I've been working for twelve hours straight, L.'

'Let's get you a coffee then.'

———

They sat across from one another in a cramped coffee shop. Lamont watched Layla sip her drink like she was dying of thirst.

'What the hell do they have you doing in that firm?' He asked.

'Too much. It's a nightmare. I work every hour of the day for little money, on top of studying and prepping for exams. Doesn't leave much time for anything else.'

'I can imagine.' Lamont reached out and brushed his fingertips against Layla's palm. 'It's great to see you.'

'I have a boyfriend, L.'

Lamont didn't immediately pull his hand away, but he felt a jolt of something similar to something he felt in 1997. It jarred him. He thought he had buried that part of himself, but here he was; getting in too deep with another woman who was too good for him.

'Do you love him?'

Layla laughed and ran a hand through her hair. 'Who asks a question like that?'

Lamont shrugged. She was right. It was a stupid question and the whole thing was none of his business. He was reminded of the last conversation they'd had; she'd essentially told him to come and find her when he was ready. He'd taken too long, though, and was now painfully aware of that fact.

'Tell me about him.'

'Why?' Layla's brow furrowed, and he couldn't blame her.

'Because I like you, and because you like him.'

Layla surveyed him, but after a minute, she began talking about her boyfriend; how they'd met while studying, and how it was early days, but she thought he'd be good for her.

Lamont saw it for what it was. A sign that he could never be that guy while he lived the life he did. He paid for her coffee, but knew he'd never seek her out again.

———

THURSDAY 5 JULY 2001

'So, we're gonna go out and have a big party in town.'

Lamont sat on the sofa at Shorty's place with his arms folded, listening to his friend talk. He'd been rambling for ages, so Lamont was thinking about other things, namely the state of the streets.

Gunplay and gang warfare had broken out on a whole new scale. Several West Indian gangs were warring with several English ones. Lamont had interceded for Colin Leary last year. Using Marcus and Shorty, he'd spoken with the aggressors, and they'd eventually agreed to leave Colin alone. Unfortunately, other conflicts had sprung up, and the people involved didn't have his diplomacy.

'L, are you listening?'

'Yes, you're having a birthday party in town and you want me to be there. Heard you loud and clear.'

'What's the problem? Why do you look so emotional?'

'I'm worried.'

'What's new there then? All you do is worry, Teflon.'

Lamont resisted the urge to roll his eyes. He'd never grown used to the nickname, but it didn't bother him as much.

'The streets are nuts. There's the beef Marcus had with Mori, and now the Yardies are going crazy, shooting at people in broad daylight. There's tension. Don't tell me you can't feel it out there on those streets.'

'I don't care. Anyone comes for me, I'll drop them myself. You know I don't play.'

'There's no profit in it. We're here to make money, remember? Warring with Yardies who have nothing to lose is ridiculous,' replied Lamont.

'Yeah well, Ronnie and them other boys aren't gonna back down, so unless you're gonna weigh in and organise sit-downs, stay out of it and keep it moving.'

Lamont wished it were that easy. He had a bad feeling about the Yardies, and he was preparing for them to make a move against him. He was rising in stature and an obvious target. He remained careful about who he was around and had moved house to avoid anyone becoming familiar with his patterns.

'Just make sure you're prepared, Shorty. If things kick off, we need to move quickly.'

'Whatever. Can we go back to speaking about my birthday, please? How many people do you think I should invite? You know a couple' people will act proper emotional if they don't get an invitation. I want plenty of women there. Stace will come, but that doesn't mean I can't look. Are there any chicks you want there?'

Lamont shook his head, still thinking.

'Stop thinking about that war nonsense. No one is trying to mess with us. We're deep in the game, and we have the firepower to take out neighbourhoods if we need to. Make sure you're planning on fucking someone at my party, because you know women will be pointed in your direction.'

———

'You're worried then.'

Lamont and Marcus sat in Marcus's ride in the Hood. It was early evening, but the weather remained ridiculously warm. He was shirtless, his muscled build on display, whilst Lamont wore a white vest and shorts. He was still sweating, and the heat made him irritable.

'I don't understand why no one else is. The Yardies are coming after crews. People are getting robbed and chopped up. They don't care about the rules. All they care about is anarchy.'

'Do you wanna take them out?'

Lamont laughed. 'That's a great idea. Kill a few of them, then spend the rest of my life watching out for Yardie triggermen. It's nothing for them to sneak into the country and come after me.'

'If they try, I'll kill them. All of them. You never need to worry while I'm here.'

Lamont grinned. They had an up and down friendship, but Marcus's loyalty had never wavered. He still went on robberies, but also had a few people selling drugs for him, so there was always money coming in. He wasn't in the same bracket as Lamont, but had enough for what he needed.

Lamont was constantly trying to get him and Shorty to consider investing their money. They weren't interested, though, so he left it alone.

'Yes Marcus!' A voice called out. Lamont looked to see who had spoken and his blood ran cold. He recognised the posture immediately, the wild hair and the scar on the face. The man slowed his Mercedes to a crawl and hopped out with the engine still running, music pumping from the speaker. Like Lamont, he wore a vest, his corded, wiry muscles on display. He looked at Lamont with cold brown eyes, then slapped hands with Marcus, who had climbed from the car.

'Yes, Ricky. What's happening?'

'Nothing much. Looking to chill for the evening. Just driving around trying to get into trouble.' Reagan's eyes flickered toward Lamont again. The two men stared one another down, neither budging. Marcus noticed.

'Ricky, this is my brother Lamont. People call him *Teflon*. L, this is Ricky Reagan. I'm sure you've heard the name.'

Lamont resisted the urge to cut his eyes to Marcus. He knew full-well Lamont knew who Reagan was. He felt sixteen again, waiting outside the door as Rochelle closed it on him to spend time with Reagan. His jaw tensed, but he controlled his thoughts. He wasn't going back. He would never be that person again.

'Have we met?' Reagan awkwardly shook his hand.

'Years ago,' replied Lamont. Reagan kept his eyes on him a moment longer, then turned back to Marcus.

'Have you spoken to Lennox lately? I've been trying to reach him.'

'He's out of town. Should be back in a few weeks.'

'If you hear from him, tell him to bell me. Might have a job for him. In fact, you can take it if you want. Someone needs to go missing. Ten bags.'

Marcus grinned. 'I'll check you tomorrow and we can talk.'

Reagan cut his eyes back to Lamont, who hadn't stopped staring. The man who had been responsible for everything he was now.

'Delroy's mentioned you a few times. He thinks you're the second coming,' Reagan's tone was hostile. Lamont figured he was jealous. Delroy hadn't slowed down his recruiting campaign over the years. Recently, he'd sent his son to talk with Lamont. He'd had chilled around Winston Williams over the years, but it was so transparent that he was recruiting for his father. Lamont still wanted to work for himself, but Winston was cool, so he didn't make an issue.

'He's never mentioned *you*,' said Lamont. Reagan's eyes flashed, but he didn't move. His eyes flicked to Marcus then back to Lamont.

'I'll see you around, Teflon.'

Climbing back in the Mercedes, Reagan took off down the street. There was a short silence after he left.

'Fucking hell, L . . . I thought you were over that Rochelle mess?' Marcus, laughed. Lamont didn't reply, his attention on the spot where Reagan had stood, his thoughts filled with rage and an anguish he tried pretending wasn't there.

———

TUESDAY 10 JULY 2001

'Would you, though?'

Lamont closed his eyes. He was in another borrowed car with Shorty and they were waiting at some traffic lights for the light to turn green. Shorty sat at the wheel, animated, bopping his head to *Mobb Deep* as he tapped on the steering wheel with both hands.

'It's not important if I would or not,' replied Lamont.

'For fuck's sake, L. I'm just asking a question. Why you gotta kill shit all the time?'

'Because you'll end up getting yourself in trouble.'

'I'm just asking a question,' Shorty repeated. 'Would you bang Bill's missus? Yes or no?'

'Fine. Yes I would,' said Lamont after thinking about it for a moment. Shorty laughed. Despite Bill supplying them with drugs, Shorty couldn't help mentioning his wife at every opportunity.

'I thought so! I've seen her looking at me like she wants a piece. I don't think Billy is hitting it right.'

'That's between them. Focus on business.'

'You need to have some fun once in a while. You're too damn serious, man.' Shorty shook his head. He turned up the volume on the music and rocketed ahead when the light changed.

It didn't take long for them to arrive at Bill's. A few random faces milled around outside, staring at the pair when they pulled up. Lamont had seen a couple of them around before, but there were a few faces he didn't know. True to form, Shorty waded through the crowd like it wasn't even there. Lamont followed suit. No one made any move to stop them.

Bill's woman answered the door again, smiling widely. Her cleavage was prominent in her tight tank top, and Shorty openly leered.

'Nice to see you lot again. Bill and his brother are downstairs in the basement. I'll take you down to them.'

'You're looking sexy today,' Shorty piped up. She giggled, reddening.

'Thank you. C'mon, before Bill comes up.'

They followed her down to the basement. Lamont shot Shorty a look, but he ignored him. He planned to tell Shorty to curb this one. Bill's woman was flirty. He didn't want any lines crossed, especially with the man who was giving them their supply.

The basement was already cramped. Bill's woman didn't hang around after showing them down. In the room stood Bill, Jonny, and two others Lamont hadn't seen before. He didn't know what they had been talking about before they showed, but the second Bill saw them, everything stopped.

Lamont's instincts were going haywire now. He didn't know why Bill had requested the meeting, but the whole setup was unnerving. He searched the faces of the men surrounding Bill and Jonny. They looked unfriendly, but they weren't giving anything away. He forced himself not to look at Shorty, hoping his partner would be ready if things went bad.

'Nice to see you, boys.' Bill shook their hands. 'Wanted you to meet someone. This is Daz.' He motioned to one of the men behind him. Daz was taller than Lamont, with golden blonde hair, blue eyes and an easy demeanour. He wore a jacket over a t-shirt with some jeans and was beaming. 'Daz does a lot of business for me. He's one of my best.'

Daz nodded, almost preening at all the praise. Bill watched him for a moment.

'He *was* one of my best, anyway, until he started shitting in the pot.'

Daz's face paled but before he could move, Jonny grabbed him by the throat and drove his knee into his stomach. Daz slid to the floor, coughing and retching. Jonny kicked him repeatedly, spewing curses as he tried to cover up.

'Daz thought he could steal from me, and I can't have that. Do you understand?'

'Not entirely,' said Lamont. 'Are you trying to accuse us of something?'

The beating stopped. The whole room was silent, save for the whimpering and snivelling of Daz, crumpled on the dusty floor of the basement.

'Should I be?' Bill's voice was deadly.

'No, you shouldn't.'

'Good. I'm not trying to accuse you of owt. I'm showing that this isn't how to do business. Don't bite the hand feeding you. I've got a good feeling about you lot, but I'm getting old and sometimes I'm wrong. Had a good feeling about that one too.' He kicked Daz in the back.

'There's no mercy in this shit,' said Shorty, nodding at the beating in front of him.

'Definitely not. There can't be. I'm not a bloody soft touch and if I take a shot on some guy like Daz here,' Bill kicked him again, 'then I expect him to make the most of it. Not to cheat me.'

'That's understandable.' Lamont understood the message Bill was trying to share with him. Stepping forward, Shorty kicked Daz in the head and began whaling on him with hits. Jonny and the others did the same as Bill smiled with approval, looking at the scene like a proud father. He glanced at Lamont, who fought to keep his expression neutral. He wouldn't let Bill see that he had affected him.

CHAPTER TWENTY

Saturday 21 July 2001

LAMONT CLIMBED out of the shower, tripping over his own feet. He'd stupidly had a nap when he was supposed to be getting ready and now he was pushed for time.

Shorty had messaged him twice saying he was in the taxi. For a person who was always late, he was a stickler for the punctuality of others. Hurrying to the wardrobe, Lamont hastily ironed a white t-shirt and jeans. He wasn't sure which clubs they would end up at, so he opted for shoes. Popping his watch on, he heard the taxi beeping from outside.

'Yes, L!' Shorty grinned, his eyes red and slightly drooping. K-Bar sat up front with the taxi driver. He nodded in Lamont's direction as the taxi drove towards town.

'How much have you drank?' Lamont asked Shorty.

'Half a bottle of Henny. Hit the spot too,' Shorty replied. The driver frowned but didn't turn around.

'Make sure you get some water in you. If you start falling all over the place, I'm leaving you.'

'Forget that. I'm lean but I'll still out-drink you.'

The taxi let them out on Briggate. K-Bar tried paying the driver but Lamont cut across him, handing the driver a twenty.

As they approached the club, they heard the thumping sounds of Garage tracks along with the excited shrieks of the crowds. They headed inside; the atmosphere overwhelming. There were flashing lights, scantily clad women and enough goons to start a riot. Shorty was a thug, but he had charisma and people enjoyed being in his company.

K-Bar and Blakey had organised the party, and Lamont had paid. While Shorty began slapping hands and flirting with every girl in sight, Lamont hovered around the edges of the party, talking with the few who approached him. He was happy for Shorty to get all the attention.

'Why are you so quiet?'

Lamont smiled when he saw Xiyu walking towards him, dressed to impress in a plum-coloured shirt, blue trousers and expensive shoes.

'Finally, a friendly face,' laughed Lamont. 'How long have you been here?'

'Couple of hours. I had business here earlier.'

'Everything go as planned?' asked Lamont. Since bringing Xiyu into the fold, he'd never failed to fill his pockets come payday. He didn't know the specifics of what Xiyu did, but whatever it was, he did it well. Shorty and his clique still had issues with Xiyu, openly calling him *Chink* and trying to undermine him. He seemed to take it in his stride.

'You're going to have another good week.' Xiyu winked.

'I'll need it after paying for this party.'

Lamont and Xiyu watched Shorty pouring champagne down his throat as the crowd cheered him on.

'He's living it up,' said Xiyu.

'He's earned it. It's his birthday party after all.'

'I hope he remembers he's representing you.'

'I'm not his boss.' Lamont looked at Xiyu.

'Whether you want to admit it, L, everyone knows this is your team.'

'I don't,' said Lamont. Xiyu smirked.

'Ask yourself this: does Shorty make any important decisions?'

'We make them together.'

'And, if it was just Shorty making them, would things run just as smoothly?'

'It's hard to say.'

'You're right, L . . . it's hard saying that I'm correct.' He took a smug sip of his Martini.

'I don't need to deal in hypotheticals. This is Shorty's night and short of getting locked up, he can do whatever he likes.'

'I thought Marcus would be here.'

'He's handling some business.' Lamont said no more and Xiyu knew not to ask.

'How long are you staying out?'

Lamont checked his watch. 'Not too late,' he motioned towards Shorty. 'He'll probably be out until the crack of down. I'll be in long before that.'

'I'll probably finish this and go.' Xiyu motioned to his drink.

'Why? It's still early.'

'I haven't slept in nearly twenty-four hours, L. I just wanted to show my love to the *birthday boy*. I bought him the expensive champagne that he's currently spilling on the floor.'

'Just let him have his shine.' Lamont as always, played mediator.

'He's welcome to his shine,' Xiyu locked eyes with a girl walking by. She smiled at him and he smiled back. 'I'll get my own. Catch you later, L.' He moved towards the girl. Lamont chuckled.

'Mate, don't you think it's getting crowded?'

Lamont turned to the sweaty man in the generic black t-shirt and trousers. His name tag announced he was the Bar Manager.

'Pardon?'

'The VIP. There's too many people squeezing in. Who is this guy? They're acting like he's a bloody pop star or summat.'

Lamont smirked at Shorty being referred to as *Pop*. He doubted Shorty was even aware how many people were trying to gain access. His tongue was firmly down the throat of a random girl. Lamont couldn't see Stacey, Shorty's girl. He wondered if she'd shown up.

'I don't wanna jeopardise the licence if something kicks off,' the manager went on. Lamont tuned him out, thinking now might be a good time to leave. Xiyu and his companion had vanished.

At that point, Lamont spotted an older figure watching him from across the bar. He couldn't place the man, but there was something strangely familiar. The look on the man's face was speculative. He was tall and thin, with hard-faced features and cool eyes. A minute later he was gone, swallowed up by the crowd.

Lamont frowned, looking for K-Bar to let him know he was going when he heard a commotion.

'Get off me!'

A man was pushing his way through the crowds. Lamont didn't recognise him at first, but when he saw the jagged scar and the wild hair, he realised who it was. Ricky Reagan forced his way to the middle of the VIP section, eyes narrowed. Lamont wondered if angry was his default mindset or if it appeared that way because of his scarred face. Looking around, Reagan spotted him and bounded over.

'What's happening?'

'Just having a few drinks. We're celebrating,' said Lamont. Three young goons appeared behind Reagan, each giving him a hard stare.

'Can anyone join, or is it a private thing?'

'By all means, stay and celebrate.' Lamont said with a small smile. The previous meeting around Marcus had irritated him, and he'd vowed to control his emotions around Reagan in the future. Reagan's face darkened for a moment, but he nodded and bullied his way to the bar.

'What is he doing here?' K-Bar appeared at Lamont's side.

'Looks like he wanted to party with his good friend Shorty,' said Lamont dryly. K-Bar chuckled. Everyone else seemed to have gotten over Reagan's brusque interruption, going back to having a good time. Lamont's desire to go home abated. He ordered a bottle of water from the bar and chugged it, waiting.

It didn't take long. Twenty minutes later, Reagan stood near a booth telling loud stories to his cronies and a few stragglers. Waving his arms wildly and gesticulating for effect, he knocked into a man walking from the bar, causing him to spill his drink.

'Oi, watch it,' the man said. Without hesitation, Reagan hit him in the face. Lamont had a first hand-view and even he winced. Reagan was slim and slightly shorter than Lamont, but his power was evident. The man crumpled to the floor in a heap. Reagan grabbed a nearby bottle, ready to strike the man while he was down.

'Ricky, don't do it.' He vaulted forward and got in his way.

'Get out the way, let me teach that bitch a lesson!'

'It's not worth the aggro. He's down, just leave it.'

'Is he your fucking man or summat?' Reagan shoved Lamont, causing an audible gasp from the gathering crowd. His eyes were red, almost popping out of their sockets.

'I'm just trying to look out for you. It's not worth the trouble,' Lamont tried again.

'Fuck you. I don't need your help. I ain't ask you to play *Mother Teresa*, did I?'

The crowd watched the exchange. Lamont stared Reagan down, the intensity from his gaze almost palpable. Reagan wiped his nose, more cautious now. His crew of hyenas grouped closer to him.

'Move,' said Reagan. Lamont ignored him. He saw the bouncers approaching, but then someone else pushed through the crowd.

'I know that's not my brother you're pushing.'

Shorty stood next to Lamont, his voice radiating complete and utter danger. He met Reagan's eyes, not backing down an inch.

'Stay out of it, Shorty. This don't concern you.' There was noticeably less bass in Reagan's voice now. K-Bar and Blakey stood with Shorty, eyeing Reagan's goons with disdain.

'If it concerns L, it concerns me. I don't even know why you're trying to beg it and be at my party, anyway. Fuck off.'

'You fuck off. Don't get lairy because you've had a few shots and a little dick rub, you little punk,' snapped Reagan.

Shorty moved forward. One of Reagan's hyenas blocked his path. Shorty caught him flush with a right hook so clinical it was heard over the music. He stepped over the crumpled thug, ready to rush Reagan, K-Bar and Blakey moving as well.

'Enough.'

Lamont didn't raise his voice, but it had the desired effect, and everyone froze. 'Back down. We don't need the situation getting any worse.'

Noticeably bristling, Shorty kissed his teeth but stayed where he was as the bouncers ushered Reagan and his cronies out of the section. Everyone stared at Lamont with awe. Most hadn't even noticed him at the party, and none had ever seen anyone impose their will on either Ricky Reagan or Shorty.

Walking towards the bar, he got the attention of the shell-shocked staff.

'Champagne for everyone. Get that music back up,' he ordered, handing his platinum card to one of them.

———

'He's dead.'

It was the day after Shorty's birthday. Lamont lazed on his sofa watching him pace the room.

'Shorty, calm down.'

'Nah, he's dead. He violated. The guy was ready to fight you, and then he wants to step to me? I don't care about his rep. I'll handle him and his team. Me and K will do it. Or Marcus.'

Lamont understood Shorty's frustration. He took his reputation seriously, and the fact Reagan had tried speaking down to him was a blow. Lamont was thinking about the bigger picture, though.

'Reagan works for Delroy, Shorty. We can't go up against that power.'

'Course we can! Delroy's an old man. Reagan and his other son Eddie are the best he's got. We topple them, the other's will drop too. Delroy can get it too if he steps in, the fat prick.'

'You're not thinking clearly.'

'My head is always clear when there's killing to be done. You know that. Let me off the leash on this one. He tried to punk you too, remember?'

'He made himself look pathetic. He crashed your party, nearly got beaten up, then got dragged from the club.'

Shorty didn't speak, his muscled arms folded. He breathed hard, nostrils flaring.

'Anymore drama from him and he's gone. You better speak to Delroy and tell him to get him under manners, because it's open season right now, and people are being shot at for less.'

For days, Lamont considered Shorty's words, and hoped Reagan didn't do anything to make things worse.

So far, 2001 had been Lamont's most profitable year yet. Bill and Jonny were giving him more and more drugs and responsibility. Crack and heroin remained his biggest earners, but he made good money from other drugs too.

Lamont's investments were tiding over nicely, and he was in an excellent position. There was so much scope on Chapeltown at the moment though, and Lamont needed the gang wars to end. And quickly. He kept close to home, working through his people, making sure everything was in place. Lamont had considered taking another trip abroad. He'd travelled a little over the years, but never for long, needing to be close to the Hood just in case something happened. Lately, it seemed that would happen more than ever.

Lamont's phone rang.

'Hello?'

'Ring me back from a phone box.' Shorty hung up. Lamont sighed and grabbed his keys. Driving to the nearest phone box, he put a pound in the machine and dialled Shorty's number.

'What's up?'

'Madness, blood. I was at Jukie's having a drink. Do you know Neville?'

Lamont did. Neville was a Jamaican who ran with a vicious gang. He had met him a few times, but they'd never clicked.

'What about him?'

'He got stabbed. Some youths ran up and tussled with him, ended up poking him like three times. There was blood everywhere.'

Lamont's jaw tensed, and he tightly clutched the receiver. This wasn't a good situation.

'Is he dead?'

'I dunno. The kids ran off. The old man called an ambulance and people just dipped. I was the first guy out of there. I was strapped, and I wasn't waiting around for Police.'

'Wait, you had a weapon?'

'There's war, Tef. You need to get one too. I'll check you tomorrow. I'm laying low tonight.'

There was a click and Shorty was gone.

———

After hanging up, Lamont made a few more phone calls to get an idea of what had transpired. It was early days though, and no one knew much.

Neville was alive, but in intensive care, and no one knew if he would pull through. After mooching around for a while and stewing on the situation, he called Marcus.

'I heard Neville's already dead,' were the first words out of Marcus's mouth when he stepped into Lamont's house later. He went to the kitchen and made himself a drink. Lamont trailed after him.

'He's still alive. At least I hope he is. Who did it?'

'I heard it was Brandon. You know the name?'

Brandon was a tearaway a year younger than him, who was making a name for himself as a knucklehead. He'd heard his name in connection with the current conflicts, but hadn't paid him much attention. Everyone wanted to get ahead. It was hard to keep up with every new face.

'Why?'

'Dunno. Brandon's not as deep as you, but he's making good money selling crack. Maybe Neville thought he could set him up.'

'What's Shorty's relationship with Brandon?'

'You know what Shorty's like. He gets on with everyone until he doesn't. Him and Brandon are basically the same guy.'

Lamont mulled this over. He was putting the pieces together in the way he believed an outsider would look at the situation. Neville and Shorty weren't enemies, but they weren't friends either and that would be enough to get people looking in his direction.

'I might need to reach out to some of Neville's people.'

'What for? Why are you taking this so seriously?' said Marcus, frowning.

'They're gonna say Shorty set up Neville.'

'How the hell do you know that?'

'Because, it's too convenient. No one really knows how this crap started, but Shorty is definitely cool with the English lot. Neville's people are going to know this and they're gonna move against him. I guarantee it.'

'You don't think you might be looking too much into it, L?'

'Possibly. But, I'm willing to take the risk. I'll tell you right now that if a hair on Shorty's head is harmed, I'm in it. Whoever touches him, I'll wipe them off the face of the earth.'

Marcus grinned. 'I like the fire, L! When you get like this, you're like a different guy. Like when you boxed Tower that time. I heard he's still locked up.'

'Forget Tower. I need you to come with me to speak with Neville's people.'

'Who we looking for then? Courtney?' asked Marcus. Courtney was Neville's boss, and a cool guy to deal with most of the time. Lamont knew that wouldn't be the case now.

'Yeah. We'll take your car. Give me a strap too, just in case.'

CHAPTER TWENTY ONE

Monday 20 August 2001

IT TOOK a few hours and several phone calls to find Courtney, but they met him in the back of a house in Chapeltown. The spot was teeming with West-Indian men, talking in loud voices and eyeballing Lamont. He would have felt more nervous if it wasn't for Marcus's presence. Marcus strolled through the spot like he owned the place, daring anyone to say something. No one did.

Courtney sat in the kitchen, talking on a phone, pausing every two seconds to shout at an older woman who stood over a stewpot. He signalled for them to wait, telling the person on the phone to ring back. Washing and wiping his hands, he greeted them both.

'How's Neville doing?' Lamont got to the point. Courtney's jaw tensed. He was a squat man, wearing a loose shirt and jeans.

'Bad. Doesn't look like he'll make it.'

Lamont glanced at Marcus, but he was focused on Courtney.

'What does that mean for Shorty?'

Courtney rubbed his eyes. 'Was he involved?'

'Course he wasn't. He's had no dealings with Neville.'

'This boy Brandon. He knows him?'

'I don't know the extent of their relationship,' said Lamont. Courtney smirked, but it was strained.

'You talk nice. Smooth. Women probably chase you down the street.'

Lamont didn't reply. Courtney took a sip of a foul-smelling drink he hadn't noticed before. The old woman continued cooking, pretending she wasn't listening.

'My people think Shorty was involved. I can't keep them back on this.'

'Can't, or won't?' Lamont asked. Marcus straightened, his eyes hard.

'It's war. My people are getting killed out there. Brandon ain't the only one doing it. What am I supposed to think?'

'You're supposed to think that Shorty has nothing to gain from setting up Neville. There's a lot of money on our side. We don't need the drama.'

'No one needs drama. Sometimes we find it anyway.'

Marcus moved forward, scowling. Lamont waved him off, his eyes remaining on Courtney.

'Do your investigation. You'll find that Shorty had nothing to do with it. You have enough on your plate with Brandon and the others. You don't need more aggravation.'

'You threatening me now, boy?'

'My name is Lamont, not *boy*. I don't need to threaten to make a point. Enjoy your day.'

––––––

'You handled that well.'

They were back in the car. Marcus had his weapon within reach. Lamont had a pistol too. He was still getting used to it, but in the current climate it was likely necessary. Lamont didn't like how the meeting had gone. The Yardies seemed determined to blame Shorty, and he wondered if they'd orchestrated the attack themselves.

'You think?'

'No weakness. Those Yardies smell that shit. You handled it the right way. They know Shorty didn't have nothing to do with it.'

'So, they're looking for the excuse.'

'Course. Shorty's cool with the kids they're shooting at. It would send a message if they could clip him.'

'Shorty needs to stay hidden then. If he comes out, it might give them a reason to touch him. I need your people all over this. I know you've got connections amongst the Yardies, but I'll pay you well.'

Marcus shook his head.

'You're my brother. Fuck the Yardies. My people will be ready; don't doubt that.'

Lamont was relieved. Shorty and K-Bar had teams of shooters to call on, but Marcus's men were ruthless. If things escalated, they would need them.

———

THURSDAY 23 AUGUST 2001

Days passed. Brandon's house was shot at, as was his mother's house, and the house where his baby mother lived. Luckily, they were abandoned. The word was that Brandon had fled Leeds, avoiding the Yardies and the police.

Shorty chafed under his forced stay, wanting to get back out onto the streets. Lamont had heard nothing from Courtney, but Marcus and his team remained on standby.

He was at home flicking through the channels when Marcus called.

'Someone sprayed one of Shorty's spots.'

Lamont sat up. 'Did they get anyone?'

'There was no one there. It'll be Courtney's people definitely. I'm gonna do some digging. Stay indoors and I'll have someone outside watching.'

Marcus was gone. Lamont sighed, feeling the beginnings of a headache. The Yardies needed to be dealt with. It meant wading into the war between them and the English youths, but Lamont didn't have a choice. He needed information. Taking out a spare phone, he dialled Shorty's number.

'Yo, L. I'm not waiting around like some little bitch doing nothing. The big man told me what happened. It's on.'

'Shorty, relax. This whole beef, what did it start over?'

Shorty kissed his teeth down the phone, making Lamont's head hurt more.

'Money. A few Yardie's were working with Keller and Mali. Summat went wrong with the deal, and Keller and Mali got ripped off. They tried getting their money back, but it didn't work, so they did a drive-by. It went wrong, and they hit the wrong guys. Suddenly there's a war, and no one's backing down.'

Lamont mulled that over. He'd heard about that shooting in passing, but hadn't known the specifics.

'And Brandon?'

'He's the hitter dudes used. He disliked them Yardies, summat to do with how his dad treated his mum, so he was running around like *Rambo* doing stupid shit. Now, he's stabbed the wrong person, and he's on the run.'

'Didn't you consider telling him to stop?'

'For what? He's not a kid. He knew what he was doing. It was just a dumb plan.'

Lamont couldn't argue with that.

'Let the big man handle this. Stay out of sight. please.'

Shorty grumbled before hanging up. Lamont drank some water, massaging his forehead. He knew why it had all started, and it was even more of a mess than previously.

The police were already making encroachments into Chapeltown. He didn't want them poking around his activity. He needed to end the war, and he needed to do it quickly.

———

Marcus checked his gun, looking to Charlie in the driver's seat. He had his eyes on the road, totally in the zone. In the back, Sharma was ready to go. Marcus wished Victor could have rode with them, but he was still in recovery after a previous job had gone awry.

Marcus had spoken with Shorty, who all-but begged to go on the mission with them. He was an excellent soldier, and they'd worked together in the past, but Marcus would handle this problem himself.

'I'm going straight for Courtney. Keep everyone else at bay and secure them in the room. If we're not gone in ten minutes, I've got a crew on standby, who will come in and spray the house. Cool?'

Both men nodded. They pulled up down the street from Court-ney's spot. It was early evening and still warm, but there was no one outside to make an issue.

They headed for the garden, Marcus behind Sharma, Charlie covering their backs. At a nod from Marcus, Sharma kicked in the door. They heard immediate noise. Marcus surged through with his shotgun, hitting a man who'd tried going for a weapon. He headed for the kitchen where Courtney and another goon were having a conversation. The goon went for a knife, but Marcus was quicker, the butt of his shotgun crushing the man's jaw. He crumpled to the floor. Marcus aimed the weapon at Courtney.

'Sit down.'

'Tall-Man, what the hell are you doing? You can't rush into my house like this.' Courtney's eyes were wide, locked on the shotgun.

'Sit down, or I'll sit you down,' replied Marcus. He heard scuf-fling sounds and moved position to allow him to see the door. Courtney waited a beat, then slid into a seat, his hands and lip trembling.

'What is this about?'

'Who sent shots at Shorty's spot? Mess me around, and we'll kill all of you.'

'You wanna start another war? You know who I am? You'll all die.'

Marcus's eyes bored into Courtney's. Courtney broke eye contact a moment later, sighing.

'We've known each other for years. You know how I get down, and you know I don't care who you send after me. Who sent shots at his spot?'

'Look, he's called Goodison. He went after Brandon's people, then he sprayed Shorty's yard. I didn't tell him to do it.'

'We spoke. You knew that Shorty had nothing to do with Neville getting stabbed, and you still went against me anyway?' Marcus cocked the shotgun.

'Tall-Man, please! On my mother, I had nothing to do with it.'

'You didn't stop it. Gimme his number and a location. Now.'

Courtney scribbled the address on some paper and gave it to Marcus. He put it in his pocket, keeping his eyes on Courtney as he did so.

'I'm gonna take care of Goodison. You're gonna put the word out that Shorty had nothing to do with what happened. Understand?'

'You think you can tell me what's gonna happen? I am an elder, and you're a kid. You cannot come into my house and start telling me what I'm going to do.'

'If you don't, I make a call and put a kill-squad into play. They'll kill everyone connected to you, family or not. If you wanna do the same to me, then cool. I'm ready to die.' Marcus again met the older man's eyes. 'Tell me if anything in my face suggests I might be joking.'

There was a long silence, punctuated by whimpering sounds from the living room. Marcus tightened his grip, wondering if his team had been overwhelmed, and if he would need to fight his way out. Courtney finally nodded, letting out a deep breath.

'I'll put the word out. People will know that Goodison went into business for himself. We will not harm Shorty.'

Marcus surveyed the man, wondering if he could trust him. He considered just killing him right there, to send a message to the rest, but gave him the benefit of the doubt. He wasn't joking about the kill-team. They would murder Courtney's family first, and save him for last if it came to it.

'I hope we can work together in the future. Put your hands on the table.'

Marcus searched him for a weapon, then checked the unconscious goon and made to leave the room when Courtney spoke again.

'What about Brandon? You protecting him too?'

'Brandon who?' said Marcus, leaving the kitchen. Half a dozen men were laid out on the living room floor, Sharma and Charlie securing them. Marcus grabbed their weapons and put them into a sports bag.

'This shit ends here. Me and your boss have spoken. Don't make me come looking for every one of you.'

Marcus walked out first, followed by the others.

FRIDAY 7 SEPTEMBER 2001

Lamont was in the passenger seat as Shorty drove, rapping along to some mediocre tune that he couldn't get enough of. It had been a few weeks since the strife with the Yardies. Courtney kept his word and put it out that Shorty had nothing to do with Neville's stabbing. It had been touch and go, but the Yardie gunman had survived, and was now in recovery. Brandon was abandoned and left to deal with the Yardie's. His death was messy and highly publicised.

Lamont had spoken with Marcus, and they had organised a loose truce for now, both sides agreeing to back away. Delroy and a few other influential kingpins had helped to give it a sense of credibility, and for now, there was peace. He didn't know how long it would last, but he was making the most of it.

Delroy had spoken with him a few days ago, wanting to know if he changed his mind about working for him. He'd also wanted to make sure there wouldn't be any further problems between Lamont and Reagan.

'We're here.'

Shorty and Lamont climbed from the car, and Lamont followed his friend into the garden. They knocked, and Bill's wife answered. She smiled at Lamont, but her eyes lit up when she saw Shorty. Lamont resisted the urge to roll his eyes when they hugged. He didn't know what they were playing at, but it was foolish.

'Bill's waiting.'

They made their way to the office, and Bill's wife returned to what she was doing after grinning at Shorty. Lamont elbowed him, causing Shorty to scowl.

'What was that for?'

'You know what it was for. Don't do anything that will jeopardise this arrangement. Please.'

Shorty shot him a dirty look as they knocked on the office door. Bill was alone which was a surprise. Normally his brother Jonny watched his back. Lamont filed that information away. Bill had his feet up, a beer in his paw, eyes on a large football screen. He didn't even move when he saw them.

'Nice to see you lads. Enjoying the weather?'

Lamont and Shorty nodded. They didn't need the small-talk. Lamont had been wary of their supplier ever since they'd watched him beat one of his workers half to death. He didn't understand why he'd wanted to send them a message, but he'd ensured that Marcus knew where the supplier lived, just in case.

Lamont hoped there were no pending issues. The supply was excellent; they paid promptly, and there was always a healthy reserve in case they needed more. He had other suppliers he could work with as a backup, but Bill and Jonny were convenient. He didn't want to ruin that flow if he didn't have to. Business had exploded, and everyone was making enough money to where they didn't need to kill each other. It wouldn't last. It never did, but it was enough for now.

'I don't like it when it's too hot. The missus always wants to go to the beach and all that crap. I keep telling her to just go on holiday without me, but she keeps talking bollocks about *romance*. Do you know what I'm on about?'

Shorty laughed.

'My missus keeps trying to get me to go away with her. No time for that shit.'

Lamont didn't reply. Women came in and out of his life, and he made no effort to keep them. From time to time he thought about Layla, wondering if he should have admitted how he felt. The fact she had a boyfriend irked him, but the man was lucky. There was something special about Layla, and Lamont knew she would go far.

'What about you, L? A pretty boy like you must have the women going crazy.'

'I'm afraid not. Just looking for Ms Right I guess.'

Shorty snickered, and Bill shook his head.

'Make sure you're not spending too much of all that bloody money you're making on them. Anyway, let's get to business. This shit with the bloody Jamaican lot. What's going on?'

'There was a beef between them. It was sorted.'

'Why were people shooting at your mate there?' Bill jerked his thumb toward Shorty, who had tuned out the conversation, watching the football.

'He was in the wrong place at the wrong time. It's sorted. That I can assure you.'

'Those guys are crazy. They robbed one of my spots and stole five boxes. That's five kilo's I now have to make up for, you know what I mean? I'm running a business, same as you. I can't be doing that all the time.'

'Bill, I understand your concerns, but I'm confused about why you're talking to us about it.'

'I'm talking to you because you're my link to those guys. When I hear about shootings and stabbings and people thinking they're gangsters and trying to do silly drive-by's, I'm gonna run it by you lot, especially if you're in the middle of it.'

'There are no problems anymore. It was a misunderstanding that spiralled out of control.'

Bill flicked off the TV, causing Shorty to kiss his teeth. He turned to Lamont.

'I like you, L. So I'll take your word for it. I'm gonna need you to take two extra boxes, though, to help me out.'

Lamont and Shorty exchanged a look, then he replied.

'Fine.'

———

'Shorty, find a buyer for the extra drugs. I want them moved as soon as possible.'

'I'll sort it. Do you wanna explain what that was all about?'

'The Yardie's targeted Bill, so he's sniffing around to see if we're involved.'

'Why would he think that?'

'Because the Yardie's are black, and we're black, so he's lumping us together. I don't know if he has any other black people he deals with, but he's assuming we're all connected. He gave us the extra drugs to see how we'd react. It could even be a sweetener so we call them off.'

Shorty mulled that over as they pulled up at the red light.

'Do you like dealing with him?'

'He's convenient. On a personal level, I don't like him, and I think he knows it. Speaking of personal, what are you playing at?'

Shorty cut his eyes to Lamont. 'What are you talking about?'

'I'm talking about you hugging up on Bill's wife and making eyes at each other. Have you slept with her?'

'Nah, we're just messing around and flirting,' replied Shorty. Lamont noticed he didn't meet his eyes.

'Please keep it that way. I don't like to tell you what to do, but you can understand why fucking the wife of the man who supplies us might be a bad idea, right?'

'I'm not daft. Stacey would kill me anyway.'

'Okay. Drop me at my place then. I've got a meeting with Martin tomorrow.'

———

'Everything is going well.'

Lamont sipped a cup of coffee and listened to Martin drone on. They were in Martin's office, and it was sweltering, the cramped quarters causing both men to sweat. On the desk between them were various pieces of paper highlighting profits and graphs.

'What about the houses? Are we ready to invest?'

Martin nodded. 'Are you sure about the location? With the way things are in your neck of the woods, investing in property may be a bad idea. You've got a bloody gang war.'

'The gang war is over,' replied Lamont.

'How do you know?'

Lamont had no intention of sharing this information. Martin was aware Lamont was connected to crime, but didn't know the full extent. He trusted Martin, and they had made money together since their initial introduction, but there was a limit.

'Just take my word for it. I want to invest in Chapeltown, so make it happen.'

'I will. You're the boss, and I'm here to help you stay rich. You're talking about a massive investment, however. You have a good thing going. You're invested in a few businesses, and they're steadily making a profit. The barber's especially has taken off over the past year. But, is it worth the risk?'

Lamont wasn't sure. He understood Martin's position, but he'd had the idea to invest in property over a year ago, and he'd taken his time, doing his research, imploring Martin to do all the legwork. Now, he could do so. He was investing over two hundred thousand pounds. This was a large portion of the money he had earned in his life as a drug dealer, and if he lost it, it would cripple the way he currently led his life. Martin was right to be cautious.

'Yes. It's worth the risk. If it works, it'll set me up for everything else I need to do. Is the company in place?'

'Yes. I've registered the company, and the office space and address are all sorted. Levine has looked over the figures and paperwork, and you can't be touched on this. Have you spoken with him about your plans to invest?'

'He's my solicitor, not my money manager,' Lamont replied. He had in fact spoken with Levine, and like Martin, the man felt that he shouldn't invest his money in such a manner. It concerned him that two of his pillars were so against him doing it, but he had to try.

'Okay. I'll get the ball rolling and start buying up houses.' Martin wiped his forehead with a handkerchief. Lamont slid to his feet and patted the man on his damp shoulder.

'Stay in touch.'

Lamont left the office, saying goodbye to Martin's secretary. The suit he wore was too tight, but he liked to make the right impression when he went to see Martin, and blending in was essential. When he left the premises, he took off the suit jacket, then unbuttoned the top two buttons of his shirt and loosened his tie. A woman walking by smiled at him and he returned it. The rest of his day was free and clear. He needed something to distract him from Martin's warnings, deciding to get a drink. Heading to a nearby coffee shop, he ordered an iced tea and took it outside. He'd taken a seat at one of the coffee shop tables when he glanced to his left. He froze.

Layla strolled along the path, hand in hand with a smiling man. She hadn't seen Lamont, too busy giggling at her partner and leaning into him.

Lamont felt a rage take over, the likes of which he hadn't felt in years. He forced himself to stay seated, keeping his head down and gritting his teeth as Layla floated by. He knew she had someone, but seeing it firsthand was something different. He wondered if seeing her was a sign he shouldn't invest his money. Layla had moved on, and he knew that he could have made her his woman if he'd asked. Layla had liked him, but Lamont had been in too much of a funk to see what was right in front of him. Now it was gone.

He glanced up at them, watching them walk down the path, icy rage still filling his veins. Lamont's jaw clenched, and he sipped his drink to distract him. Nothing worked. Layla was more beautiful than ever, and he didn't know if it was because he couldn't have her that he felt this way, but there it was.

Finally gaining his composure, Lamont dialled a number, holding the phone to his ear.

'Shorty? Wanna go out tonight? I need to drink. A lot.'

CHAPTER TWENTY TWO

Friday 17 May 2002

'Are you enjoying yourself, L?'

Lamont sipped a glass of champagne and smiled at Martin.

'Yeah, I'm good.'

Martin smiled, drinking his own drink.

'Good. Tonight is all about you.'

'No. This is your thing,' Lamont insisted, taking another sip. He wore a light grey shirt with trousers and expensive shoes. His hair was neatly lined up, and he was clean shaven, save for his tapered sideburns and moustache. Lamont was the poster boy for a man who had made it. He had on a Rolex he had treated himself to, and some Calvin Klein aftershave. He felt fresh, but out of place.

It had been a long year. The drama on the streets fluctuated from calm and happy to end-of-the-world critical. There was little middle ground, and some crews seemed to look for any reason to fight each other.

Lamont had focused more on legitimate ventures, making a great profit with his housing venture. This was only blighted slightly by a failed investment in a pub. On the whole, he had no financial concerns.

Martin had organised a party to celebrate their latest venture, a gym. He didn't know any of the people Martin had invited. Apart from Xiyu, none of his people were there. He didn't know who to talk to, so he'd spent most of his time skulking in the corner, nodding to the music.

The party was in the backroom of a club on Call Lane. Martin had booked it and organised everything from the liquor to the DJ. Lamont liked some songs, but wasn't feeling the vibe. There were women scattered around. Several had made eye contact, but he wasn't interested. He wanted to be by himself, not surrounded by people he didn't know. He felt strangely flat. Xiyu had been next to him, until he had spotted a woman and promptly disappeared with her.

Draining his glass, Lamont placed it on the bar and made for the exit. Martin stopped him.

'L? Where are you going? You still need to say a few words.'

'Relax. I'm just getting some fresh air.' Lamont moved through the main room, nodded at the bouncers and stepped outside.

It was almost midnight. Breathing in the cool air, Lamont leaned against the wall and looked at the sky. He liked the moment. The moon was out, but the sky was bereft of stars. Shrieking laughter brought him back down to earth. Spotting the cause, he froze.

She was more conservatively dressed than back in the day, wearing a pair of tight-fitting trousers with a navy blue top. Her hair was straight, just how he remembered it, and her face was flawless. She laughed at something one of her companions had said, then looked straight at him. Her mouth parted into an almost comical *o* shape, and she stopped. Her friends noticed. There were two of them. Both pretty. Both vivaciously dressed. Next to her, they were wallpaper.

'L?' She stepped toward him. Lamont did his best to look cool, but his heart hammered in his chest. It had been five years, but she looked as good now as she had then.

'Hey, Rochelle.' Lamont met her eyes, still trying to portray confidence. This was a woman that had seen his inner depths, though. She had crushed him in a way no woman ever again could. Lamont often wondered how he would handle seeing her again.

He'd considered tracking her down, seducing her, leaving her in the lurch as she had done him.

Now, face-to-face, he regressed back to that pathetic kid he had once been. His knees were weak, his throat tight as he took a deep breath.

'What are you doing here?'

'I'm in there,' Lamont pointed at the club. 'We're having a party. It's a business thing.'

'What kind of business thing?' Rochelle tried her hardest to sound non-committal. Lamont could pick things up in her body language now, that he'd been too inexperienced to pick up on before.

'We opened a gym. Guess you could call this a launch party.' It surprised him at how easily his words came. Her friends looked from the pair to each other, trying to work out what was going on. He doubted Rochelle had ever mentioned him. *Why would she?* He had been unmemorable.

'That's great, L. That's really great,' Rochelle said brightly. Lamont noticed she still hadn't introduced him to her friends. He met their stares, then turned back to her.

'How have you been?'

'I've been well. Just working hard. You know how it is.' Rochelle ran a hand through her hair, then rubbed it against her trouser leg.

'Yeah, definitely.'

One of Rochelle's friends coughed. She took the hint.

'Sorry. Lamont, these are my friends, Bronie and Tenika. Girls, this is an old friend, Lamont.'

'Old friend, huh?' Tenika looked Lamont up and down, her eyes suggesting that she knew exactly the type of *friend* he had been.

'Nice to meet you both.' He evaded her stare. There was another moment of silence, everyone watching the other.

Outside a bar across the road, a woman was screaming at a man as the bouncers tried to separate them. Despite not knowing the situation, Lamont seized the distraction, watching as the bouncers moved the commotion down the street. He mentally tried to compose himself. He needed to be in control. Seeing Rochelle had changed his night. He needed to put some distance between them. Fast.

'Do you want to come in?' Lamont motioned to the club. He could have kicked himself. Rochelle blinked.

'We shouldn't. It's your party.'

'Stay and have a drink. We have the bar all night.' Lamont motioned for them to follow, his head and heart not on the same page. Martin was chewing his nail when he walked in.

'Where the hell were you? What's going on?' he eyed the women.

'I told you I went for fresh air. Ladies, this is Martin Fisher, my business partner and close friend. Martin, this is Bronie, Tenika and an old friend of mine, Rochelle.'

Martin shook hands with the trio. He led Bronie and Tenika to get drinks, leaving Rochelle and Lamont stood, trying not to look at each other. Lamont couldn't help it. Some women never lost their mystique.

'L, while we're here, I want to say sorry, for—' Rochelle started.

'Don't worry about it.'

'No, I have to—'

'I made an error, and I learned the hard way.'

Rochelle looked at him for a long moment, then nodded.

'I understand.'

'Did you ever pursue the teaching gig?' He changed the subject. Rochelle shook her head.

'I had to grow up. I was promoted, but I'm still working for the same company.'

'Well, we all have to work,' Lamont babbled. 'How's Mia?'

'She's doing really well. She's engaged, and she has a son. He's almost two.'

'That's good. Are you seeing anyone?' Lamont didn't know what possessed him to ask. Rochelle blinked, but quickly recovered.

'Not at the moment.'

Lamont nodded. 'I see.'

'You don't believe me, do you?' Her eyes narrowed. Lamont shrugged.

'It's none of my business. Doesn't matter if I believe you.'

'Fair enough. How's Marcus?'

'Still doing what he wants, when he wants.'

'That does not surprise me. I'm glad I don't have to listen to him screwing my little sister anymore,' Rochelle laughed. Lamont laughed with her.

'Those were some awkward nights.'

'Plenty of awkward nights back then.' Rochelle met his eyes. He relaxed. Rochelle was beautiful, but equally nervous. That gave him strength. Tenika walked over with a drink for Rochelle, and they talked.

The rest of the night was a blur, but he didn't leave Rochelle's side, and she didn't seem to want to leave his. Soon, they were both drunk. Lamont's shirt stuck to him and he had to keep moving his arms to avoid the perspiration showing. Rochelle remained next to him, smiling goofily, looking more like she had back in the day. He put his arm around her waist, pulling her close, pleased when she didn't move away.

'Where are you going after this?' He slurred in her ear.

'I don't know . . . Home I guess,' Rochelle whispered back.

'Yeah? Whose home?'

Rochelle giggled. 'Don't think you're gonna get me drunk and take advantage.'

'You're already drunk. So there's no need,' Lamont countered. She nudged him.

'You're trouble, L. you were always trouble.'

He laughed. Tenika watched them. She walked back over, Bronie trailing.

'We're gonna take off now. Are you coming?'

Rochelle hesitated, and Lamont made a split-second decision.

'Ring her later. I'll make sure she gets in.'

Tenika looked to Rochelle, who giggled.

'Make sure you look after her though. I know who you are,' Tenika warned. This piqued Lamont's interest, cutting through the alcohol haze.

'What do you mean?' he asked. The pair were already walking away, though. Rochelle linked arms with him.

'What now then?' she asked, eyes twinkling.

———

They took a taxi back to Lamont's. The taxi driver tried to make conversation, but they ignored him. Giving the driver a tip, Lamont led Rochelle inside.

'This is a nice place,' she remarked, sitting in the living room. It was decorated in shades of light blue. There was a TV/video player with an extensive collection. In the room's corner was a Hi-Fi, and a large amount of CD's.

'Can I get you a drink?' Lamont offered. She shook her head.

'I think I had enough.' She crossed her legs. Lamont watched.

'You haven't changed a bit; I thought you would have learnt how to be subtle.' Rochelle giggled. Lamont shrugged. He headed to a wooden drinks cabinet and poured some brandy. He finished it and placed the glass on the table.

'I never thought I'd see you again.' Lamont looked directly at Rochelle. She shifted in her chair, but maintained his gaze.

'And now you have.' She laughed again, but it sounded forced.

'I was determined to put you behind me, but, I always wanted to speak to you. To find out about what happened that day.'

Rochelle wiped her eyes.

'Did you bring me here to rehash the past? You didn't want to discuss it earlier.'

'What if I changed my mind?'

'If you did, then I think I should go home.'

'You're not going anywhere.' The authority in his tone unnerved Rochelle for a second. It was the same attitude he'd displayed the night they slept together.

'Are you going to keep me here against my will?'

'How could you sleep with Ricky? He's a prick.' Lamont ignored her and poured another drink.

'You don't even know him.'

'I didn't then, but I do now. I know all about him. You picked him over me.'

'What are you talking about? I told you I had baggage, but you kept pursuing me anyway. Yeah, I had something going with Ricky, and it was awkward, it was all-consuming, and it made me that miserable bitch you used to stare at on the sofa. But that was then. I don't want to go through it all again. Can you understand that?' She sighed loudly, closing her eyes. Lamont finished his drink, then licked a stray drop of alcohol from his top lip.

'I'm sorry. I just, that day . . .' It was his turn to sigh.

'Can we just forget it? Please?' Rochelle's voice was almost pleading now. He nodded.

'Consider it forgotten.'

They sat in silence. Rochelle fidgeted with her handbag whilst Lamont stared at the empty glass on the coffee table. After a while, she rose.

'I'm going to go. This was . . .' She was about to lie, but couldn't. Instead, she gathered her handbag and started for the door, expecting Lamont to stop her. He didn't, still analysing his glass. Shaking her head, Rochelle was at the front door when he spoke.

'I loved you.'

The words were barely above a whisper, yet Rochelle heard as if he had shouted in her ear. She paused, her hand resting on the front door handle. Turning, she re-entered the room. Lamont was still looking ahead.

'What did you say?'

He glanced at her, eyes wet and slightly bloodshot.

'I said, I loved you. I was a stupid kid, but I loved you. When I saw Ricky at the door, it crushed me.'

'You loved me?' Rochelle sat back down without realising.

'I did. I don't think I even knew until you closed the door on me that day. I had nothing to compare it to.'

'I didn't—'

'Of course you didn't know. I was a mess. I had nothing going for me. You were extraordinary. I wanted to tell you I wanted a relationship. Figured you'd laugh, but I was going to do it anyway.'

'Why?' Rochelle's voice was hushed.

'Because even if you'd rejected me; even if you laughed, at least I would have had closure. I suppose him answering your door was closure too.'

Rochelle's eyes glistened.

'I'm sorry,' she whispered.

Lamont smiled. 'You have nothing to be sorry for. I was a silly kid. I learnt a lesson that day. About giving too much of myself to someone. I owe you for that.'

'That's not a lesson, L.' Her expression seemed pained.

'Really, then why are you single?' Lamont countered.

'There's nothing wrong with being single.'

'When you look like you, it makes a man think; makes him wonder what damage someone could have done.'

'I'm leaving.' Rochelle again stood, but this time Lamont grabbed her arm.

'Let go of me.'

'No.'

'I'll scream if you don't.'

'Scream then.' Lamont pulled her towards him. 'Go on then . . . scream.'

She struggled but Lamont was too strong, holding her arms tightly by her sides.

'Let go of me!'

Lamont paid no attention, his eyes calmer now. Gazing at Rochelle, he pressed his lips to hers. A delicious electric tingle shot down her spine. She no longer resisted. It took a moment to realise he had let her hands go. His hands grasped her hips, and he slowly darted his tongue deeper into her mouth. They broke away, panting, eyes meeting, hearts frantically beating.

'Like I said; you're not going anywhere,' said Lamont, and then he kissed her again. This time, Rochelle was more than ready. She let out a gasp as he pressed her against the wall but she didn't break the kiss. Her soft hands cupped his cheeks, tilting his head as she kissed him deeper. Lamont's hands travelled down her back, palming her arse.

Rochelle's body felt like it was on fire. This was not the Lamont she had previously dealt with. The awkward teenager whom she'd guided was gone. In his place was an assertive, worldly man who knew exactly what he was doing. He attacked her neck with a viper's precision, leaving a tingle everywhere he touched. They writhed on the floor, undressing each other. Holding her arms above her head with one hand, Lamont traced her body with the other, his mouth engulfing a delicious breast. He dipped lower, his tongue touching her belly button, then going beneath her pelvis. Kissing at the insides of her thighs, Lamont took his time. Rochelle's head snapped back with such force it banged against the wall. She tried to cry out, but her voice caught in her throat.

As Lamont explored her with his mouth, a whirlwind of emotional pleasure cascaded over Rochelle. She couldn't believe this was happening. She grabbed his hair, her fingers tangled in his coarse black curls. She felt it manifesting, bubbling to the surface and until, finally, she reached her peak.

CHAPTER TWENTY THREE

Saturday 18 May 2002

MORNING CAME. Rochelle opened her eyes, taking a moment to gain her bearings. She didn't immediately recognise where she was, light snoring to her left startling her. Lamont laid half on his side in a deep sleep. Rochelle watched him, thinking about the night before. The sex had been spectacular. After they had caught their breaths, they headed upstairs to repeat the act. They took their time, exploring one another's bodies.

Last night it all seemed perfect. Sleeping with Lamont had seemed the most natural thing in the world. Now, she felt awkward.

Climbing from the bed, Rochelle quickly dressed. She had everything on but couldn't find her shoes. Silently cursing, she hurried downstairs. The shoes were next to the table. Rochelle was about to put them on when she sensed another presence.

'Going so soon?' Lamont stood in the doorway clad only in some brown pyjama bottoms, his arms folded. She hadn't even heard him enter.

'Busy day, lots of things to do. You know?' Rochelle said in a fake, hearty tone she didn't recognise.

Lamont nodded. 'I understand.' He smiled, but there was no warmth in his tone or eyes. Rochelle knew that he sensed what was going on. She didn't need to break it down for him. Instead, she just stared. The vulnerability again flared in Lamont's tired eyes. Rochelle opened her mouth to speak, but she couldn't get the words out.

'How's things ended with us . . . I'll always regret it, L.' It wasn't quite what was on her mind, but it was true.

Lamont nodded.

'Call me if you ever want to talk,' he said listlessly. After putting his number in her phone, they walked to the door and shared a brief hug. Surprising herself, Rochelle leaned in for a kiss, only for Lamont to angle his head so she caught his cheek. She could smell herself on him and for a second, she squeezed tightly.

'Take care,' Lamont's voice was mechanical. Rochelle didn't know who she was seeing now. She'd thought sneaking out would be best for Lamont. He had truly changed, though. Lamont wasn't that sensitive little boy anymore, and it was because of her. With a regretful smile, she left.

TUESDAY 21 MAY 2002

Lamont drove home, switching lanes as the sky slowly turned from amber to black. The day had been a busy one of running around making sure that everything continued running smoothly. Louie though, had been silent.

Since Lamont began working with Bill and his brother, he hadn't seen Louie as much. He still supplied him, and even sent Shorty to have a word with the kids working for him, making sure they didn't take liberties. Dialling Louie's number while stopping at some lights, the phone rang but there was no answer. As the light turned green, Lamont called Shorty.

'Send someone to see the old man.'

'For what?' scoffed Shorty. Lamont could hear voices and loud music in the background.

'We haven't heard from him or his team. They should be done with their work by now.'

Shorty kissed his teeth. 'I'll send one of my gunners round. You better hope he's not in there watching *Quincy*, because I'll smack him up personally if he is.'

Laughing, Lamont hung up and headed home. Inside, he checked his phone for messages and changed out of his clothing. After a quick shower, he made himself a cup of coffee and plopped down on the sofa, picking up the book he'd started reading earlier. His mind was too wired. It was common nowadays. Even when he was at home, away from all the drama, it was difficult to switch off from the streets. He put the book to one side, watching the end of a football match while he finished the coffee. He made food, then just picked at it for a while until he finally put it to one side.

Lamont was antsy and didn't know why. He was insulated, and he had a good team working for him. Financially, he was fantastic.

Lamont could have laughed. He had money and respect. Mostly, people left him alone, but it felt hollow sometimes. Lamont thought back to the second-hand clothes and the constant ridicule. Now, he had the world at his feet. Maybe it was time to act like it.

Heading upstairs, he put on a new pair of jeans and a black designer t-shirt. He looked down at his dad's old watch for a moment, feeling strangely confident, as if the old man's strength was flowing through him. Spraying on some aftershave, he headed outside to the taxi he had pre-ordered.

As always, the town centre was heaving with people out on the prowl. Lamont slipped through the crowds into a bar, ordering a glass of whisky. He sipped it quickly and ordered another, his eyes flitting around the bar looking for a distraction. He caught the eye of a few girls and thought of Rochelle for a moment. He wondered if he had done the right thing in dismissing her, resolving that he had. A girl that had been watching him since he walked in, again caught his eye, motioning for him to walk over. Shrugging, Lamont did.

'Lamont,' he said straight away. She smiled, appreciating his forwardness.

'Kari.'

'What are you drinking?' Lamont led her to the bar. She was nearly as tall as him, with a lithe frame and short, dark hair. She ordered a glass of white wine, sipping it as she met his eyes.

'Who are you with?' He asked. Kari giggled.

'I'm by myself tonight. I just wanted to do something different.'

'I can sort of relate,' admitted Lamont. They sat in a corner of the room by now, the pulsating House music slightly muffled.

'Are you in here with anyone?'

Lamont shook his head. 'This was very spur of the moment. It's not like me.'

Kari made a face. 'Are you one of those people that plans out every moment of their life?'

'I can be. Last thing I want is to end up slipping.'

'How's it working out for you?' Kari surveyed him over the rim of her glass.

'It feels weird.' Lamont shook his head again. 'Forget it. We don't need to get this deep.'

'I want to.' Kari sidled closer. She smelled amazing. Some women just had a naturally adult scent that made him think of rough sex rather than flowers.

'Everything in my life is going well. In terms of financial security and job security, I'm set. I've made some big moves that have put me in a good position.'

'And what? Now you're waiting for the other shoe to fall?'

Lamont nodded.

'Maybe you just need to relax.'

'Why do people always give that generic advice? It means nothing,' snapped Lamont. She made a face.

'Sorry, I wasn't trying to annoy you.'

'Nah, I'm sorry. Wigging out on the prettiest girl in this place won't make me feel better.'

Kari was all smiles now.

'I'm glad you realised it.'

'Realised what?'

'That I'm the prettiest girl in this place.'

They locked eyes. Lamont felt the pull, two parts of his brain arguing with each other. One side was telling him to put the moves on Kari. The other told him to go home and get his thoughts in order. She continued staring. She had a pretty face. Thick, luscious lips, the sort Lamont hated in his younger days but cherished now. *He was definitely a mouth man.*

She wore a dark shade of lipstick that seemed to shine under the club lights. He moved towards her, only to be cock-blocked by his vibrating Motorola. Mumbling a swear word, he pulled out the phone and answered.

'L, where you at?' Shorty's voice boomed over the speaker, causing Lamont to move the phone from his ear for a moment.

'You don't need to talk so damn loud. I can hear you.'

'Where are you? This ain't a drill.'

Lamont stood.

'What's going on?'

Kari looked at him, confused.

'It's Louie. Meet me at your place. We need to talk.'

———

Shorty paced up and down outside Lamont's house as he climbed from the taxi. He glared at Lamont, Blakey hovering nearby. The pair blended in with the night sky around them in their dark attire. Blakey nodded at Lamont, who returned the gesture.

'Did you find him?' asked Lamont.

'Yeah, we found him all right,' Shorty's tone was sulky.

'If you think I took the piss in the taxi, I—'

'Fuck the taxi. He's dead.'

Lamont blinked foolishly. 'Who's dead.'

'Louie.'

'What?'

Shorty rubbed his face.

'Sent Blakey and one of my other dudes, like you said. They banged on the door for a bit, shouted through the letter box, but no one answered.' Shorty shot a look to Blakey, who took it as his cue.

'We were about to jet, but Larrie thought he heard the TV. We kinda broke in, and—'

'You broke into his house?' Lamont interjected.

'We wore gloves. Don't worry. Anyway, when we were inside, it smelt funky. We went into the living room and there he was.'

'How did he look?'

Blakey made a face. 'How do you mean?'

'Did he look like he died by himself?'

'There was no one else there,' said Blakey, completely misunderstanding.

'He means, did someone else kill him, you prat,' sniped Shorty. Blakey hung his head.

'He looked like he was sleeping. We couldn't see nothing out of the ordinary, but we didn't stand around having a look.'

'Did you call an ambulance?' Lamont continued his questioning.

'We just kicked out. He was dead, so we just hurried out of there.'

Lamont held Blakey's stare for a moment, then motioned for them to come inside. He strode into the living room, reaching for his phone. He stared at it for a second, mumbled something, then picked up his keys, passing them to Shorty.

'Drive to a phone box. Can't make this call from the house.'

Shorty started the engine and flew down the street, ignoring Lamont's request to slow down. A few minutes later they found a phone. Lamont rummaged around in his pocket, then looked at his companions.

'Either of you two got any change?'

'I don't carry copper,' said Shorty, as if this were an adequate response.

'Here.' Blakey reached into his pocket and pressed a damp fifty pence piece into Lamont's outstretched hand. He thanked him and hurried towards the phone box. He spoke for less than a minute and then went back in the car. Shorty drove them back to Lamont's.

'Marcus is gonna tell one of his guys to make the call. He's gonna check first, make sure there's nothing connecting him to us.'

'Bloody hell, I didn't even think of that,' said Blakey.

'Shut up. We're talking now,' Shorty snapped. Blakey's mouth immediately closed.

When they were back at Lamont's, he took out a bottle of brandy and poured three shots, handing the other glasses to Blakey and Shorty. Without a word, they held them aloft a moment, paying silent respect to Louie, then drank as one. Wiping his mouth, Lamont poured another.

'You're driving us back, B.' Shorty held out his glass. Lamont topped him up, and they repeated the procedure.

'When was the last time you saw him?' Lamont asked.

'A month ago. I didn't even deal with him direct anymore. I left his people to K-Bar and Maka.'

'I haven't seen him since the last time we were there,' admitted Lamont, wondering why he felt guilty. He thought back to the first conversation he and Louie shared; where they admitted they were there because of women. Lamont wondered if it would upset Auntie when she heard the news about her ex. Kari flitted into his mind. She'd gone out looking for a good time and he'd left her without even getting her number. Some lucky guy was probably with her now.

'No reason for you to, I guess. He was a nobody. Everybody knows that.'

'Still, he got us started. Who knows where we'd be if it wasn't for him.'

'We'd have got somewhere regardless, fam. You can't keep hungry dudes like us down.'

'Damn right,' said Blakey.

'Shut the fuck up. We're talking here. In fact, go wait in the car. I don't need you repeating shit to impress little girls in town.'

Abashed, Blakey slunk out to the car without protest.

'Why do you talk to him like that?'

'Who? Blakey? He likes it. Do you think Louie will have anything connecting us?'

Lamont shrugged. 'My instincts tell me no, but it's worth it to double check. You just never know.'

Shorty nodded. 'I get you.' He again topped himself up.

Lamont wasn't sure if it was Shorty's third or fourth glass, but he still clutched the bottle.

'What's up with you?'

'What do you mean?' Shorty made a face as he guzzled down the liquor.

'If I didn't know any better, I'd think you were grieving.'

'Grieving for who? Louie?'

Lamont said nothing. Shorty kissed his teeth.

'Fuck him. Yeah, he started us off, but so what? We were running him by the end.'

'Then, why are you upset?'

'I'm not upset!' bellowed Shorty. Lamont glanced at him, his eyebrow slightly arched. A second later, Shorty took a deep breath. 'It's just . . . That was how it ended for him. Dead on a mouldy sofa in a piece-of-shit house.'

'So?'

'So, that's not how I wanna go out. I ain't saying I wanna live forever, but I wanna leave in style,' Shorty poured yet another drink, topping up Lamont after. They both drank in silence, no more words needing to be said.

CHAPTER TWENTY FOUR

Friday 7 June 2002

IT WAS A POOR TURNOUT.

That was the main thought on Lamont's mind as he hung around after the service for Louie ended. He was with Shorty. No-one else from the team bothered to show. None of the kids Louie dealt with had turned up. Just a few old people probably looking to get drunk now that the service was over.

Louie had a sister who'd organised everything. He offered to help, but she hadn't let him, saying it was something she needed to do. He hadn't even known Louie had siblings. Lamont had learned Louie's parents were also dead. The similarities between the pair were uncanny, and he was trying not to look too deeply into it.

Shorty had been subdued throughout the service, not speaking to anyone and even now that the service was over, remaining close to Lamont. After they found the body, Shorty had admitted to Lamont that they'd found money at Louie's place. Thousands of pounds, which appeared to be profits from the drugs sold. He'd done nothing with the money. By the sounds of it, he'd stopped doing anything, no longer wanting to take care of himself. Lamont had initially suspected foul play, but no one else had a hand in Louie's death.

'Are you all right?'

'I don't like funerals,' replied Shorty.

'Who does?' Lamont recalled his parent's funeral. He and Marika had sat stiffly up front with Auntie as the service went on. Everyone looked sympathetic but mostly it seemed staged, like the so-called mourners were just acting for non-existent cameras. They told him how sorry they were, patting him on the head.

Lamont told himself he wouldn't cry during the service and he kept his word. Even when Marika had cried, shouting *mummy* when she heard her mother's name mentioned. Lamont held her, feeling her tears soak his suit.

The after-party was full of debauchery. Some of the same faces that had told Lamont how sorry they were, now drank liquor and danced like they were at a party. Auntie had been right in the middle of it, shimmying away to catcalls and wolf-whistles, Lamont relegated to the corner to watch as she lapped up all the attention. He'd seen a gleam in her eyes that night that he hadn't understood.

'This, though . . . this is pathetic. There's about twelve people here if you don't count the alcoholic crowd that are just waiting to get drunk. Look at them.'

Lamont spotted them. The laggers. Shuffling around in borrowed suits. They looked shaky, eyes darting all over place, constantly licking their lips. This little service would be the highlight of their week, and the chance to get a nice drink.

'I know. It's sad.'

'Damn right it is. Don't let me go out like this, L. When you bury me, make sure there's music and people dancing and shit. *Tupac* or summat.'

'*When?* Are you planning on going somewhere?'

'You never know.' Shorty shrugged. Lamont was about to question this, when a car pulled up outside the church and three men climbed out. He recognised one of them. It was the same man he had seen looking at him at Shorty's party last year.

The men glanced in their direction, then made a beeline for Louie's sister. The man at the front spoke to her for a few minutes, his face full of concern. Lamont was too far away to hear, but she was sniffing and nodding. The front man gave her a brief hug, then headed in his direction.

He was surefooted, his back straight, wearing a white shirt, khaki trousers and boots. His dreads were even longer than K-Bar's and his face was thinner than his frame, his cheekbones almost jutting out at sharp angles. He glanced balefully at Lamont, then shook hands with Shorty, his goons following suit.

'Nice to see you here, Shorty.'

'You too, Leader. Didn't know you and Louie were cool like that.'

At the mention of the name, Lamont stiffened. This man had murdered Craig and destroyed Levi's life. He fought to keep his face neutral as Leader turned now, his hand outstretched.

'You must be the one they call *Teflon*,' he said in his heavily accented voice. His eyes glittered.

'That's me.'

'I've heard a lot about you. Heard you're a good person to know.'

'I don't know about that,' Lamont replied, not breaking eye contact.

'He's chatting shit,' Shorty interrupted. 'Teflon is the man out here. Get to know.'

Leader nodded at Shorty's words, a look passing between his men.

'Maybe we can all do some business. I knew your people. Years back. You probably don't even remember.'

'I remember.' Lamont hadn't taken his eyes from Leader.

'Sometimes you have to put people in their place, make sure they don't step out of line.' Leader smirked. 'I'm sure you under-stand that.'

'I'm sure I do.'

Leader nodded.

'I'll see you both around. Give my love to Levi if you see him.' Leader strolled away, laughing with his goons in tow.

'What was that about?'

'You tell me,' snapped Lamont. 'Since when did you get so pally with him?'

'Leader? I wouldn't call it pally saying hello to the dude at a funeral.'

'Do you remember what he did?'

Shorty kissed his teeth. 'You still crying over that shit that happened years ago? L, this is the game we're in. Craig was a fool, and so was Levi.'

'So they deserved what happened to them?'

'They rolled the dice and fucked up. You can beat yourself up about it, but they knew what they were doing. We all play this game. You need to realise that, because you can't pick and choose. Leader gets that. That's why he's around and they're not.' Shorty moved from Lamont, leaving him standing alone.

——————

Shorty had accumulated a few different hideouts over the years, but had a main spot where he stayed most of the time. It was a mess, with computer games, pirated DVD's and CD's everywhere, along with the lingering smell of weed.

As if on cue, Shorty lit his spliff when he took a seat, sighing loudly. With his freehand, he unbuttoned the top two buttons of his funeral shirt, dumping the suit jacket on the sofa next to him.

'Hit this. It's better than the shit we used to put out.'

Shrugging, Lamont took a small burn, coughing. He hit it again then passed it back to Shorty, who laughed.

'Didn't think you actually would. What's the drill?'

Lamont laughed himself. He'd indulged in a few drinks at the after-party, and his head swam. Thinking back to when he first met Louie, he spoke.

'Remember a few years ago, when we first started, and you heard me and Louie talking?'

Shorty frowned. 'Summat about a girl, wasn't it?'

'Her name was Rochelle. She was the sister of a girl that Marcus used to deal with. Dunno if you ever met her.'

'Wait a sec, are you talking about *Bad Rochelle* from the ends? You smashed that?' Shorty's mouth hung open. Lamont again nodded. 'Gimme some skin!' He slapped hands with Lamont. 'Why didn't you tell me?'

'I didn't tell anyone. Marcus only knew because Mia told him. It didn't end well. Turns out she was fucking Ricky Reagan. I stopped by to talk to her and saw him there.'

'Wait, so she played you?'

'We were never a proper thing. I was just into her. Probably more than she was.'

'Is that why Reagan wigged out on you at my party that time?'

'I doubt he even remembered me. I was a nobody.'

Shorty killed the spliff and cracked open the bottle of brandy, half-filling two glasses, then topping them up with Coca Cola.

'Why are you telling me this now?'

'Because I need to talk about it. That funeral hit me harder than I realised. Louie left nothing behind. No one cared. Even his sister just went through the motions. You're my brother, and I needed to get it out. I saw Rochelle out recently, and I slept with her again.'

'Why would you do it to yourself?' Shorty kissed his teeth.

'I needed closure.'

'*Closure?* Are you a girl?' Shorty rolled his eyes. Lamont laughed. It was typical Shorty.

'I was serious about her. I brought her back to my place, and we fucked. The next day she left.'

'Just like that?'

Lamont nodded.

'I'm surprised you didn't propose to her.'

'I'm not that bad.'

Shorty continued laughing, his drink shaking. Things grew hazy after that.

—————

Waking with a groan, Lamont found himself face-down on Shorty's sofa, head pounding. Closing his eyes again, he swallowed down the nausea, then gingerly rose. Stumbling to the bathroom, he splashed cold water on his face until the cobwebs cleared, looking at his bleary reflection in the bathroom mirror.

Wiping his eyes, he left the room. His phone rang. Lamont checked the low battery, intending to charge it when he got home.

'Yeah?'

'Lamont? It's Paul. I live next door?'

'Hey, Paul. What's up?'

'I'm not sure if you're aware, but it looks like someone has broken into your house.'

'Are you serious?' Lamont pressed the phone to his ear.

'The front door is definitely open, but I'm not sure. I've called the police anyway, so get here as soon as.'

'I will. Thanks a lot.' Lamont hung up, glad he'd had the foresight to share his personal number with the neighbour. He headed to wake up Shorty, his mind racing. Shorty was already up and in the kitchen. He was staring into space, frown lines etched into his forehead.

'Bro, are you okay?' Lamont asked, forgetting his situation for a moment.

'Rochelle . . . I started putting pieces together when I woke up. Didn't really register when you were telling me last night.'

'How do you mean?'

'She's thingy's bitch.'

'What do you mean? Who's thingy?'

'Leader. Rochelle is his girl.'

'Bollocks,' scoffed Lamont. 'She works in an office. How would she even know Leader?'

'She's from the Hood. If she knows Reagan, why wouldn't she know Leader?'

'Even if she does, what's that got to do with anything?'

'Leader approached you yesterday. Remember? When he was talking shit?'

'Yes, I remember, but you're not making any sense.'

Shorty sprang to his feet, rubbing his forehead. Lamont watched him in disbelief. He didn't have a clue what was going on.

'She fucked you because of him.'

'What?'

'Leader told her to get close. He's after you. That's why he was at the funeral.'

'He was paying his respects to Louie.'

'Are you hearing yourself? No one respected Louie!'

'Why are you shouting?'

'Because I'm vexed. That dude is coming after you. He's supposed to respect this shit. He knows who I am.'

'So this is about you?'

Shorty waved his hand. 'It's about all of us.'

Lamont blinked, wetting his lips, still trying to catch up.

'Rochelle wouldn't do that.'

'What, like she wouldn't fuck you and Ricky Reagan at the same time? Grow the fuck up, L. This is the street.' Shorty paused. 'Wait, did you say you took her back to your place?'

Lamont froze, realising exactly why Shorty was asking.

'Yes,' he replied, his voice subdued. 'A neighbour rang me just now. Someone broke in.'

'Leader. He expected you to be there. C'mon, I'll call K and we'll go over.'

———

Lamont remained deep in his thoughts as K-Bar drove them to his house. The connection between Rochelle and Leader seemed ridiculous. He and Leader had spoken for the first time yesterday. The more Lamont considered things, the more twisted things became. He recalled seeing Leader at Shorty's party last year. That alone added weight to his words.

How would Rochelle have engineered a meeting, though?

Lamont's stomach twisted in a knot. His phone vibrated and when he looked at the screen and saw Rochelle's name, he thought he was dreaming. Hesitating, he answered.

'L?'

Lamont didn't speak.

'L? Are you there?'

'Why are you calling me?' The phone shook in his hand as he tried to control his growing anger. He hadn't learned a thing, even after all these years.

'Look. I . . . what happened . . . I'm sorry. Please believe me. This thing with Leader is complicated. He found out I knew you and he was asking questions, and then he found out we slept together.'

'You told him?' Lamont wanted to trust Rochelle's words, but they were lost in his growing rage.

'No! Bronie told someone. They told him. I swear, I haven't been like that with Leader in years.'

Lamont laughed. He felt Shorty looking.

'You should be pleased.'

'Pleased? Why?'

'Even after all these years, your bargaining tools are still working. What are you after now? Money? You fucked me once, and now you've screwed me over once again.'

'No! I swear this is the truth.'

'No, this is the truth: you made one mistake. I am not the little punk you slammed the door on four years ago. When you run into your boyfriend, tell him that.' Lamont hung up, breathing hard. Shorty surveyed him, but didn't speak, a tense silence lasting until they arrived.

Lamont saw people milled around his house. K-Bar remained, but Shorty went with Lamont and they strode toward to the house. The front door was wide open and visibly damaged. An officer in the garden was making notes in his notepad when he saw Lamont. He blocked his path.

'Can I help you, sir?'

'No, you can't. I live here, officer,' said Lamont. This piqued the officer's interest.

'You're Lamont? *Lamont Jones*?'

'That's correct. What happened?'

'I was hoping you could tell me. One of your neighbours heard a disturbance and called us. They advised they saw men running from the premises and climbing into a large car.'

'Can I get inside please? I would like to see the full damage.'

'And I would like you to please answer my questions.'

'You haven't asked me any questions,' snapped Lamont. 'Also, you don't have the right to stop me entering my own premises.'

The officer cleared his throat. He was young, probably a fresh recruit, with sparse blonde hair around his chin and grey eyes. He sized Lamont up, watching Shorty in the background.

'I haven't established who you are,' he said, as if he'd scored a telling point. Instantly, Lamont showed the officer his driving licence.

'Satisfied? Now, move out of the way.'

'Watch your tone, mate.'

Shorty stepped forward.

'Did you hear what he said? Move out the damn way so he can see the damage.'

'This doesn't concern you, sir,' the officer said to Shorty.

'Nah, it doesn't concern _you_.'

The crowd watched the exchange. Already at boiling point after his talk with Rochelle, Lamont was just as ready to fight as Shorty. Thankfully, an older officer wandered over.

'What's going on?'

'This is Lamont Jones, sir,' The younger officer gestured to Lamont. 'He wants to get inside.'

'So, let him. It's his place.'

His face reddening, the officer moved. Lamont and Shorty hurried inside, their feet crunching on broken glass. Lamont went straight to the living room, his stomach plummeting when he saw his CD's and DVD's all over the place.

He knelt down and began picking up the chess pieces that had spilled to the floor. He'd collected all the black pieces when the older officer walked in.

'Any idea who could have done this?'

'I was out all night. I have no idea.' Lamont rushed upstairs. Thankfully, there was no damage.

'We'll need some details, and you'll need to come to the station to give a full statement,' the officer said when he came back downstairs.

'No.'

'What do you mean?'

'I'm not pursuing any charges. I don't know what happened. You can see I was out. There is no reason for me to go to the station.'

'But . . . Mr Jones, sir, don't you want us to catch the guys who did this?'

'I doubt you could,' said Lamont scathingly. He hadn't meant to be so harsh, but he was barely keeping hold of his temper by now. The older detective scowled. He stowed his notepad and made for the door.

'Fine then. You're on your own.'

———

Shorty waited while Lamont got his things together. Blakey had been summoned, and would stand guard until the door was fixed. Lamont's mind was all over the place as he stuffed clothing and essentials into a sports bag he used for the gym.

Rochelle's betrayal stung. He was sure that the night had meant more. To find out she was setting him up, was galling. It wasn't until they drove away, that Shorty finally spoke.

'Blakey will drive my car back. You need to ring Rochelle back.'

Lamont shot him a blank look.

'Why?'

'To get answers.'

'About what?'

Shorty's brow furrowed. He glared at Lamont.

'About Leader. This is war now.'

———

'She's not answering.'

Lamont and Shorty stood by a phone box in the Hood. He had tried ringing Rochelle three times, but she wasn't picking up. After the way he had flipped out on her, he wasn't surprised.

'Right, come on. We're gonna drop off your stuff, then we're gonna go out looking. I'm ringing Marcus.'

––––––

Later, Lamont and Shorty headed out and hit the gambling spots. It was evening now, and the games were just getting started. People would be there the rest of the night, hoping to take the tables. In a back room, they smelled fried food cooking. The ever-present stench of weed and alcohol was in the air, but the pair barely noticed. Shorty stopped to question an acquaintance. Lamont made his way to the furthest table, tapping someone on the shoulder.

'Can I have a quick word?'

'What is the problem?' Trinidad Tommy asked.

'Leader,' said Lamont, once Trinidad had left the table with him. A man moved straight away to take Trinidad's place, sitting at the table and picking up the cards. 'I need to find him.'

'Why?'

'It's important.'

'Leader is nasty. You should stay away from that kind of person. He will get you in trouble.'

'I know what I'm doing,' said Lamont, which was a lie. He kept recalling the way Leader's guys had thrown the chessboard to the floor. The chessboard his father gave him. Rage coursed through his veins. He wanted to hurt Leader and Rochelle for what they had done to him.

'I don't think you do. I know what you are, and what you're not. Don't let people get you into something you're not ready for.' Trinidad looked past Lamont at Shorty.

'Thanks for your time,' Lamont held out two twenty-pound notes to Trinidad.

'What is this for?' he looked offended.

'For your time. I made you lose your place.'

'I don't want your money. I just want you to listen,' said Trinidad. Lamont folded the money and stuck it in Trinidad's shirt pocket.

'The money is the only thing I can guarantee. Thank you for your time.'

CHAPTER TWENTY FIVE

Thursday 13 June 2002

'You hear anything?'

Shorty and Lamont were on Grange View in Chapeltown. Shorty slouched in the car, Lamont leaning against the bonnet talking to Marcus Daniels. Marcus stifled a yawn, his face ravaged with tiredness. Lamont didn't know how long he had been tracking Leader, but he hadn't found anything either.

'Leader's people are being quiet. I've got contacts but all they're telling me is that Leader is shady and no one's really fucking with him.'

'How can none of them have seen him? Someone's lying,' interjected Shorty.

'Maybe. If they are, no one is saying anything.'

'What about that bitch you used to lay with? Nothing there?'

Marcus shook his head. 'I haven't seen Mia since I dumped her. I went by the house, but Rochelle doesn't live there anymore,' Marcus rubbed his forehead. 'I can't believe she's involved in this shit though. Never expected it from her.'

'Did you know she was with Leader?' Lamont asked.

'It's not a secret.'

'You should have told me.'

Marcus laughed.

'How was I supposed to know you were gonna bang her again?'

Lamont couldn't argue. No one had expected to see Rochelle, least of all him. He wondered how she learned about the event, and how she would have approached if he hadn't stepped outside.

'Anyway, I'm gonna keep looking. I'll get with you later.' Marcus touched Lamont's fist, nodded at Shorty, and left.

'Back to square one then I guess,' said Shorty. Lamont wasn't listening though. He had a plan.

———

'I hope you're here to take me up on my offer,' were Delroy's first words as Lamont was shown into his office. It was a small house at the top of Louis Street that was heavily protected. Delroy had turned the living room into his office, which had a desk, chairs, a sofa and a large TV. There was a computer in the corner but Lamont was positive he didn't even know how to turn the thing on.

'I'm here to talk about something else.'

Delroy signalled to him to take a seat.

'You're wearing that watch well. Your dad would be proud.'

'Thank you.' Lamont looked down at the battered watch, feeling his heart swell for a moment. He focused on Delroy.

'You called this meeting. I don't think it's because you just wanted to chat.' Delroy waved his hand.

'Do you know Leader?'

'I know a lot of Yardies.'

'So, you do.'

'Why are you asking?'

'I need to find him.'

Delroy coughed.

'Why?'

'I need to finish something he started,' replied Lamont. Delroy digested that one.

'I'm gonna send someone to get food. Proper homegrown stuff. Do you want some?'

'I ate before I came.' Lamont recognised a stalling tactic when he saw one.

'Fair enough. So . . . You're after Leader. Must be big. You look different from last time.'

'How did I look last time?' Lamont was intrigued.

'On top of the world. Focused. I've been keeping tabs on you, Teflon. I'm sure you expected that.'

'I did.'

'This Leader thing. I've got a lot of influence over that side. One phone call to the right people, and I'd find him.'

'But?' Lamont prompted. Delroy smiled, but it didn't meet his eyes.

'But, you rejected me. As much as I respect the way you do business, helping you doesn't benefit me.'

'So, let's make it a business deal. Name a price.'

'I don't need money.'

'I bet that if your workers started giving you less profit, you'd have something to say about it,' Lamont pointed out. Delroy chuckled.

'Let me put it another way then; I don't want *your* money. I want you to work for me. If you can't do that, you're useless to me. Good luck, though. I'll tell Winston you asked after him.'

'Please do.' Lamont clenched his fists, taking a deep breath. He shook Delroy's hand and moved toward the door.

'Teflon?'

He paused. Delroy grinned.

'How does it feel to not be winning anymore?'

He left.

———

Days passed. Lamont remained indoors, everyone else coordinating to keep things running smoothly, and hunt the renegade Yardie. He made enquiries into where Rochelle could be, but she had disappeared. He recalled their conversation. He'd ripped into her on the phone, and though he didn't regret what he said, he wished he'd shown more patience. She could have led him to Leader.

Pausing the *Sopranos* episode, Lamont went to freshen up. He was tired of sitting around. Shorty had left him a loaner, an old Peugeot that belonged to an associate of theirs. He was driving Lamont's Lexus to keep up appearances.

Driving to the Hood, Lamont parked around the corner from Shorty's hideout and walked in. Downstairs, all the lights were off, but he could see lights coming from upstairs along with the sound of soft music.

'Shorty?' He called. 'Are you about?'

Knocking once on the master bedroom, Lamont entered. He heard *TLC* playing in the background at the same time he saw the bare breasts of Bill's wife. She gave a gasp when she saw Lamont and covered herself. Lamont's eyes flitted to Shorty, shirtless and grinning. No one spoke, as TLC crooned about a *Red Light Special*. Lamont shook his head, but couldn't think of the words.

'I'll be downstairs,' he said finally, 'when you're done with your business.'

———

'What the fuck are you playing at?'

Half an hour later, Bill's sheepish-looking wife had been sent home in a taxi. Shorty reclined on the sofa, smoking a spliff, still beaming.

'What did it look like?'

'It looked like you pissing around and fucking things up, that's what it looked like!'

'Why are you shouting?' Shorty frowned.

'Why are you screwing the connect's woman is a better question.'

Shorty grinned again. 'It just happened.'

'No, it didn't. How long has it been going on for?'

'I've hit it twice. It's nothing.'

'And Bill? The second you get bored with her — which we both know you will, she'll run and tell him.'

'Fuck Bill.'

'For a guy who loves money so much, you love to fuck with business.'

'This is about business is it?' Shorty let out a harsh laugh.

'Of course it is.'

'Business is messed up because of you. You got played by that bitch Rochelle, and now the team are chasing Yardie ghosts.'

'Leader planned this. Not me. No one saw it coming.'

'You sure? Because Leader knew what he was doing. He saw that you were pussy-whipped and sent her to get you.'

Lamont's temper flared. He was determined to wipe the smug look off Shorty's face.

'I've been cleaning your messes for years. You would have been in prison years ago if I hadn't held your hand and kept you out of trouble,' he snarled.

Shorty opened his mouth to reply, but Lamont's phone rang, distracting them. Seeing Rochelle's name on the screen, his stomach plummeted as he answered.

'What do you want?'

'I heard you've been looking for me?' cackled Leader, his voice muffled on the line.

'I have.'

'You should have stayed at your spot then. I went to see you and you weren't there.'

Lamont remembered the scattered chess pieces. His hands shook with humiliation and rage. He was still furious from the argument with Shorty, and now he had to deal with this fool.

'Tell me where you are. I'll come to you.'

'Stop talking. Your bitch lent me her phone.' Leader paused and Lamont heard whimpering in the background. 'You wanna come get her, it's gonna cost you five hundred thousand.'

'Go fuck yourself.'

'That's your choice then.' Leader hung up. Lamont flung down the phone. He rubbed his face.

'What happened?' Shorty asked.

'The joker wanted half a million for Rochelle.'

'When he rings back, talk nice. Try to set up a public meeting, and we'll take him out.'

They sat quietly, the tension from their short argument abating. Lamont thought about Rochelle. He'd definitely heard a female in the background. Leader could have been screwing with him, but he was sure it was her. He kicked himself for not negotiating. He was incapable of staying calm and was allowing emotions to cloud his judgement.

Rubbing his face again, Lamont blew out a breath.

'Shorty?'

Shorty glanced at him.

'I'm sorry. I shouldn't have said that stuff to you.'

'You're my bro. Don't worry about it. We both said shit we shouldn't have.' Shorty patted Lamont on the shoulder, and they settled in to wait.

Hours passed with no call back. Shorty ordered enough Chinese to feed several families. Evidently screwing Bill's wife had left him with an appetite, because he tore his way through the food whilst Lamont picked at his, drinking two glasses of brandy. His head pounded from the stress. Laying on the sofa, he began drifting off when his phone rang again. He answered it without checking.

'Yeah?'

'L, where are you?' Marcus sounded worried.

'I'm with Shorty, why?'

'I . . . Look, I'm gonna give it to you straight. Police just found Rochelle in Harehills, with her throat slit. She's dead.'

CHAPTER TWENTY SIX

Thursday 20 June 2002

LAMONT SAT, drinking, hiding from the world. No matter what had transpired. No matter what Rochelle had or hadn't done, her death had left a hole. He had believed he was over his feelings, but the sorrow over her death, manifested with the guilt, was driving him over the edge.

Shorty and Marcus were out trying to find Leader, publicly slapping people around to put their point across. He no longer cared what people thought. He could have talked to Leader, negotiated, arranged a meeting, asked for her to be left out of it. She could have left the Hood; free to pursue her dream of becoming a teacher. It wasn't meant to be. In the two days that passed since her death, the police had questioned him. They'd searched her phone and seen the call to Lamont before she was killed.

At one crucial point during the questioning — a medley of *no-comment's* — they showed him a picture of Rochelle's body, her head practically decapitated. The image stayed with him, plaguing him along with a single question: *Was he an effective boss, or was he too weak to lead?*

Lamont kept thinking of the world he'd willingly strode into. That had been because of Rochelle too. It all related to her. The desire to be better than Reagan had led him to where he was. Right now, he couldn't stand any of it.

———

Another day passed. Lamont consumed cups of the horrible instant coffee that Shorty kept. He was going crazy sitting inside. Showering and throwing on some clothing, he made some calls and located an address for someone he needed to speak with.

———

'L?'

Mia gawped, surprised to see him. It had been far easier to track her down than her sister. Mia had changed from the old days. The beauty was still there, but buried under too much makeup and clear signs of grief. Her eyes were heavy and her black clothing was rumpled.

'Hello, Mia.'

'What are you doing here?'

'I wanted to give my condolences. I'm sorry about what happened to Rochelle.'

'Come in.'

Lamont took a seat while Mia made them hot drinks. Soon, they were sat in awkward silence. The living room was cosy, stuffed with furniture, kids toys and family photos. He studied Mia's partner, but didn't recognise him.

'Why is my sister dead?'

Lamont considered what to tell her. The police had interviewed him, but he didn't know if they had spoken with her.

'Do you know Leader?'

'What does Leader have to do with anything?' Mia froze.

'He killed your sister. Don't ask why. You can't tell anyone about this, especially the police. I'm telling you because you have a right to know.'

'What am I supposed to do, L? You can't drop a bombshell like that and then not say anything! You're talking about my family here.'

'The police won't catch Leader. I promise you, he will be brought to justice, one way or another.

Mia ran a hand through her hair, putting her untouched drink on the table. Lamont did the same.

'Remember the old days? The four of us in that living room, talking shit and drinking?'

Lamont nodded.

'You were so good for her, L. I'm not just saying this. Rochelle was never happier than in those moments when she'd be sitting and talking with you.'

Lamont swallowed down the lump in his throat.

'She broke my heart back then.'

Mia glanced at him, her eyes tearing.

'She broke her own heart too. Now, she's dead.'

He held her as she cried, determined not to shed his own tears. The need for vengeance grew. Leader was responsible for so much sorrow. Levi had ended up in prison, Craig and Rochelle had lost their lives because of him. Lamont made a silent vow to end him by any means necessary. It had gone far enough.

———

'Nice to see you again. Heard you had a bit of trouble with the police,' said Delroy as Lamont sat down in the office. He nodded. His face was drawn, and he was in no mood for small talk. Delroy recognised this and straightened up.

'I want Leader's location.'

'We've been through this already. I want—'

'Help my people find him, and I'll buy exclusively from you instead of my current supplier.'

Delroy took his time replying, a telltale gleam in his eye.

'Are you sure about this?'

'Do you agree?'

Delroy scratched his lip.

'Let me make a few phone calls, and we'll talk numbers.'

————

'He's in there.'

Lamont sat in the back of the car, Shorty next to him, Marcus and K-Bar in the front. They were parked down the road from a terraced spot in Keighley.

Delroy had acted swiftly, finding Leader's location and stressing that he moved around a lot, so they would need to hurry. Lamont rounded up his people, and they had put the plan into place.

No one replied to Marcus's redundant statement. This time, there would be no escape.

'Should be any minute now.'

As Marcus spoke, a black van pulled to a stop outside the spot, and four men surged toward the house. From their spot, they heard multiple bangs and loud noises, then watched as they dragged Leader from the spot, struggling. Lamont's jaw tensed. He wanted to jump from the car and attack the man that had caused so much trouble, but he waited.

'Drive to the spot. We'll meet them there.'

————

Lamont loathed the fact that Leader wasn't scared. They were in the basement of an out-of-the-way spot Marcus had set up. It was soundproofed, packed with weapons and tools designed to coerce information from people.

The floor of the basement was covered in plastic. Leader was trussed to a chair, his glittering eyes focused on Lamont.

'You got lucky.'

Shorty smacked him in the face, the hit making a dull slapping sound. Leader's head jerked back, but he kept smiling, showing blooded teeth.

'Does the truth hurt?'

'Maybe I need to hit you this time.' Marcus stepped toward Leader, but Lamont stopped him.

'You're going to die.'

The room was quiet, all eyes focused on the Yardie killer. He stared insolently at Lamont, blood trickling down his mouth, staining the t-shirt and tracksuit bottoms they had found him in.

'I don't fear death.'

'I think you're lying. Regardless, it doesn't matter. These lot are going to rip you apart, and you're going to know that it wasn't worth it.'

'I took what you loved. That makes it worth it. Teflon . . . the love-struck boss, happy to fuck *Shelly* after so many years. You loved her, but her pussy belonged to me. Nothing can change that.'

When Marcus moved forward this time, Lamont didn't stop him. The power of his uppercut toppled Leader's chair. He jerked on the floor, coughing, moaning in pain as K-Bar and Shorty steadied his chair before punching him multiple times in the stomach. The tools came out. Lamont was desensitised to the sounds of Leader shouting in pain, or the retching sounds. He didn't care. The image of Rochelle's battered body was prevalent in his mind.

'Stop.'

Leader hunched over now, saliva and blood covering his clothes, his right eye closed and his lips bust. He glared at Lamont, no longer speaking.

'When you die, the world will immediately forget you. No one will avenge you. You killed the woman who loved you. Your team betrayed you. You got the better of me, but I still won the game. Enjoy your last few moments.'

Signalling to the others, he stepped back as they pulled guns. Leader's screams were louder now, yet drowned out by the sounds of the bullets. They shot him in each leg, then Marcus put his gun to Leader's stomach at point-blank rage, firing twice. His body jerked, then he was still. With a glance to Lamont, Shorty put his gun to Leader's head, and pulled the trigger, ensuring the job was finished.

For a few minutes, no one spoke. Lamont kept his eyes on

Leader, waiting, hoping the image of his destroyed body would replace Rochelle's, but it didn't. Finally, Marcus spoke.

'K, take L home. We'll clean up here. Make sure someone is watching his spot, then we're all gonna lay low after this.'

———

MONDAY 24 JUNE 2002

Lamont lay on his sofa staring up at the ceiling when there was a knock at the door. He opened it, surprised to see Xiyu, who carried a six-pack of Red Bull energy drinks in one hand, and two bottles of water in the other. Lamont led him into the house. Xiyu handed him a drink, opening one himself. They drank silently for a moment.

'How are you doing?' Xiyu asked.

'I'm fine.'

'You don't need to lie. I spoke to the guys. I know about Rochelle, and I know she meant a lot to you.'

'I got her killed.'

'No, you didn't.'

'I should have negotiated with Leader.'

'Leader would have killed her, regardless. He wanted to get to you. She knew what she was doing.'

'I slept with her and it was magical. To me, anyway. It felt real, everything about that night. The emotions. All of it. When I think of her acting through all of that, it makes me feel sick.'

Xiyu was quiet for a moment.

'Maybe she was being real. I don't know the specifics of why she dealt with a man like Leader, but things could have played out differently. This might have been her way of being with you again.'

Lamont considered that. He wasn't sure he believed it, but it sounded good. For the first time since it all started, he smiled.

'You know what's funny?'

Xiyu shook his head. 'Tell me.'

'It's amazing how much of my life revolves around women.'

They both laughed.

'There is something I need you to do.'

'I'm listening,' said Xiyu.

'Set up an information network. I want it to be as intricate as possible. Pay whoever you need to pay, but put something in place so that in the future, we're not playing catchup, or forced to make deals. I want to know everything about everyone. No matter the cost.'

Xiyu surveyed Lamont for a long moment before he replied.

'I'll handle it.'

EPILOGUE
Friday 5 July 2002

LAMONT SCANNED the room as if through someone else's eyes, hands clammy.

A single thought resonated around his head: *What would he have become if he had gone into Rochelle's house that day?*

He often tried to put himself in that mindset, contemplating what would have happened if Reagan hadn't looked at him like dirt on that day, reminding Lamont that he was superior. *Teflon's* story began that day. It was as if that was where the tape had started and no matter how robust his efforts, Lamont couldn't look past that.

And now he didn't need to.

Leader's death was a story for a while, but rival's quickly filled the void he left behind, carving up his interests and manpower. No one approached Lamont about the murder, but the right people knew what had transpired, even if they didn't know why. It boosted Lamont's reputation, giving him and his team more street credibility.

Outside, a horn beeped. Splashing cold water on his face, Lamont tidied himself and sprayed aftershave before leaving. A new model BMW 4x4 idled at the curb. Even before he reached the ride, he heard the pulsating music.

'Yes, Tef!' Shorty said over the music. Marcus slouched in the passenger seat smoking a large spliff. He nodded at Lamont, then closed his eyes.

'Are we ready?' asked Lamont as the driver set off.

'Everyone's waiting for us,' said Marcus. Satisfied, he looked out of the window as the whip rumbled down Spencer place. Lamont recalled the days when he had struggled to sell drugs around this very street. He saw the scuzzy women on the game strolling, trying to entice passing cars to stop.

Nearby were other local pushers. They seemed younger than he had been when he started. They were dressed similarly; dark hooded tops, tracksuit bottoms, and expensive trainers. He saw the hunger as they eyed the Beemer and wondered if any would ascend, or if they would stay on the bottom rung forever. He rubbed the scar on his chin, wondering what level he would finish at.

Shorty nodded his head to the beat and Marcus looked so still, he seemed asleep. The ride was void of words, and Lamont liked it. It wasn't often the two juggernauts were quiet.

Climbing from the ride, the trio walked toward the restaurant, dressed to turn heads. Lamont wore a sharkskin grey suit with a charcoal shirt, brown tie, and black shoes. Shorty and Marcus had ditched the suit jackets, wearing white shirts, black trousers, and shoes. People stared at the trio as they sauntered by like movie stars.

Inside, they were shown to a private room. K-Bar, Xiyu and several other faces waited, dressed in their finery and drinking champagne. They rose when the three entered.

The seat at the head of the table had been left for Lamont and he stood next to the chair with the regal arrogance of royalty. Reaching for a glass, he took a small sip, wetting his throat.

'Years ago, we banded together to try something new. The streets are no joke, and it all intensifies when the task is to build something real.' He paused, looking into the eyes of every man present. 'We're stronger than we've ever been thanks to the efforts of everyone in this room, and all our people out of it. That's why I wanted you all here. To thank you for staying loyal, even when things grew difficult lately.

'As long as we keep going, the money will keep flowing. Let's continue to show everyone who the dominant team is.' Lamont saw the pride etched on all the faces of the men. 'Let's eat some of this good food, smoke some cigars, and go get drunk!'

As each man held their glasses aloft, Lamont prepared himself for the future.

DID YOU ENJOY THE READ?

You can make a huge difference

Reviews are immensely powerful when it comes to getting attention for my books.

Honest reviews help bring them to the attention of other readers.

If you've enjoyed this I would be very grateful if you could spend just five minutes leaving a review (it can be as short as you like) on the book's Amazon page.

Thank you so much

GET A FREE NOVELLA

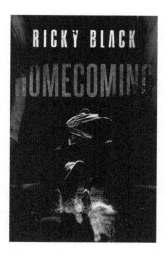

Building a relationship with my readers is one of the best things about writing. I'm first and foremost a fan of books, and getting to talk at length about them is a bonus.

If you sign up to the mailing list, you'll receive a copy of my novella Homecoming, absolutely free.

You can get this immediately here

TARGET PREVIEW

Check out the first chapter of Target, book 2 in the Target series

CHAPTER ONE

Wednesday 31 July 2013

LAMONT JONES STOOD OUTSIDE A ROOM, listening to two men discuss killing him.

'Del, he's a problem,' the first voice kept saying. It belonged to a man named Ricky Reagan.

'He's pure profit,' a second, more accented voice replied. This one belonged to Delroy Williams, a kingpin on the streets of Leeds. 'Do you realise what we make from *Teflon*?'

'He's too big. Everyone wants to buy more from his people than ours.'

'We control his supply. That means they're still buying from us. We control him.'

'Teflon's sneaky. You think he'll be satisfied behind you? He wants your crown.'

'He does? Or you do?'

Silence followed. Lamont pressed his ear closer to the door.

'What are you trying to say?' Reagan's voice rose.

'Maybe you're not happy with the way things are,' Delroy paused. 'Maybe you think you deserve a bigger slice.'

'It's not about me. It's about Teflon. Gimme the word and he won't last the night.'

'What, you wanna kill him in my office now? Is that smart?' Lamont heard the amusement in Delroy's tone.

'You're a gangster, not a businessman. Why do you need an office?'

'I'm both. That's why I'm rich. Teflon realises that. You never have.'

'Are you saying he's better than me?'

'I'm saying there's no profit in killing him. Learn to work with Teflon instead of against him. I want you on your best behaviour when he arrives.'

Lamont moved from the door and moved back down the draughty hall. The bribe he'd paid Delroy's people at the door had been worth it. He cut back around, knocked on the door twice and entered.

The office was old, particles of dust visible in the air. A large table dominated the room. The smell clung to Lamont's nostrils; stale cigarettes littering the overflowing ashtray, and the eye watering scent of white rum.

There were two chairs in the room. One, an oversized throne-like leather chair. The other, a metal contraption more suited for a torture chamber, faced the desk.

Reagan leant against the wall, feral and wild-eyed. His afro style hair was uncouth, his facial hair neater. He eyed Lamont, nodding. Lamont returned the gesture.

'Good to see you, Teflon. Take a seat,' said the dark-skinned, dreadlocked man in the big seat, Delroy Williams. Born on the Island of Grenada, he'd had fled to Britain after a murder in his home country. He ascended to power in the prosperous, bloody Eighties, resting at the top of the Chapeltown hierarchy ever since. He eyed Lamont with a toothy smile not reflected in his eyes. Lamont sat on the hard-backed metal chair. Reagan bristled behind him. He ignored him, focusing his attention ahead.

'How's business?' Delroy continued, his chair creaking beneath him. From his own seat, Lamont noticed the buttons straining on the short-sleeved shirt the kingpin wore. Other than a shimmering gold watch on his right wrist and numerous rings on his thick fingers, he showed no signs of wealth.

'Business is business,' said Lamont. It was an ambiguous reply, but he wanted to learn why Delroy had summoned him. They were both high enough up on the food chain that they worked through people. He couldn't remember the last time he'd spoken face to face with Delroy.

'Business is important, don't you agree?' asked Delroy.

'I suppose I do.'

Delroy's mask vanished. 'Tell me why I've heard things about your team then?'

'What have you heard?'

'You don't know?'

'He probably told them to say it,' said Reagan, interjecting himself into the conversation.

'You don't need to talk about me like I'm not here, Rick.'

'Don't talk like we're friends,' Reagan grumbled.

'I'm talking to your boss, not you.' Lamont kept looking ahead. Reagan's mouth twisted.

'You fuc—'

'Stop.' Delroy didn't raise his voice, but it silenced the pair. Agitated, Lamont tapped a slender finger on the table as Reagan stewed, breathing hard.

'Don't take me for a fool. Do you know or not?' Delroy continued.

'Stop talking in riddles. Just be straight up,' replied Lamont. Delroy studied him. His dark eyes flickered towards Reagan for a moment, then back to him.

'Do you want a drink?'

Lamont didn't. He recognised the intent, however and nodded. Delroy poured the remnants of the rum into a cloudy glass and handed it to Lamont. He wiped the glass and drank.

'Reagan, wait outside.'

'What for?' Reagan's voice rose.

'I'm trying to talk business with Teflon.'

Reagan didn't move.

'I should be in the room when you're dealing with him.'

'Why? Because you can handle me?' Snapped Lamont without thinking.

'What—'

'Ricky, go.'

Reagan stomped from the room, slamming the door behind him.

'Dunno why you're always aggravating him.' Delroy wiped his eyes. He looked exhausted and sounded less confident than he had earlier. Lamont wondered if it was an act.

'He's emotional. It's not my problem.'

'Until he makes it your problem. I dunno what it is with you two, but Ricky hates you. I don't think you're his best friend either.'

Lamont shrugged.

'Your people are talking shit. They're saying the supply is weak,' said Delroy, realising they were finished discussing Ricky Reagan.

'Do you have names?'

'Forget names. I don't want that crap out there, so get your people in line and sort it. Got that?'

Lamont continued to assess him. The kingpin scratched at his face with a paw-like hand, leaning backwards.

'I said, got that?'

'I suppose I do. Anything else you want to discuss?' Lamont asked. Delroy eyeballed him.

'We've got something coming in a few days. Save it for the drought. We'll tell your people when it's here.'

————

'Someone's been talking.'

Lamont slumped in the passenger seat as Shorty drove away from Delroy's at speed, loud music pumping from the ride. It was a new mixtape by some brash kid Lamont wasn't familiar with. All Shorty's music sounded the same though.

Lamont rubbed his temples, his head pounding. The car was stuffy and the smell of weed overpowering. He turned off the music.

'Oi! What are you doing?' said Shorty.

'I'm talking. I don't want to shout over whatever rubbish this is.'

'Ask then. Don't just reach for my shit,' snapped Shorty. A small peanut shell coloured tank of a man, he would bring drama to anyone who wanted it. Brutal and animated, he kept himself in ferocious shape by spending far too many hours training and working the bars in the park.

'Listen then, please. The big man's upset that we said his product was weak.'

'It is, so what's he crying about?'

Lamont shook his head. 'That's not the point. I don't want people talking out of line.'

'People are feeling the pinch, L. We're not making the same off this weak shit. You need to run that to Delroy.'

'Leave the supply to me. While we're paying wages, I want no one talking out of turn. Sort it.'

Shorty cut his eyes to Lamont, not liking the bite in his friend's tone.

'Fine. It's handled.'

'If anyone complains, tell them we'll make it up on the next go around,' said Lamont.

'How? With more crap?'

He didn't bother responding.

———

'Same old then?'

Shorty had dropped Lamont off at the Park Row apartment of Xiyu Manderson. Known as *Chink*, his nickname came from his light eyes and facial features, inherited from his Chinese mother. He'd grew up poor in Meanwood. Bullied by the tough kids of his neighbourhood, he learned to stay out of sight, developing a skill with numbers and gaining recognition as a proficient mathematician.

Chink and Lamont had become friends in their teens, and he'd followed Lamont into the drugs game, using his talent for figures to help them gain a foothold. He was smart with his money, and his home represented this. It was spotless, bereft of even the slightest dirt. The furniture combined *The Baroque* with a few modernists pieces such as Andy Warhol. The windows were wide, all-encompassing, the walls various shades of white and cream. A solid bookshelf displayed various self-help books and history tomes.

'The quality will be shit again.' Lamont rubbed his eyes, sinking into the plush, linen sofa. Chink watched.

'You need to sleep.'

'I will. I thought you needed an update,' Lamont stifled a yawn.

'And Shorty couldn't tell me? Where is he, anyway? Outside smoking ganja?'

Lamont grinned. Shorty and Chink worked alongside each other, but their differences were clear. Shorty was rough and tumble; direct, keeping immersed in the streets. Chink moved behind the scenes, weighing up the profits and flushing them through careful investments.

Chink thought Shorty was a thug, and Shorty believed Chink was a spineless pretty boy. Lamont did his best to keep them apart unless necessary.

'He dropped me here. Had something to do.'

'It was his people spreading those rumours. You know don't you?'

'I know.' Lamont was fully aware it was Shorty's guys talking loosely. Shorty didn't respect Delroy or his team, and it was filtering down to the lower ranks. The thought of the drama made his head hurt more. He hoped he had suitable painkillers at home.

'So, tell him. Make him run his crew better.'

'Shorty's fine. Be on hand to coordinate.'

'I know the drill. We're overpaying for crap gear, though. It barely stands up to a cut, and Shorty's people aren't the only ones with complaints. Clients aren't happy.'

'They're still buying.'

Chink's eyes narrowed. 'Yes, they're still buying. Is this how it's gonna be? We let Delroy keep diluting the product and wait for our clients to go elsewhere?'

'I've got it covered,' Lamont muttered.

'Do you? Because we already had one venture fuck up. Or did you forget Party in the Park?'

Lamont hadn't forgotten. The plan had been to set up a team of dealers to distribute drugs in the park, and to supply after parties that sprung up after the annual event. He'd had everything in place, but the weak product meant that the buyers copping the drugs opted to work with different dealers.

'Chink, I said I have it covered,' Lamont repeated. He rubbed his head. The headache felt worse now.

'What is with you?' Chink asked.

'Nothing.'

'You look like shit. Something's happened.'

Lamont took a deep breath. 'I got into it with Ricky Reagan.'

Chink grimaced.

'Was that smart?'

Lamont shrugged.

'Did you tell Shorty?'

Lamont smiled. Chink had a habit of asking questions to which he already knew the answer.

'What happened?'

'He kept interrupting when I was talking to Delroy, so I put him in his place.'

'You and your vendettas.' Chink shook his head. Lamont didn't want to talk about Reagan. He didn't want to talk about Shorty or any of it, even though he needed to. He needed to stay on top of the situation, but he couldn't bring himself to care right now.

'I'm tired, Chink.'

'Sleep.'

Lamont looked at him. 'You know what I mean.'

Chink sighed. 'Why do it then?'

Lamont pondered Chink's question. It gnawed at him daily. He took a deep breath, marshalling his thoughts.

'People depend on us to get paid. We used to control everything. Now, it's like a fucking machine. And we're just going along.'

'You don't think you have power?' Chink raised an eyebrow.

Lamont shook his head. 'That's not what I'm trying to say, but, I can't keep making excuses for the life I'm living. Something has to change, and soon.'

'Like?'

'People used to listen,' said Lamont, needing to get the words out. 'Now they don't. Our world used to be about money. Now everyone has something to prove.'

'Didn't we too? Maybe that's the problem, L. You made it. Cars, money, that mini-mansion you've got. There's nothing left to prove.'

'How can I live like that, though? How can anyone live like that? With nothing to prove. No order.' Lamont paused, his voice filled with emotion.

'What happens if I stopped playing by the rules? Does this thing we built fall apart?'

'Is that why you do it? To stop it all tumbling down?' said Chink.

Lamont couldn't answer.

———

That night, Lamont struggled to relax, drifting into a fitful sleep just after four. When he woke, his head still pounded. He dragged himself to the shower, letting the scalding water beat down on his head and shoulders. He closed his eyes, willing the thump of his brain to cease. It was to no avail. He could have stayed in the shower all day, but readied himself instead.

Lamont had several missed calls from his sister, Marika. He stowed his phone and drove to his makeshift office, the backroom of a barber shop on Chapeltown Road. It was almost eleven now, and the barbers was in full flow.

The premises were reasonably sized, with four barber chairs and a tidy waiting area with weathered leather seats. The walls were adorned with flashy pictures of the different hairstyles available, along with a handwritten price list. There were magazines, and an entertainment system in the corner. Sky Sports News results flashed along the bottom of the muted TV. Loud reggae music played and several of the older guys waiting were nodding their heads.

Lamont greeted them. Trinidad Tommy, the manager, approached, his lined face cracking into a smile.

'Trinidad, everything good?' asked Lamont. The man nodded.

'The crowd will be here soon. You sleep? You look tired.'

'I'm fine.' Lamont excused himself to his backroom office. It was much smaller than the main area, with only a heavy wooden desk, computer chair and several filing cabinets. He looked over the paperwork from his legal ventures and met people to talk business here. Cautious, he ensured it was swept for listening devices, just in case.

Sinking into his chair, Lamont opened the drawer, taking out an open packet of Pro Plus. He dry-swallowed two, glancing at the most valuable thing in the room as he wiped his mouth. It was a battered old chess set. The board was marked, the pieces chipped. He loved it though. It reminded him of the good times. Fingering several pieces, he put them down and started to work. He pored over several statements, his mind drifting in no time.

'L?'

Rough hands shook Lamont. He woke. Trinidad stood over him, concern in his eyes.

'Are you okay? I was seeing if you wanted any food.'

Lamont stood, yawning.

'No thanks. I'll get something from Rika's.' He wiped his eyes.

Before leaving, he took another two caffeine tablets. As he started his car engine, his eyeballs throbbed. He blinked, pulled out and drove to Marika's. She lived in Harehills, but wanted to move after several incidents with her neighbours. He parked outside and strode in. Marika's place was small, but comfortable, the living room stuffed with toys and pictures of her children, Keyshawn and Bianca. The professional photographs were probably more expensive than the drab furniture. As always, the place was clean.

'Oh, now you wanna turn up?' She looked up from the TV show she was watching. 'I've been ringing you all day.'

'Have you got any paracetamol?'

She fetched him water and a few pills.

'Coffee?' she asked. Lamont nodded.

'Please. Black, no sugar.'

He plopped on the sofa, closing his eyes. Minutes later, he heard the cup being placed next to him.

'Do you want any food? I can warm something up.'

'Sounds good.'

Lamont closed his eyes again, relaxing to the sounds of his sister clattering around in the kitchen. When the food was ready, they ate, talking as they did so. They had their difficulties, as all siblings did, but the love was still strong.

'Why didn't you reply before? I rang you loads of times.'

'I had things to tie up. How much do you want this time?'

Marika pouted.

'How do you know I want money?'

'Don't you?'

'That's not the point.'

Lamont laughed, putting his plate on the coffee table.

'If you say so.'

'I know you've got it, anyway. You lot are killing it on the streets.'

'Says who?'

'Everyone. Keisha told me the other day that Ricky Reagan kept calling out your name.'

Lamont's stomach plummeted. During the day, he had fleetingly thought about the conversation he'd overheard. He'd always known Reagan didn't like him, but the fact he was so open about killing him was unsettling. It remained another reason to make sure he had all the angles covered.

'Is he trying to beef with you?'

'Don't worry about Reagan,' Lamont said, wondering if he could take his own advice.

————

Shorty sat in the dingy gambling house drinking straight glasses of Hennessy. He'd procured a table in the corner, enabling him to see all the comings and goings.

The gambling house was rife with the pungent smell of sweat, mingled with weed and beer. It was nearly midnight and loud, the music playing in the background drowned out by people talking. It comprised four playing tables, and a few smaller ones. Men crowded the tables, seated on wooden chairs with ripped, cheap leather seating.

There was a backroom with a pool table where the younger crowd congregated. In his corner spot, nobody troubled him. He wanted it that way.

Lamont took a few steps into the gambling house before greetings and requests from all around besieged him.

'Lamont!'

'Yes, L!'

'You good, man?'

Lamont had to buy the bar before being allowed to move. He trudged across the room and sat across from Shorty.

'Bloody vultures,' he muttered.

'You love it. How come you wanted to meet here? This ain't your scene.'

Lamont drunk his beer and ordered another one.

'Not like you to drink and drive,' Shorty added. Lamont was a stickler for rules.

'I took a taxi. Dropped my car off.'

'What's going on then?'

Lamont sipped his drink, froth gathering around his mouth. He rested his elbow on the table which creaked under the weight.

'Did you talk to your people?' he asked. Shorty expressed his disapproval by kissing his teeth.

'Why are you stressing? Forget Delroy.'

'Shorty, we talked about this.'

'We don't work for that fat motherfucker. We can say what we like.'

'While we work *with* Delroy, we stay quiet. Things are going on in the background. There's a plan in place.'

'What plan?'

A heavy hand clapped down on Lamont's shoulder before he could reply.

It was Reggie, one of the old crowd. Once a big deal in the streets, he was now an elderly man whose clothes hung on his frame. He had never planned for the future and had no money saved. It was a sad reality.

'Lamont! How are you?' Reggie's hearing was going, meaning he tended to shout.

'I'm doing well, Reg. How about yourself?' Lamont shook his hand.

'Life is hard. These young ones don't respect their elders. Not like you, Lamont.'

'Sit down with us. Have a drink.'

Reggie indulged and Lamont slid to order him a white rum from the bar. Shorty glared at the old man. Reggie had clutched the same pint for hours. Shorty had seen it too many times. Reggie would stay all night for free drinks now.

They listened to his tales of the old days, his peeves about life and its disappointments. They started a game of dominoes, Reggie and one of his pals versus Lamont and Shorty. The wily pair decimated them. Shorty was decent, but Lamont was useless and Shorty wasn't pleased about it.

'Stop messing about. You'd be trying harder if it was chess!' he kept saying.

They left, drunk and poorer. Reggie and his pal had taken them to the cleaners. Shorty wouldn't shut up about it.

'We didn't win a single round. That's ridiculous. You need to stop reading all the time and practise.'

'Piss off. You made me pay for it, anyway. Reggie and his white rums cleared my pockets too.'

'Dunno why you even bother with him. He's washed up. We can't use him anymore,' said Shorty.

'He's an example of how not to turn out. There's a lot to learn from Reggie and his era.'

'Sounds daft.'

Lamont didn't reply straight away, watching Shorty try to light a cigarette.

'Whatever. Where are you going now?'

'I've got a girl on Hamilton Avenue I'm gonna wake up.' Shorty touched fists with him. 'I'll get with you tomorrow.'

Lamont watched him stagger down the street. 'Catch you then.'

ALSO BY RICKY BLACK

ABOUT THE AUTHOR

Ricky Black was born and raised in Chapeltown, Leeds. He began writing seriously in 2004, working on mainly crime pieces.

In 2016, he published the first of his crime series, Target, and has published four more books since.

Visit https://rickyblackbooks.com for information regarding new releases and special offers and promotions.

For my Family. For MyMy.

Keep inspiring me. Keep pushing me.